LAMPLIGHT

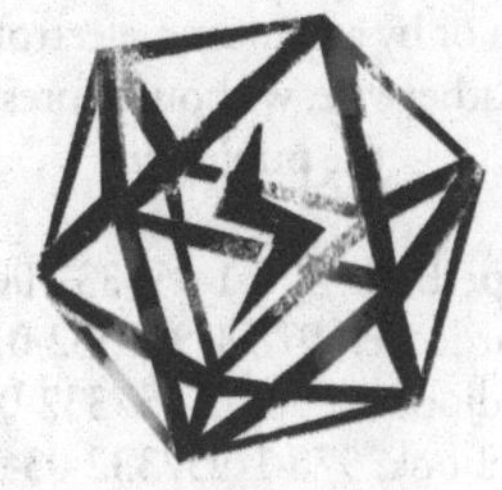

A. DAVID BARRETT

Dedicated to:
My wife and my world, Gabrielle.
And my Grandfather,
Gary Grant Mundt Sr.
Wish you were still here.

Preface

The journey I took to write this first novel was a strange one. I set out to write a story based on a dream of mine, and it quickly grew into something completely different. That in itself was okay; maybe for the better. It had its hardships and moments I felt I should just give up and delete every single file. It also had its moments in which I felt as if it was turning out exactly as planned, and I was proud of it.

But, eventually, it got to the point where I felt good about it again; something to be proud of. If it wasn't for the constant encouragement of my wife, Gabrielle, I do not think I would have finished this novel. If it weren't for the help from my mother and friends along the way, it wouldn't have turned out the same either.

Writing a novel is something I believe everyone should do if they have a story they want to tell. In the end, isn't that what life is about? I believe that the stories we tell will define who we are.

I think, though, overall, I wanted to write a story I think my grandfather would have enjoyed reading. And I want to thank you, my steadfast reader, for enjoying the story I wanted to tell.

Rest easy, Grandpa.

Chapter 1

An Unfair End

30th March, 1888
Whitechapel Borough, London, England
12:00 a.m.

The deep carmine of the fresh blood pooled out in all directions around the woman. She lay twitching in the muck and the dirt of an alley made of worn cobblestone, tucked away from the prying eyes of guardian angels. Her short, raspy breaths filled the midnight air as she struggled to fight the darkness that beckoned to her. The beaming shadow of a full moon illuminated the tears that streaked down her face. With each moment that passed, more of her life force drained with each new heartbeat from the long slash across her throat. A shadow was cast upon her body from a man in black, donning the night as a veil to hide who he really was.

"Do you hear that?" said the man.

He waited for her response, even though he knew there wouldn't be one. She tried to speak— to scream— but all that escaped her weakening lips were gurgles of anguish.

"All of the noise has faded," the man said. "It is finally becoming quiet."

The woman twitched, arm stretching to its limits as she reached for her locket. She strained, fingers curling as she feverishly attempted to grasp her last good memories to bring with her into the abyss.

"We can't have that," said the man.

He walked over to her and kicked the locket out of reach, sending it off to the side. It clattered as it struck the wall, short-lived sparks arcing in different directions as it did so.

"I take no pleasure in what I do," the man said before pausing for a moment. "Well, actually, I do. But, alas, you my dear are the first of my victims."

He returned to pacing around his prey, eyes locked onto her fading ones. A new tear streaked down her waxy cheek, mixing with the filth on the ground.

"Too long have I waited in the shadows as the tainted bloodlines of the great and magnificent King Arthur hunt me down." The man said in a mocking tone. "But with you, my lovely one, you will be the thing that turns the tides on the cattle that dare to go against my will."

The man crouched down next to the woman on the ground. His form cut off the beauty of the moon and pitched her in the blanket of death. She took in a few more labored breaths as she bled out.

In the blackness, he spoke. "I have to thank you, my dear poppet. With you and the gift you give me, the world will finally burn."

CHAPTER 2
Never The Same

1st April, 1888 - Fools Day
Whitechapel Borough, London, England
5:00 p.m.

Small swirls of my exhalation curled and billowed in an arc upwards as I reached for the lamplight. Clumps and piles of ashen snow were pushed up in corners of doorways and along faded brick fences, hiding from the wind. The cold, piercing April air made for a miserable night shift. Leftover snow flurries often changed to ice-cold sleet, making one take extra precautions. The Tesla bulb seemed to pull away from my grasp, making me strain to turn the incandescents into place. I swore quietly to myself as my fingers slipped once more, frustration beginning to overtake my actions. Stepping up one more rung on the ladder, stretching one last time, the connection was complete for the amplifying process.

"You know, this just seems counterproductive. It takes forever to go up and down all the streets," I said aloud to myself. "To think that I will have to go back around in six hours to turn them back off."

"Then why are they doing it?" a voice asked, causing my footing to slip on the ladder.

The unexpected voice startled me, causing me to wobble back and forth on the ladder. Regaining my balance and gathering my composure, I turned my head towards the feminine voice. To my surprise, it came from a gentleman about the age of thirty. He wore a bowler hat, plain dark clothing, jet black hair and a wiry black mustache. He had thin lips that seemed to disappear as he pursed them and eyes that were beady like a bird's. I felt a severe disease as he stared at me, not blinking for long seconds. As he stood there, he was leaning against a cane that, at first glance, seemed normal the longer I looked at it, the more I was sure that it was anything but that. The handle was made of an amber-colored substance with imperfections and bubbles floating around what looked like a lock of hair. The shaft was black and carved to look like a bone, most likely a femur.

"Excuse me, what did you say, sir?" I asked.

"I asked, then why are they doing it?"

"Honestly, I still don't know much about it, but it's a new technology that we are implementing. It's called Wavergy, a bloody brilliant thing if you ask me. The one thing that seems foolish to me, though, is that I still need to ground them, like regular conventional wiring. But that's technology; always a work in progress."

The man gazed at the blinding light for a minute, shifting his weight onto his cane. He then looked back at me. "Who came up with all of it?"

"Nikola Tesla. He helped with all these technological updates to the city. It feels like we are in the future compared to a few years ago; millions of pounds have been invested in his wireless electricity research. I helped convert all the old oil-burning street lamps to these new grounded, wireless electric ones."

"Interesting. How does it work?" he asked.

"They use the generated energy from the Tesla coil substations placed throughout the city,"

"I see. And is this Tesla native to England?"

"No, he isn't. From what the newspapers have told us, Nikola Tesla came to England about three years ago to work with the Crown. They offered him quite a bit of money to help with his inventions and bring about the electric age in Great Britain. In turn, he created the Tesla Electric Association company, or TEA for short, as a tribute for the help with his research and inventions."

"Well I see I have found an expert on the subject. So, where was he before this, before he came here?"

"Well, a year before he came to England just a few years ago, in '85, he immigrated to America. He was born in the Austrian Empire, but needed to go somewhere he could work on his ideas; his inventions."

"These seem like modern wonders of the world. Amazing. Simply amazing."

"It really is. But what I find even more bizarre is that you'll still find some parts of London and other parts of Great Britain using the old oil lamps. But they are few and far between, mostly in the outlying villages and pub-only towns. Parliament wanted to connect everyone to the new age of electricity; the new age of light," I said.

I climbed down the ladder rung by rung, keeping my balance, trying not to topple over. Once on the ground, I straightened my jacket and smoothed out all of the wrinkles from the night's work. I offered my hand. "Me name's Davey. Sorry for talking your ear off. What's yours by the way? Where are you from?"

The man reciprocated as he took my hand, "The name is Herman, Herman Mudgett." He said in a calm voice, continuing, "That's quite alright; I am here from the United States myself for some business. I did know half the reason Nikola left, but I definitely did not know as much as you. It was very informative." He let go of my hand and looked around. "I was just wandering around town, trying to find out what you folks do for fun around here," he said, a smile curling on his face.

"This time of night, you won't find much, but during the day, there are plenty of things to do," I said, feeling a little uneasy. "There is the museum, where I happen to also work. They have a few new exhibits coming soon, so if you're in town long, that might be an exciting thing to see."

"I might try that; thank you, kind sir. Best of luck and good fortune to you. I will take my leave now," said Herman.

The strange man started off down the road, cane clicking against the stone as he did so. His body eventually being absorbed into the foggy haze of the ever-encroaching darkness, disappearing from my view altogether.

When I couldn't see the man anymore, I looked around at the dirty, worn cobblestone ground, thinking back on the peculiar interaction. The night often felt like it came to life out of the corner of my eyes, making me feel the need to keep an eye out for anything lurking in the dark pockets of shadows which spread throughout every intersection. Every twist, and every turn lining the emptying, twilit streets.

What a very odd fellow, almost creepy. Nightmare stuff, that is.

I, as usual, ended my route as a Sparker in the Spitalfields Market area in Whitechapel early in the morning. All the other chaps that ran the other lines didn't like this area very much, so I usually got stuck with it because not too many blokes would mess with me. Wondering just how early in the morning it was, I reached into my breast pocket and pulled out my brass pocket watch. The faceplate reflected off one of the lamplights, revealing a design of Atlas, the titan from the old Greek legends. Sometimes I felt like him because just as he was tricked into holding the heavens on his shoulders, I too eventually held the weight of a world on my back. The watch, a gift from my wife Marie for my twentieth birthday, was still in pristine condition. It often reminded me that the tales we tell define who we are.

I am getting old, well maybe in experience.

Curious about the time, I pressed the button at the top of the watch, which opened the faceplate, and saw that the clock read 9:15 p.m. I looked around one last time and decided that everything looked about right for the time of night.

Turning on my heels, I set off in the direction of the British Museum. Along with being a Sparker and policeman, my night watchman duties included checking on the museum, just to see if there was anything suspicious going on. Mainly, my duties were to go around, making sure nobody tried to break in. I wasn't quite sure how much longer I was going to be working that job on the side though; everything else was enough to keep me busy.

I focused as I made it to the museum in a little over thirteen minutes, passing dark, hopeless alleyways and smog-riddled intersections. Along the way, I watched as a few drunkards stumbled out of sleepless pubs and horse-drawn carts pulling tarped piles containing God only knows what. The ladies of the night beckoned to the godless men tempted by a warm bed and a perceived loving heart. Wisps of fresh snow floating carelessly through the air, reflecting the warm light from the Wavergy lamps, like little beacons of hope guiding anyone through the dark to where they are meant to be.

The museum's courtyard was one of the very few places left in London that still used the old style oil lamps outside its large doors for light. I breathed in a deep breath of cool crisp air, looking around at the Greek style columns that held up the roof of the museum.

Fancy that. I don't think I be needing to go to Greece to see columns like these; they're right here!

The structure was a marvel of imagination and architecture, standing tall and defiant to the ever-developing future. Lit oil lamps stood surrounding the front entrance and around the building itself, keeping away the things that lurk in the night. One would think that the museum would want to be leading the way in embracing the future by implementing Wavergy, but alas, I believe they know that things will never be the same from this point on.

"Oi," said a man walking up towards the entrance of the museum.

Surprised, I turned my head in the direction he was coming from. He was close enough to me to allow for a close look at him. The clothing he wore seemed like it was patched together, only being held to each other with single strands of thread. His head's thinning forest of hair blended in with the snow that had piled in the streets around us. What he lacked for in follicles on top of his head, he made up for in the beard on his face. It seemed to stretch two feet down his front but was thick and full. I locked eyes with him before I tore myself away to look at my pocket watch.

I took it out to check the time before asking, "Hello? Who's there?"

"Ye be open still?" Barked the man.

"No, are you daft? Do you know what time it is, mate?" I asked.

The old man looked at me with a kind of confused and concerned look. He then glanced down, patting his body up and down as if he was checking for his own watch. "I do not, young man; no need to be gobby. Do ye have the time?"

"It's 10:07 p.m. What are you doing here at this time of night?" I questioned as I opened my watch once more.

About six feet behind the old man was a horse drawing a cart, hoof digging at the ground for something to eat. I started to get a little worried, not knowing what I should expect.

"Aye, 'tis late. I been traveling for three days straight. I needed to get this here to you," he said.

What could he mean, 'to me?'

"To me? Or to the museum?" I asked.

The old man chuckled. It turned to a short coughing fit, then finished with a few grunts. "To the museum, of course, that's what I mean. Why would I be looking for someone in particular?"

At the last thing he said, a twinkle in his eye formed. It was quick and faint but quite visible. I tried to sneak a peek around the man to catch a glimpse of what lay on the cart. A canvas tarp was stretched across whatever it was, one corner flapping in the gentle midnight breeze.

"I suppose that'd be a little odd, wouldn't it? What is it then? What do you need to bring here at such a late hour?" I asked.

"Aye, best to tell you then. Not too long ago, I was going through the fields on me farm, getting ready for the upcoming planting season. Me wife and children were playing down by the cove that runs along the shoreline portion of me land."

"How far have you traveled, old man?" I asked, curious as to where he was referring to.

"That need not matter. Please let me tell ye," he said. "They came along a cave that I was sure I had never seen before. I soon realized that it was low tide that revealed it that early morn. Me wife yelled hard for me to come over and see what lay inside. I climbed down the rocks and through the sand to the entrance of the small cave. Looking inside, I could make out a reflection off a little puddle. I squeezed through the cave entrance, narrow and jagged, opening into a larger cavern the size of a small room. In the right corner of the cave lay the puddle that I had seen from the outside. The light seemed to shine off the surface from no natural source. Thinking it was odd, I looked to the right of the puddle and saw some chests. All but one had shown signs of severe weathering from the waves over many years."

He certainly has a lot to say. It's almost as if he is lecturing me about this.

I cut him off once more. "That's what you have underneath there? Underneath that tarp?"

Sounding frustrated, he cleared his throat violently, coughing raggedly. "Please son, let me finish."

"Okay, sorry, sir."

"I walked closer to have a look, and noticed that the trunk was as new as a fresh layer of dew on a field of wheat. Me sons and I got the chest out into the sunlight, and it seemed to light up from the rays beating down upon it. Knowing it was something important, I tried to open it but the damn thing wouldn't budge. So, me sons had told me of this museum that they had seen when they came to university. It felt like the right thing to do," said the old man.

He was wheezing from talking so much. He stood for a moment as he tried to catch his breath from his long-winded explanation.

"Well, that's certainly an interesting story old-timer, but it seems to me like you are trying to tell me rubbish on account of it being April fools day," I murmured, chuckling from the tall tale.

"Do not be confused youngin; this be the truth. I swear on me own family graves. I got the feeling it need be here that this trunk goes," explained the old man.

"What's your name, old man?" I asked.

"Me name doesn't matter. All that matters is that you take this now. Its time is done with me," he said.

With his breathing under control now, he seemed to visibly relax before my eyes. The old man pulled the reins on the horse, having it trot closer to me, its hooves clopping abruptly on the cobblestone, like drunkards slamming cups down at a pub waiting for another round. He turned the horse and cart around so the back door of the cart was pointed towards me. Reaching for the latch, he guided the door with his hands carefully towards the ground. He looked at me with an impatient stare, hands now in the air near the trunk.

"Ye gonna help or not?" He barked.

His question startled me, making me uneasy once more. I reached up to the trunk handles and helped him heave it down. To my surprise, the trunk was quite light in my hands. From its looks alone, it seemed like it would be rather heavy. I set it down, and I dusted off my hands on my trousers. Looking at him, I said, "You just want to leave it here? What am I to do with it?"

"It's up to you now to do what you will; it's not my concern anymore. The weight has been lifted off me shoulders." The old man sighed, peace slowly creeping back into his eyes.

He turned around, reached down to grab the gate and flipped it up into place. His calloused and overworked hands made sure the worn latches were securely in place before he hobbled his way to the horse in the front. He slowly embraced the beast's head with his palm and murmured softly, "Time to go, old girl. You did a very good job. Very good."

The old man turned to the seat of the cart and heaved himself onto it. It rocked back and forth from the added weight of the man, eventually correcting itself. He started off down the path, horse pulling the cart along behind.

He made it a dozen or so feet down the road before I yelled out, "But old man, what is your name?"

Turning around one last time he yelled back, "Gregory. Gregory Merlinus."

CHAPTER 3
It All Begins Here

A light breeze weaved its way past the feet of the knights and their horses. It pushed the kicked-up dust, giving it a small adventure of excitement and awe. The tent's door flap rippled with the persuasion of the fresh new air.

"Arthur, could you go fetch a pail of water?" the man asked, handing him a bucket.

"Yes, master; right away, master," Arthur said, taking it from his master.

Turning, he jogged out of the tent with haste to be quick with his retrieval. The intense sunlight sharply lit up his eyesight as he broke the barrier the tent flaps created. The dingy camp was cramped, packed tight with other tents and stable posts for horses to be left at when the riders took a break or the night off. The dirt road broke through the mess of the camp leading and winding to the towering gate of the stone castle up the slope on the slight hill. Arthur tried to be careful as he ran between men in full chainmail outfits and other young squires leading their masters' restless horses, each of them equally worn from the constant fighting they endured on and off the battlegrounds.

"Excuse me, sir; sorry, sir. My apologies sir," said Arthur as he jumped out of the way from being trampled by the heavy hooves.

He made it to the gate relatively unscathed, wiping his forehead in relief, sweat and dust coming free upon his sleeve. A few lonely clouds covered the sun, causing shade to blanket the courtyard that lay before him. It was sparse but large, and what lay beyond the gate was home to a few fruit-bearing trees, some benches and the well in the center off to the left. Some farm life, a few horses and donkeys, were tied up next to the gate entrance. They lazily ate at the small amounts of grass still standing from the onslaught of gnawing teeth. Arthur walked underneath the first fruit tree and leaned down to snatch a ripe apple off the ground. Bringing it to his face, he scrutinized the skin, looking for imperfections or marks of intrusions. After an intense interrogation, he lifted the ruby red apple to his lips and took a bite. His teeth dug into the skin with ease, causing it to crack as he took part of it away.

"Oh, right, the water," he said aloud to no one in particular.

Taking a few more quick bites of the delicious apple, he flung the core off to the side, hoping it landed in front of the animal that deserved it the most. He then turned his attention to the well close to him. It was built of small jagged rocks, which were stacked waist-high, jutting out at strange angles. But, since Arthur was still so short, the well still towered up to his chest. The rope used to lower buckets down the well lay next to it in a small heap, guarding it like a cobra ready to strike. Next to that was a splintered and loose-looking pail, barely held together by the rusted metal bands that surrounded it.

He tied the rope to the handle of the pail, whistling, imagining he was a snake charmer as the rope moved in his hands. Arthur finished and tied the rope off on a protruding root that was cut off, sticking out from the ground next to the well. He pulled himself up over the top of the well wall and regained his balance as he sat down on the rim for another adventure. As he started to lower the bucket down into the strange darkness, a cool gentle breeze picked up from deep below as it ruffled his hair. In the sky above him, the clouds left the sun, happily going about their own business and allowing rays of light to shine down upon him. Arthur looked back down the well to see if the pail was near the bottom, hands clasped around his eyes to see better.

To his surprise, a splinter of light shone directly down the well, reflecting off something in the bottom. Squinting, he tried to make out what it was but to no avail. He gave it some thought before lowering the bucket the rest of the way. He tugged on the root to check if it would come loose before grabbing onto the rope to lower himself down. A few seconds passed as he tried to lower himself, feeling his weight strain on the rope as he repelled below.

The bottom of the well opened up into a large, wet cavern covered with whispering shadows. The bucket stopped a foot off the ground, so he decided to jump the rest of the distance. He took a few deep breaths before leaping, splashing down into a small puddle that came up to his ankles. He shook the water from his shoes as he walked out of the small pool of water.

The sun shined down into the cavern, reflecting off multiple surfaces, glistening as it lit up even the darkest parts of the cave. The young boy took a look around, awestruck by the beauty of the cave around him. His eyes fell upon a magnificent sword peeking from a rocky prison at the far end. Small arcs of electricity reached out from the silver blade, snapping back as quick as lightning.

"Whoa, Master would be very pleased if I could get him that sword," Arthur said.

He walked over to the monument of metal and stone and put his hands on the hilt of brown leather. He felt a deep sense of purpose as he pulled the sword from the stone.

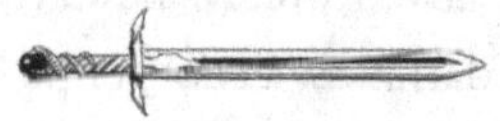

2nd April, 1888
Spitalfields Borough, London, England
10:31 a.m.

I rolled over gently onto my back and blinked a few times, sluggishly, lids still heavy with the night's short rest. I took in the dusty morning light from the billowing curtains that stretched across the linen covering Marie and I.

Her beauty never ceased to amaze me. Even after seven years of marriage, her face was always the sweetest dream I could ever wish to wake to. I felt her shoulder-length blonde hair flutter across my arms and chest as we lay there. It tickled, but I ignored it, sneaking a peek at her face as I always did.

Her soft skin was as radiant as a spring meadow, but her smile could cure any form of mental ailments. Light brown freckles dotted her face that moved and danced as her lips arced up in a smile. Her cute button nose wiggled as she scrunched her deep brown eyes shut for a moment.

"You know Marie, I had the strangest dream last night. Very odd, and I'm not sure what to make of it," I said, rubbing my eyes vigorously with the palms of my hands.

"Hmm, dear? What was the dream about?" whispered Marie as she purposely rolled over to look at my face, arm stretched across my chest.

"Well, it was about me working at the museum, like any other normal night," I started. "But this old man came by. He had a horse-drawn cart and a magical trunk that he got from a cave, really odd," I said.

Magical trunk, how ridiculous.

"Then it turned into me seeing a kid trying to fetch a pail of water for his master like it was back in medieval times. Very detailed, almost like it really happened."

"Well, honey, whatever it means, it's over now. You're here, and as far as I know, your shift last night wasn't anything special," she said.

Marie reached over and ruffled my hair with her hand with a smile growing on her face. I reached for her hand and pulled it close to my lips, giving them a light kiss. I held them for a moment longer, wishing that the feeling would never end.

"I suppose, prolly should get up and get going. Times a wastin', and we have things to do today. Thomas took my shift this morning to turn off all the lights. I had a long night at the museum," I said.

Marie rolled off of me, allowing me to sit up and roll my legs over the side of the bed. Hearing a thunk, I realized the heel of my foot hit something underneath us. Wondering what it could be, I reached down to the floor with my hand to feel for anything. My fingertips felt the cool metal handle of something, immediately prompting me to want to pull whatever it was out.

I sat back up and glanced over to Marie with a look of intrigue that shifted to confusion. I became worried, not knowing if there was anything else I couldn't remember. She returned my gaze with confusion and concern of her own.

Why is this here of all places? It's actually real? Why didn't I leave it at the museum? It certainly doesn't belong to me, and I'm not sure why it's here.

I lowered myself to the ground and sat down on my knees next to the bed. My knees popped as I leaned forward and pulled the trunk toward me, looking at it from top to bottom. As a whole, it was about four feet long by two feet wide by one foot tall. It was made of a beautiful, sturdy mahogany stained a deep rusty brown. The ornate hinges, latches and handles were forged from polished bronze or copper. Unclipping the latch, I opened it to see what it held. The top of the chest was littered with papers, with a single envelope on top. Picking up the envelope, I saw that it was sealed with wax in the design of a dragon and the word Scion underneath. I grabbed the envelope and peeled it open, pulling the paper out to read what it said.

> Greetings worthy descendants, noblemen and noblewomen, sons and daughters, I bid thee well. I, Arthur Pendragon, am scribing this letter on the ninth of October of the year five hundred and fifty-six... There is but a single task I need thee to do, for as I was unable to accomplish mine self. There is a great evil that befell my kingdom, one for which we, I, were unable to defeat. Tis up to you now to defeat that which plans for our destruction. I am but of the mortal coil and will not live to finish this task. For which my dear friend Merlin will see to it that this reaches the right person. When you grasp the sword, you will understand the task at hand. Tis a man that will help you, located at St Bartholomew the Great. May God have preserved this priory so that you will complete this task. He will be of blood to Taliesin, my faithful bard and records keeper. He will know what to do next. I bid thee good luck, and may the almighty God save our souls.
>
> Sir Arthur Pendragon

"Sir Arthur Pendragon? Like the one from the knights of the round table?" I said as I looked at Marie.

"What do you mean?" she asked, taking the letter from my hands.

"This can't be. He says in this letter that I need to meet with someone that belongs to the St. Bartholomew church. Apparently he will know what I need to do."

I glanced at Marie as she turned the paper around in her hand. The old parchment crinkled as she looked at it once more.

"But Davey, the paper is blank," she said incredulously, showing me the sheet of parchment again.

"No, it isn't Marie; it says so right there," I said, pointing at the handwriting.

Marie looked at me with a puzzled look, turned her head to the side and let out a nervous chuckle. She asked, "Are you sure? All I see is a blank piece of paper. Did you hit your head last night?"

"I honestly do not know Marie."

What are the odds that someone will be at the church and know what the bloody hell is going on?

Letting out a chuckle of my own, I shifted on my knees and looked back down at the sword laying gracefully in the soft red velvet. The sword, which looked like a double-edged one, was about three feet long from the hand-guard to the tip of the blade. Looking closer at it, I noticed the hilt was made of a dark brown leather wrap starting at the pommel and interwoven with a single dark, almost ruby red stripe crisscrossing to the top near the crossguard. The pommel was what I guessed to be a dragon claw clutching a red stone the size of an apricot.

Reaching for the sword, I said to Marie, "The letter says all I need to do is grab the sword."

With a flash of light, thousands of memories flooded my mind. Hundreds of lives coalesced into one object, ready to tell me anything and everything I would ever need to know. I could feel the lives and thoughts of people I had never met but somehow knew very intimately.

"Bloody Hell!" I yelled.

I let go of the sword and jumped to my feet. It landed on the velvet bedding it was previously resting upon, settling back into place.

"What is it!?" said Marie, startled by my sudden movement and yelling.

"I know what I need to do! The letter was right," I said.

"What letter? It is blank!" she yelped.

"I just needed to pick it up! I need to find him!"

"Find who, honey? What are you saying? You're not making any sense." She shrank as she spoke, eyebrows furrowing with fright as she pulled the linen closer to herself.

"Don't be worried Marie, I know what I need to do!"

I reached down and gripped the sword before jumping to my feet. I knew I was already running out of time. The clock was ticking, and he was already behind by a thousand or so years. I needed to find the current relative of Arthur's bard to understand what to do next.

Before I got too far, I realized I couldn't show up to the church without clothes. I went back into the bedroom and grabbed some trousers, a white button-up shirt and my jacket. My need to keep up a decent appearance urged me to check in the mirror as well for a second or two. I ran my fingers through my black hair, which seemed to be getting lighter over time, to make sure it sat well on my head. But alas, it was to no avail, so I gave up in my endeavor. My mustache seemed to be growing well, so I decided to leave it alone except for curling the ends upward. I then threw on my shoes and hat as I ran out the door.

"Davey?" Marie called out to me again.

I was already too far away to respond.

I ran down the streets, cutting through large crowds of morning workers. They were clumped together like a swarm of gnats after a fresh spring rain, coalescing en masse. I checked my grip on the scabbard of the sword, wanting to make sure she was still there even though I could still feel her between my fingers.

I jumped out of the way of horses pulling carts, carrying anything from manure to freshly made coffins on their way to meet their new owners for years to come. I skirted past corner bakeries that had fresh meat pies and loaves of bread baking in the thick morning smog. Immediately after the wonderful smells of food, my senses were assaulted by the stench of raw sewage. It seeped from burst plumbing lines mixing with the aroma of rotting food in piles that lay under the windowsills of second-story houses. I could almost see the walls bowing outward from being cramped with as many family members as the number of sardines you could fit packed into a can.

I could hear the constant humming and crackling of the coil substations spread throughout the east end. Busy, loud chatter from young homeless kids in the streets begging for money to buy food also filled my ears. I tried to shake all of this from my mind because I knew I had to get to St. Bart's soon so I could learn more. It was unclear to me as to why the urgency took over for my common sense, but it was not something I could control at the moment. I just couldn't shake the feeling of imminent despair and hopelessness that came with the thousands of memories now floating in my consciousness.

Farringdon Borough, London, England
1:00 p.m.

I was relieved to finally have made it to the church as I ran up the walkway to the front door. I glanced at my pocket watch as I ascended, hands stretched across its face as it read 1:00 in the afternoon.

On either side of the sidewalk loomed three wireless lamp posts made of wrought iron. The weathered oil lamp heads were converted to new *Wavenergy* not long ago, bulbs pulsing with incandescence. The first and second lampposts stood guard around a stoic granite bench about one yard long as the other was right next to the door itself. I knocked on the heavy wooden doors, waiting a minute or two and tried again.

An older man answered the door, metal squealing as he did. He looked me up and down before asking, "What's your business here today, young man?"

"I need to see someone. You'll never believe me, but I just need to see someone in particular." I chuckled, shaking my head. "I don't know his name but he was related to someone named Taliesin; I don't know his last name. I know it's a long shot, and it sounds crazy. But I need his help."

I grimaced as the clergyman looked at me with what I could only imagine as pity. I must have sounded like a crazy person.

"My son, why don't you come in and take a seat. I'm not quite sure what you're on about, but I think Father Hubert may be able to help," smiled the clergyman.

"Alright," I said.

I followed him inside through the large double doors. As I crossed the threshold into the front hall, I looked up and around to take in the church. The towering archways were accented by secondary archways, flowing above to protect the captivating windows which let in the radiant afternoon light. The church's nave was lined with chairs all along either side leading to the altar. I gazed at the cross on which Jesus was hung, wondering if this type of situation had happened before. If Jesus himself had seen this kind of event unfold. The clergyman led me to the rows of chairs that lined the left side of the nave and asked me to have a seat.

"Let me fetch Father Hubert for you. I believe he is around here somewhere. He will be able to help," the clergyman said, smiling.

I looked down at the chairs, picking one on the end of the front row. Still grasping the sword in my right hand, I realized I had forgotten I was still carrying it. It was so light, and my mind was in other places so it probably just seemed that way.

I must have looked like a loon running around holding this. I'm going to have to find a way to keep this strapped to me instead of carrying it around.

I heard a shuffle of shoes coming from the right and looked up at a slightly older man. He had well-kept hair, combed back and starting to gray while his face was clean-shaven except for a small mustache and goatee. His robes were well-fitting and pressed, giving off the impression he took pride in his appearance.

He certainly is well dressed for being a priest.

"Hello young man, I am Father Hubert Jaschob. How may I be of assistance?"

As he spoke, I looked straight into his eyes; they seemed very familiar. It was odd. I couldn't put my finger on it. It felt as if I had met him, or maybe someone from the many memories he may have been related to a long time ago.

"Hello, my name is David. But most people call me Davey. This is going to sound really absurd, very looney, but I feel there is no one else to talk to. Last night I came into possession of a trunk from a farmer." Rubbing my neck, I continued. "Inside the trunk was a letter saying I needed to come here and find a relative of someone named Taileisen."

He clicked his tongue and let out a slight chuckle. "Well, Davey, it actually is a little more believable than you might think. To be blunt, I am the one you seek."

"Really?" I asked.

"I am related to Taileisen," he said, taking a seat. "You see Davey, my family has worked here for over six hundred years. My father, and my father's father, and very many before him, have been protecting a secret, waiting for the right person to find their way here."

I was dumbfounded. It was all true. All of it. I didn't believe it at first. I mean, I know that I touched a magic sword and saw memories of past relatives, but I assumed it was all rubbish.

He continued, "When I was a child, my father was a clergyman devoting his life to serving God as well as Ordo Aequitatis. The Ordo was created by none other than King Arthur. For many years Arthur and his knights kept the order in the kingdom until evil arrived. He was known as Jakobus the Reaper, an evil sorcerer. In the aftermath, the knights of the round table failed to defeat Jakobus before he disappeared."

"Is the order still around? Do they still go by Ordo Aequitatis?" I asked.

"Yes, it is still around. But now, the order is simply referred to as The Keepers. After The Keepers were formed, they continued to hunt down Jakobus but to no avail. Eventually, the knights began to age, and King Arthur became too old to continue on the mission, so Merlin came to them with a solution."

"What was that?"

"Eventually after trial and error they found a solution, enchant thirteen items that the knights hold dear. In turn, they would pass them on to later generations to find when Jakobus returns to wreak havoc and mayhem on the world."

This all seemed like rubbish, just like what the old man said to me.

"What happened to all the knights then? Or at least their relatives?" I asked.

"In the centuries since its creation, many of the order's lineage have been lost to time. In the last hundred years, the order has been trying to track down the current generation of The Keepers to train and prepare them for the time when evil returns."

I sat for a second, thinking, taking in all of the implications of this revelation, the possibilities of all the things I thought I knew about this world. At this point, I realized I was looking down at the sword, now in the palms of my hands. I looked around at the lamps letting off a golden glow, bathing things in a light that seemed to make everything come to life.

Noticing Hubert taking a seat next to me, I looked over at him and said, "What do I do next? Why did this sword show me everything?"

"See Davey, the time has come. Jakobus has returned. That was one of the effects of enchanting the items. It only activates when he returns." I kept my eyes on the sword in my hands as he continued. "By the looks of it, you seem to understand what's going on. In fact, it's very interesting that Excalibur found its way to you. That's a very good thing; you are an important person."

"I'm skeptical. Am I really related to King Arthur? I mean, I am unsure of the whole thing, but I never thought my family was part of something that important," I said with a shrug.

"Well, I assure you it's all true. Since my father passed the torch down to me, I have been helping search for all the descendants. You see, the sad thing is, we do not know where they are. Most of the lineages, sometimes called legacies, have run away to be free of their destiny, or they just gave up."

"Well, who is left? Where are they?" I asked.

Father Hubert clicked his tongue once more. He looked down at the floor of the church, worn and familiar. Then he gazed at the crucifix, looked back at me and said, "That's the thing. We haven't had much luck in a while. It's actually a difficult thing to do when they don't even know who they are."

"Then how do you do it?"

"We have a few methods of detecting them, so to say. But it's definitely not foolproof. One such way is a ring bestowed upon my family by Merlin; it glows when near others of the round table lineage. Some descendants that have used it said it holds some memories, much like that sword of yours and other artifacts. The other way is that we have noticed most of them have some sort of birthmark that looks like a scar from a cut on the palm of their right hand." Putting his chin in between his pointer finger and thumb, he said, "We actually do have a lead on one person in particular, though."

"What's his name then?" I asked.

"To be honest, we don't have a last name. But, there were reports of someone by the name of Steven having a scar of that description. Many years ago, I had the privilege of knowing another descendent by the name of Frederick. He was part of another family that lived here at the church. Both groups of people, me included, carried on the memory of all that happened all those years ago. Eventually, he grew up and moved on."

"Moved on to where?"

"He left his family and this life behind about five years ago." He paused and stroked his chin. "Yes, five years ago, I received a letter from Frederick after not speaking with him for some time. It was instructions to give a letter to his son. Frederick's son took his mother's maiden name when he left the family, so that's why we have been unable to contact him. From what we do know, he works for TEA. We think his job is in the maintenance division."

"I've heard of the company. I actually work for them as a Sparker. Late nights and early mornings are how I live. They call the coil repairmen Buzzers on account of the coils making a buzzing noise all the time. They are most definitely a strange lot. I wouldn't want to work on those bloody things; dangerous they are. I know a few from the job. I might have to ask around."

"I believe that's where we should start then: checking with TEA," he said.

I nodded and was about to turn to leave before he spoke once more.

"A word of warning for you as well, young man."

I stopped and turned to him. "What sir?"

"Jakobus does have certain people at his disposal to use freely. We currently know very little of this group."

"What do you know then?"

"We know that they are growing in size and go by the name of Harvesters. The reasoning for that particular moniker is because they select and procure the correct people and objects for The Reaper himself," Father Hubert said, shuddering at the thought. He tried to snap out of his trance and smiled. "We've been waiting for you, so without further ado, welcome to The Keepers!"

Chapter 4
What Comes Next

2nd April, 1888
Spitalfields Borough, London, England
10:00 p.m.

The afternoon's revelations swam around in my head like a dark, heavy rain front, ready to wash away the sins of the past. It overcast me and my thoughts; dark, brooding and overwhelming. I was quite unsure about the whole mess, and it seemed like a story out of children's folklore. But, it was more like the original versions of the stories, before the watered-down, palatable ones we tell now. The dangerous ones, which include dragons breathing fire and roasting the champions. Or the ones that tell of flowing rivers of blood, and children walking to their toasted and well-done death. I got the feeling that whether I wanted to or not, this was my story now, and it was my decision how it ended.

I shook my head and kept my balance as I stood above the ground on the wooden rung of the creaking ladder. I reached back to the sword to feel it was still there. I knew it was; I could feel it was, but it was more of a reassurance that I hadn't gone completely bonkers. One could say it was a nervous tick that I felt I would have for a long time.

Since getting Excalibur the day prior, I was no longer just carrying it around in my hands like a loon. Marie fashioned me a sling for the scabbard, so, once in a while, I had to check if I still had it. Realizing it was still safely strapped to my back, I started back to work.

The sun had been set for about an hour, creating a foggy haze that seemed to trap in the orange and red light lurking in between the streets and alleyways. I was almost done with my last couple of streets and started to climb down off my ladder to continue with my night. My foot was on the last rung of the ladder when I heard a man talk behind me.

"Oi, what's all this then?"

I turned to see a constable holding up a Cynder Box towards my face. It was bright and yellow, piercing through the darkness that settled into the evening.

"What's going on here, young man? Up to no good?" demanded the constable.

I covered my eyes with my hand to block the blinding light and tried to climb down the ladder just by touch. I would like to think I did a good job at it, but sadly, I would be lying.

"Nothing, sir, just doing me job. Just turning on the lights for the safety of the public," I said.

The constable held the light in my eyes for a moment longer before lowering it. As my eyes adjusted to the now darker surroundings, I heard him give a hearty laugh. "It's just me, lad! How have you been? Staying busy?"

"Bloody hell Jules, you scared me! Why didn't you just tell me it was you?" I said.

"Well Davey, where would be the fun in that?" said Constable Jules, smiling.

"What are you doing out here at this time?"

"My beat was switched to the afternoon. It's nice to see a familiar face, though."

"Yeah, if you didn't scare me like that, I would probably like it too."

"I wanted to give you a nice scare; helps you live longer." He paused before speaking again. "See any trouble so far tonight?"

I looked up and down the streets, checking for visible acts of vagrancy or any foul play that needed to be broken up. I was currently at the intersection of Hanbury Street and Brick Lane, finishing up this part of Whitechapel for my shift. I turned to look at Constable Jules and said, "Not that I can recall. But then again, isn't that the point? You aren't really a good criminal if you get caught up to no good."

"I suppose you're right, young man. So you say you're just about done for the night?" he said, shifting the Cynder Box from his left hand to right.

"I only have a few streets left; what about you, constable?"

"I'm done in about an hour. Want to meet up at the pub to get a pint tonight?" Jules asked.

I tossed the idea around in my head for a second or so. "Sure, we can meet up at The Ten Bells. Does that work for you?" I asked.

"Certainly does, but only a pint or two. Be needing to be up early tomorrow for my usual beat," said Constable Jules.

"Alright, sir, meet you there in an hour or so?" I asked, leaning over to grab my ladder from the lamppost.

God only knows I need a drink right now with everything that's going on.

"That would be grand, but please keep an eye out?" asked Jules.

I cocked an eyebrow. "I can. For what though, may I ask?"

"Some nights ago, there was an attack on a woman not far from here. She was killed, throat slit from ear to ear. If you see anything along those lines, let me know," he said.

I nodded in agreement.

Someone was murdered a few days ago? How is this the first I am hearing of it?

"One more thing. Why do you have a bloody sword on your back, lad?"

Feeling a little nervous at his question, I struggled to find an excuse. "It's just a new thing that the Sparkers are trying, don't worry about it.

Constable Jules paused before nodding his head once, curiosity brewing as he thought. He then smiled as he tipped his hat as he turned to depart. I heard his voice echo off of the empty walls of the vacant streets, "Will do Davey, keep up the good work shining light on the great streets of London!"

When he got about ten feet away, a familiar tune drifted back in my direction, bringing back memories of my childhood. The melody was slow and sweet but not without a hint of deviousness.

3rd April 1888
Whitechapel Borough
1:25 a.m.

"Now you see, the reason you knock on the watermelon is to see how ripe it is," slurred Jules. He leaned over the well-worn bar top, knowing it had more memories and pain than the years we'd been alive.

Looking off into space, I could barely feel the buzz of the ale in my system. I had too much on my mind to enjoy this time of good cheer and merry gatherings. There was too much to focus on and at stake not to worry about it every waking moment. It had been four hours, and I didn't plan on being here this long. I originally wanted to go back to the TEA depot to talk to my supervisors about the coil technicians, and find anything about anyone named Steven. But then, 'Mr. Ripe Watermelon' here wanted to have a few too many 'just one more' as we sat there. I looked over at Jules and saw his face was hovering off the bar top by about eight centimeters. I shook my head in frustration.

"I think you've had enough there, Constable. You're a little up the pole. Time to go home, don't you think?"

Jules looked in my general direction and let out a bit of a sigh while blowing raspberries, spit speckling my face. "I suppose you're right there lad, help me up, would you?"

Getting up, I straightened my clothes a little and leaned over towards Jules to help him up. I reached for his arm and pulled it to stretch it over my shoulders. The pub door busted open in a cacophony of noises that confused my senses, causing me to sway on my feet.

"Help! Is there a bobby here?" yelled the gentleman. "We need help! There was a mugging some blocks away!"

"Imma constatable. We're in trouble?" slurred Jules, lifting his head in confusion.

"You're a constable? Is there any other bobby here?" The gentleman said as he looked at Jules. "He's half-rats. He can't help. He can't even stand up!"

I looked at the man before turning back to Jules, then at the man once more. "I can help. I am a night watchman."

I'm a constable too, but I can't blow my cover just to help, so my role of a night watchman will have to do.

The man gave a sigh of frustration and shouted, "I don't care what you are, we just need some help! A lady was mugged, and she's needin' some help!"

I scrambled to help Jules back onto the stool, but he slumped over the bar top before I even let go of his arms. My body spun on its own accord as I rushed towards the man, motioning to show the way. I quickly felt my back for the scabbard to make sure she was still there.

There's that damned tick.

We both started to pant as we ran down the cobblestone streets. I took in a few large breaths of air and exhaled before I attempted to speak. "Where did this happen? Do you know who's all involved?"

The man was gasping for breath, choking down lungfuls of thick smog-tainted air. He coughed out, "It's just a few blocks down this way, there's a lady that looks like she be injured."

I have to decide if I think he's involved or not. Best to keep my guard up.

"How did you find her?"

"I was walking home from me shift and I came along these ruffians messing with the lass. I ran them off, but I think she's pretty banged up."

I tried picking up my speed to make it to the lady in time. The longer it took, the more worried I became that she would be too far gone to save. I reached around to the sword to hold on to it on my back while we ran. It bounced around and threw me off balance from the quick pace and tight turns. The street lamps lit up the doors and the alleyways that flew by with each new step. I glanced back to my side and asked the man, "Are we getting close?"

"We be only one house away, she's right up h–?!" exclaimed the man.

The man stopped without much in the way of a heads up in front of me. In turn, it caused me to hastily skid to a halt as we rounded the corner. I looked up and saw we were at the intersection where Osborn Street crossed Wentworth Street, narrowing into the depths of Brick Lane. I then checked the ground for the woman.

"There's nobody here?!" I yelled aloud.

There was no sign of the women anywhere on the cobblestone. I took a few more steps and felt my foot slap down into something. It was a sticky wet sound, sickening to the stomach. Taking a closer look, I reached into my jacket pocket and wrapped my hand around the Embyr. The handheld copper encased incandescent bulb felt cool to the touch. Even if its primary use was by Sparkers and Buzzers when they worked. It did the trick in a pinch. The version of the device I had was the original, but other iterations of the device have shown up for use by other TEA employees.

Pulling it out of my pocket, it started the grounding process that allowed it to illuminate and shed light in the darker area of the street. It had lit up the ground around us a little more than I suspected it would, allowing us to see everything.

A very large puddle of blood lay beneath my feet, miniature waves rippling back and forth as it bounced off my sole and the edge of its reach. It was accompanied by some other liquid that reeked of ammonia. I didn't need to guess to know what it was from. We could all but assume what it was.

I turned towards the man and asked, "You said she was here? How long ago was this?"

He looked down at the splotches, then back at me, "T'was just but five minutes ago. I came across the rapscallions and drove them off before I turned back around and saw the missy just laying there in pain. I told her to just hold on, and I would go get help."

I kneeled back down, moving my Embyr a little closer to the ground to look at the blood. As I did this, I noticed it trailed off south down Osborn street. I stood up and shuddered as a chill ran through me. It wasn't one from cold weather but one born from a situation that seemed like it wasn't actually real.

I looked back at the man. "I think she may have gotten up and made her way this way."

I pointed down at the faint trail of blood speckles that trailed in the opposite direction from which we came. I started down the cobblestones and motioned for him to follow me. My sword shifted and rattled as I jogged lightly.

I glanced in his direction as we continued in our search. "What's your name anyway? I never got one from you. I'm David. You can call me Davey for short though."

He looked over at me and grimaced. "Me names Steven Ledger. Steven for short. Nice to meet you, but why do you go by Davey and not David?"

"I got the nickname from my old friends in the 21st Regiment of Hussars. They called me Davey because I reminded them of Davy Crockett from the States."

"How's that?"

"They said I am the last great frontiersman of Britain, and well, I guess it just stuck."

I paused as the realization hit me. I was dumbfounded even.

Out of anyone I could have possibly met today, there was no way this was the Steven I was looking for.

I lifted my Embyr up to see his face somewhat better than I could before. With the added light, I could make out him having inky black, shoulder-length hair. There was a little bit of scruff on his neck and face but he had a well-defined and bushy handlebar mustache that stretched across his face. His facial hair was dark black, not soot-black, but perhaps a charcoal color compared to the rest of his hair. A black top hat sat on his head and he wore a tweed sack coat with off-color tweed waistcoat. Underneath all of that, he wore a white collared shirt with black trousers and brown spats.

I asked him, "By chance did you say what you do for a job?"

"One, get that blasted thing out of me face. And two, why does it matter what I do for a job? Shouldn't we be more worried about the lady?" he asked.

"Please, I'm just curious."

"I'm a Buzzer. I work on the Whitechapel area substations. If you need to know," said Steven as he started back down the street.

The light of my Embyr's glowing embrace slowly receded its protection, and the unsure embrace of the street lamps took over. I stood there for another five seconds or so, just thinking of how odd this was. Shaking my head, I started off down the road after Steven. "Hey, wait up! I'm coming!"

I caught up to him a few blocks down as he turned right onto Whitechapel High Street. We passed a few people huddled in doorways as they muttered sour somethings and some horse-drawn carriages that rattled on the uneven cobblestone. We both tried asking all alike if they saw an injured woman come this way. To our dismay, none had seen anything of the sort, not that they would have been paying attention anyway.

The trail of blood went down another block and veered to the left onto Leman Street. We followed it about three blocks down the street, eventually losing track of it completely. Stopping for a moment, I crouched and leaned over my knees and placed my Embyr in my left side pocket. I then reached into my jacket to pull out my pocket watch from my waistcoat. The springs creaked as I popped open the brass timepiece and looked at the time. The second hand chugged along like the little engine that could as the other two revealed it was three-thirty in the morning.

Where did the time go? Wasn't it just twenty minutes ago I was back at the pub with Jules talking about ripe fruit?

I glanced over at Steven and asked, "Do you think we lost her?"

"I'm not so sure we did, I think we just have to keep moving. We might happen upon the trail once more. But then again, we have been wandering around now for an hour just looking for drops of blood that may or may not be the lady's," he said, voice sounding strained.

We turned back towards the south, noticing we were near the railyard and the Leman Street Station. Looking at each other, we both nodded our heads and started off towards the station.

"Let's go check there, I suppose."

As we got closer to the railyard, the air felt as if it was as thick as water. It clawed its way down to our lungs, expanding to prevent deeper breaths as we struggled to breathe. Surprisingly, there were more people up this early in the morning than I thought would be, going to and fro waiting to take the trolley to their jobs. As we walked up the steps to the platform, I glanced at Steven and murmured to him, "You think she may have come this way?"

He looked around at the people waiting for the next trolley.

"Maybe. We can ask a few people and see what they say," I said.

I spent the next thirteen minutes asking around, trying to learn what we could. Steven didn't have to help but he did, and I was thankful. It was mostly men coming home from late night to early morning shifts and some vagrants begging for help, not sympathy. We soon realized that no one had seen a thing, and we were wasting our time. After that, we decided to look on foot again, departing the platform back to the dark streets.

"I think we may have lost her." I paused. "We probably won't find anything tonight. Maybe we should go check the hospital?"

"I don't want to just give up. I said I would get help. I said I was going to be back." Steven's voice began to falter. He stopped abruptly and walked over to a bench, taking a seat. He took off his hat and put it on his lap, forming fists with his hands and squeezing them until they became as white as the snow.

I walked over to him and took a seat on his right side, the wood creaking from the added weight. To prevent my sword from catching on the bench, I adjusted it to my side to hang slightly off the edge. Since Father Hubert explained the whole mess to me, it had been odd. I felt as if I knew him in another lifetime, just like the father. Since I wasn't sure what would be best to say next, I decided to just start talking.

"My wife works the late shift at the hospital. We might get lucky, and she may have made it there. I can check with her in the morning."

Steven didn't say anything to my statement.

I took out my watch and ran my fingers over the engraved outer shell, feeling the design more than seeing it. I popped it open and chuckled. "More like I'll check with her in a couple hours from now."

The tension from the evening came to a head, feeling as if it would bubble over and scald us. Instead, it spilled over with the rain, starting to pour from the clouds. Steven let out a chuckle that turned to a hearty laugh. He turned and looked at me, offering his left hand and said, "I think we should do a little better of an introduction. My name's Steven, Steven Ledger."

Reaching my hand out to him, I glanced down at his hand. I noticed there was some scar tissue on his palm. "The names Davey, Davey O'Shea."

There is no way this isn't the right Steven. He must be the one I am looking for.

He looked at me, rain pouring down his face. "By the way, why do you have a bloody sword?"

"I'll have to tell you another time," I chuckled.

CHAPTER 5

Coincidence

They felt the sun beating down hard on their necks, unforgiving and unrelenting as they went on with their day. It left marks to remember it by: red and hot burns on any exposed skin. With each new step, the day progressed slowly, inching along like tiny larvae looking for somewhere safe to hide. Maybe with enough hope, like the larvae, it too could blossom into a beautiful butterfly.

"Gaheris, please. I need men like you," Arthur pleaded.

Gaheris turned, "No Arthur, I cannot. I need to stay here for her. I am the only man left of the house; I simply cannot leave my mother alone. I need to go home to protect her." He continued down the uneven path, worn from full carts pulled by strained horses.

"Gaheris, wait! Please! He won't stop! He will find you and make you suffer!" Arthur took off after Gaheris, trying to catch up. "At least let me see to it that you make it back home safely."

Walking still, Gaheris said, "Okay, but nothing will make me change my mind.

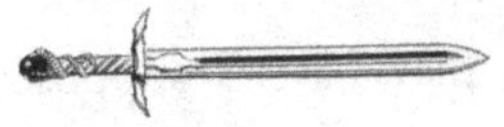

3rd April, 1888
Spitalfields Borough, London, England
11:43 a.m.

Opening my eyes, I took in lungfuls of air as I wondered why I was holding my breath. I looked around and realized I was in my bed, old and dingy but somehow twice as comfortable.

I wish these memories would tell me something useful. It was still jarring when I dreamt of someone else's life, or rather, remembered a memory that was not mine.

Lying on my side facing the bedroom door, I focused on Excalibur. It was leaning up against the armchair in the corner, somehow stoic even though it was an inanimate object. My gaze shifted to the sun that peeked through the window and reflected off the blade. The curtains flapping in the cool late morning wind broke through my trance and reminded me of everything else around me.

Marie slowly rolled over and rested her chin on my shoulder. Her caramel auburn hair tumbled down over my collarbone and onto my chest in rivers of flowing chocolate. I could hear her slow, relaxed breathing, giving me a sense of relaxation. She took a few more breaths and let out a yawn, making me follow suit.

I murmured out through a groggy state of mind, "When did you open the window? It's a little cold."

She shifted a little and let out a shallow sigh. Not one of concern or stress, but one of reflexes or pondering. Of thinking of the night prior and whatever every second brought. "I didn't. It was open when I got home not too long ago," she said. "I thought you did."

"I'm not sure. I may have. I suppose it doesn't matter so much," I said, clearing my throat. "How was your shift last night, Marie? Was it mostly quiet?"

Marie shifted slightly. "Last night was mostly uneventful, normal happenings. Mainly drunkards and pub fight victims."

I shifted myself and looked at her on my side.

She wrinkled her nose and pursed her lips. "Actually, one thing was odd, though. Early this morning, we had this strange lady come in, poor thing. She was quite banged up and injured."

I felt less tired at the mention of a woman coming into the hospital. I squirmed as I tried to sit up in bed, stretching at the same time. "What time did you say the lady came in last night?"

Marie began to sit up on the bed as well, hair slinking over her shoulders to fall gently on her chest and back. She held the linen to her chest to retain modesty, mostly because the curtains were still flapping in the wind. It caused the sheets to conform to her smooth skin, hugging her curves in the radiant morning light.

"Oh, maybe five or so?" she said, putting a finger to her lips. "It could have been four-thirty, though. Not quite sure. She was in bad condition."

All of the talking about the woman had woken me up enough to realize I should get moving. I stood up and went over to my armchair that sat in the corner. My mind drifted off with a wave of thought, swelling and pushing my consciousness further out to sea. I could hear Marie as she spoke, but it seemed very far off, muffled by the distance between the solid ground of grounded thoughts.

I have never really taken a second or two just to look at the chair I use oh so often. It had ornate claw feet, made of mahogany maybe, but I wasn't quite sure. The fabric was a dandelion yellow with a leaf and flower pattern that contrasted in a darker yellow color. It had a mother of pearl inlay along the backrest that continued through the arms. We had gotten it as a wedding gift from my mother when Marie and I got married.

I looked down, shook myself from my reverie and reached for my trousers. "What did she say happened? Was it one person? A group?"

"She was very incoherent. At one point, she had said her name was Emma Smith. She had lost a lot of blood. Everyone on staff had to come help stop her bleeding. I only just got home about four hours ago," Marie said.

As I listened to her speak, I grabbed my shirt, waistcoat, and pocket watch. After all of that was situated, I paused before opening the door and reached down to pick up Excalibur from the floor. Marie had gotten up from the cozy-looking bed and wrapped the linen around herself as she stood. She frowned and walked towards me with a concerned face, arms folded tight against her body.

"Where are you going? You left like this yesterday, and you never told me why you did that. What's going on, Davey?" asked Marie.

I had my hand on the door latch, "I have to go see the lady that came to the hospital. This man barged into the pub and needed help with a woman. He found her beaten and bloodied some ways from there." I shifted my weight a little, continuing, "When we got there, the woman was nowhere to be seen. It seems like too much of a coincidence to ignore it. But I need to check if it is her that came to the hospital."

I took my hand from the latch and walked back over to Marie. She grimaced as I leaned over to give her a peck on the cheek. I pulled away from her and smiled before making my way out of the house.

"Wha— Alright, I suppose. Please be safe then!" yelled Marie.

3rd April 1888
Shadwell Borough, London, England
12:35 p.m.

Shortly after making my way to The London Hospital, I entered through the front entrance to find the injured woman. I slowly weaved through sickened people wrapped head to toe in blankets and employees rushing back and forth trying to keep badly injured patients from getting worse. The halls were retrofitted with the brand new Tesla Bulbs, buzzing as they shed much-needed light on everything. The major differences between these bulbs and the inferior Edison ones are that they worked better with the Wavergy. It also may or may not have been because the filaments were in the shape of a lightning bolt; who knows. The hospital ran off of its own coil substation, so if the rest of the city lost power, they would not. They were located near the back of the building, just far enough away to not cause harm to someone who may get too close. The hospital had recently added a new wing to the advancement of galvanism and the use of electrical stimulation to cure fits of hysteria, among other things, in the attempt to stay up to date with the times.

I made my way to the hospital wing that held the critical condition patients while thinking of other things. As I came up to the room that supposedly held one Emma Smith, I decided to check in with a nurse to find out more info about the patient. I looked around and found the nurse near her station on that floor.

"Excuse me ma'am, could you tell me more about a patient by the name Emma Smith?" I asked.

The nurse put down the charts she had in her hands and looked at me. "Who wants to know? Are you a constable?" She leaned to glance over my shoulder with a somewhat bewildered look on her face. "And we don't allow weapons of any kind in here," she continued, clearing her throat. "Including swords."

"Yes ma'am, I do understand that. But this is not a sword, it's a– it's a big letter opener." I cleared my throat before continuing. "I'm just a concerned night watchman that was told of a vicious attack on a woman while working last night. I was brought to the scene of the crime, and upon arriving there, we realized she had taken off somewhere."

"Why do you care then?" she asked.

"Just looking out for her is all," I replied.

The nurse eyed me up and down for a moment incredulously. "Do you have any identification to prove this?"

"Yes ma'am," I said, reaching for my ID number badge.

Pulling out my dark brown leather bifold, I felt the well-worn outer shell before opening it. Inside was a lighter, brown stitching that held it all together, even after years of use and punishment. I lifted the flap to pull out my ID number card and removed it from the frail hide. I leaned in to show the nurse just as she leaned in to look. As she made sure I was telling the truth, I heard someone from behind talking about the coils located in the back of the building. After a moment, I realized I recognized the voice. I turned and saw Steven down the hall talking to the hospital maintenance men, and it sounded to me like he was yelling at them about something they potentially did wrong.

The nurse cleared her throat as she finished. I turned back to her and was greeted with an annoyed look on her face.

"Okay, looks like you check out. There was already a constable in there, though. He came by around an hour ago to ask a few questions about what happened," she said.

"Do you know if he is still here? Did you get a name when he came by?"

"Not sure. It's not my job to know where the police are. It's my job to help these poor souls."

I wonder which constable she is talking about. Whomever they are, I might want to get in touch with them to help figure out why this happened.

"Thanks ma'am. Which room is she in, by the way?"

The nurse had already looked back down at her notes, making marks here and there. Her focused eyes never moved from what she was doing, she said, "Bed number thirteen."

I tipped my head and said, "Thank you, I'll start there."

Turning away, I remembered that I had just heard what I thought was Steven down the hall. Looking in that direction, I saw he was still giving the maintenance men a piece of his mind.

"You're all a bunch of bloody idiots! Why did you try fixing it yourself? You should have just come and got one of us from TEA to fix it!"

The two maintenance men seemed to visibly rear back from the ferocity coming from Steven's shouting. One of them lifted a hand to say something, but Steven didn't give him enough time to say whatever it was he was going to say.

"Now I have to spend more time working on it! Did you know there are millions of volts coming from those machines? You could've fried yourself, or someone else for that matter!"

I thanked the nurse and walked toward him. "Steven! You should really take it easy on them. It's not their fault they don't know as much as you!"

He turned to look at me as I came walking up "Davey? You ugly son of a—"

"Alright that's enough there, Steven. What are you doing here today?" I asked.

"The staff of this somewhat fine health establishment felt the need to try and fix the Coil Substation they have attached to the back of this place themselves. Now I was called after the fact to come fix what they mucked up," he said as he turned to give the workers an angry look.

Trying to help spare them any more of Steven's wrath, I interrupted again. "It's actually quite a coincidence that you're here today. Me wife came home last night and said that a lady had been admitted. Someone that she reckoned was beat on a wee bit."

"Really?" asked Steven as he cocked an eyebrow. "By chance, did they get a name? Or where about this happened to her?"

"Yeah, I got the name Emma Smith. But she was very incoherent last night. She's apparently here still in this very hospital. I was heading that way right now if you want to come with."

Steven agreed to accompany me, but not before he chewed the workers out a little more. He grumbled as we started to the area she was kept in. As we walked down the hallway that led to her room, I felt a hand grab my shoulder. It was a tight grip that caused me to panic. Jumping in my boots, I swung around as I grasped the hilt of Excalibur. In a practiced motion that I was unfamiliar with, I drew the sword and pointed the tip at my attacker. As I did this, I realized it was just Jules.

"Bollocks!" I bellowed. "Why must you keep scaring me?! I could've cleaved your head straight off!"

"Well hello to you too, Davey. What are you doing here today? And–" he drew out the word and for about four seconds, trying to show his surprise, "Why do you have that sword again?"

Straightening, I sheathed the sword and exhaled slightly before I spoke. "We're here to talk with a patient that checked in last night, and I told you already, it's a new thing that we're trying out at TEA."

I glanced down at my feet to avoid further scrutiny after I finished speaking. After a moment, I looked at Jules once more.

Giving his eyes a subtle roll Jules asked, "You mean the lass that was mugged while we were at the pub? You went and helped in my place, didn't you?"

"I did. We searched for a few hours for her to no avail. We were actually hoping she would show up here today so we could ask her some questions about what happened to her," I said.

He rubbed at his chin. "I also have a slight recollection of something about a watermelon?"

"The watermelon doesn't matter."

"If you say so," he replied. "I was just in there talking to her myself."

I reached into my front pocket to check my watch for the time. Popping open the lid, I read it was 1:03 p.m. I looked back at Constable Jules and asked, "Were you able to get anything out of her?"

"Not much. Just a name, actually. Emma Smith. That's it though. She's right through those doors over there."

I followed his finger and looked where he was pointing.

"I will be back tomorrow to get more of a statement out of her. Let me know what you gentlemen find out." Jules paused before looking at Steven, "By the way, what's your name, young man?"

I glanced over at Steven as he began to talk.

"Me name's Steven Ledger. I actually met you last night, but you were half in the bag," he said in a matter of factly tone.

Jules clapped his hands together as he shrugged off Steven's sarcasm. "Well good luck, boys. Try not to get into any more trouble while you're at it."

He tipped his hat and started off down the hall. We turned towards the doors as I heard his footsteps echo off the walls. We pushed through the doors to see what we could find out for ourselves.

Upon entering the area with her sectioned off bed, we almost bumped into a man standing at its foot. He was wearing a plain, basic brown tweed waistcoat and brown trousers with a white linen dress shirt tucked into it with neat precision. The sleeves were rolled up to his elbows as he stood there holding the woman's charts.

What struck me as odd was the shoes because they seemed very out of place. They were as white as the ivory that was poached from an elephant.

I cleared my throat to get the man's attention.

It took a moment for us to get him to look our way as if he was lost in deep thought. When he turned to us, he held a clipboard in his hands, presumably Emma's charts. His eyes still focused on the sheets of paper, turning them over and over as if he kept doing it, all the words on its surface would just disappear.

Finally, he looked up to us and mumbled, "Oh, sorry. I didn't see you there. I was preoccupied with this." He reached out a hand to me saying, "My name is Dr. Henry."

I reached out to take his hand. "Hello, my name is David O'Shea. This is my friend Steven Ledger."

Steven tipped his hat slightly in a friendly gesture, face stretched in a mocking expression.

"We actually came by to check on the lady here, Emma Smith."

Dr. Henry broke eye contact with me, and I followed his gaze down at our hands. After a second or two longer, shaking, he let go and let his hand fall to his side. I then noticed he was clenching the charts in his left hand, papers shaking as his knuckles turned white. He then went completely still, as if he had turned to stone, like a victim of Medusa from Greek Mythology.

"Dr. Henry? Are you okay?" I asked.

Looking back up at me, he said, "Yes, I am fine. Sorry about that, I've been ill as of late. Not quite sure what it is. I apologize for that. Excuse me, I must be leaving."

Setting down the charts on the side table, Dr. Henry excused himself. He passed us and walked to exit through the double reinforced doors on the far left of the large room. Steven and I turned back towards his receding footsteps and looked at the immaculate white shoes. I felt my vision fade, shifting to a wash of gray.

Scrape, scrape

All I could sense was blackness. I could hear the wind howling as it reminded me of packs of stray dogs. Running and searching for something, food? The wind nipped as it flowed through my hair, my fingers and brushed against my skin. I could hear crashing sounds and thought it was water, maybe the ocean. I felt the heat of the sun radiate down from above, warming my skin and giving off a sense of security. I felt a hand rest on my shoulder, but I wasn't frightened by it. I just stood there, wondering what was happening and why I was there. I tried opening my eyes, but it seemed like I couldn't; there was just blackness.

Scrape, scrape

I shook my head and tried to focus on the here and now. My eyes shifted from where Dr. Henry was standing to Steven and the still form of Emma. Steven cocked an eyebrow before returning his gaze to her as well.

"Well, he was a bit odd to say the least. What do you think that was all about?" I asked.

"Not sure, definitely strange though," Steven replied.

I turned back towards Emma Smith and took a couple steps closer. Trying to stay somewhat quiet, I picked up her chart and started to read it.

The patient received a slash or tear atop the right ear as well as blunt trauma. She also received damage to the peritoneum. The extreme force used in her internally also caused some organs to rupture internally. It is believed that she did not try to solicit the men she claimed to assault her, nor was she under the influence of any kind at the time of the attack.

After reading the chart over for myself, I flipped between it and the x-ray attached to it. All thanks to Nikola Tesla's advancements in electricity, a man by the name of W.C. Röntgen was able to develop this life-altering technology to aid in the diagnosis of major trauma. I handed it to Steven so he could have a look for himself as I focused on Emma. I took a few more steps towards her and lightly put my hand on her shoulder, hoping that would stir her awake.

"Emma? Are you awake? Can you hear me?" I asked.

Seeing her eyelids flutter slightly, I gave her a gentle shake. Her eyes slowly opened as her left one did more than the right. It was like seeing someone take in their surroundings for the first time, like a newborn. Nothing around her looked like it made sense, everything disorienting.

"He– hello? Who are you?" Asked Emma.

Her question was groggy and laced with pain. I reached down for her hand with gentle fingers and grasped it. My hope was that it would help keep her focused on us, right here and now.

"Hello Emma, me names Davey. Are you feeling okay? Is there anything I can get you?"

She roused more. "I'm so thirsty. My mouth is so dry."

"Do you need some water? I can go get some," I said. I looked back at Steven. "Can you fetch me a glass of water?"

"I'll go get one," Steven said as he exited the room.

"Emma, while he gets some, can you answer a few questions for me?" I asked.

She nodded her head gently on the pillow, a small moan of pain escaping her lips. "I can try."

Before I could ask anything, I heard the floor creak behind me. I turned to see Steven walk back into the room carrying the glass of water I asked for. He handed it to me carefully, trying not to spill it.

I brought the water over to Emma and held it close to her lips. She shook as I tilted the glass slowly, not wanting her to cough from swallowing it too quickly. After she was done drinking about half of the water, I pulled it from her lips and placed it on the bedside table next to her head.

I gave her a moment to finish swallowing the last of it before asking anything else. "Can you tell us what happened last night? I know all this is a little much, but we need to know as much information as possible so we can help."

I could feel her hand tightening around mine, squeezing as tight as a noose. She went into another rough coughing fit that I feared would undo all the doctors had done for her. After a few seconds, the coughing died down, and she slowly turned her head in the direction of my voice.

She opened her eyes again with a little more focus and said, "I don't know what happened. I was walking home, minding me own business, when I started to hear whistling."

Her breath quickened, and I could see tears well up in her bruised and puffy eyes streaming down swollen red stained cheeks. I just kept holding her hand because that was all I could really do.

"I knew what the tune was, I've heard it before. Me mum used to whistle it when we were children. I just don't remember," she said.

Her eyes went distant as she began to hyperventilate. She sobbed as she tried to choke out the words that were trapped in her throat. It was as if a boa constrictor was wrapped tight around her neck, not giving in. Her lips tried to squeeze out the tune, but she gave up after a few notes, coughing more. I could somewhat recall the tune. The answer was stuck on the tip of my tongue, like a distant memory or lost thought.

I put my other hand on top of hers and said, "It's okay Emma, you hear me? It's all okay. We will find who did this. Please calm down a little. This isn't good for your current state of health. Can you do that for me?"

Her breath slowed slightly, shuddering like a steam engine skidding to a screeching halt. She tried lifting her arm to her face to wipe away the mess that started staining her face. I grabbed a towel from the bedside table and reached up to help wipe it away. The coarseness of the fabric sounded rough as it cleaned her face of tears, even as I tried to be careful.

She let out another shudder as she began to talk again. "I think it was more than one person. At least two. I could hear the footsteps echo on the alley walls and quicken on the cobblestones. I started to pick up my pace because I was getting scared. Then all of a sudden, I felt something hit the back of my head." Tears started to form again in her eyes. "I was on the ground before I could scream for help. They just kept kicking and punching. For a second or two, I got a look at them. Somewhat of a look at least."

"What did they look like?" I asked.

"One was very tall, and the other was large, I think. I blacked out for the worst of it. I just couldn't feel my body at some point. Like I was finally going to see mum again."

The tears really began to come this time. I could almost feel her regret and sorrow roll down in waves down her cheeks. I lowered my hand from her face and found hers again, squeezing to help her feel comfortable.

She looked at me once more and said, "I think I remember something else."

"What is it?"

"One of the men had on gray shoes. It was dark in the alley, but they were as gray as the soul of Satan. White enough to believe his lies, dark enough to know better."

I squeezed her hand some more before letting go.

She closed her eyes once more and mumbled, "They would not understand now any more than they understood then. I just wanted to live somehow."

I leaned in closer to make out what she had said. "What does that mean?"

She opened her eyes again and said, "Nothing. It was nothing. Something I told someone once." She looked over at Steven. "Do I know you? You look awfully familiar."

Steven stepped closer, still clutching her chart in his left hand. "You do ma'am. I was the one that drove off all the rapscallions. I tried to go get help, but upon my return, you weren't there." He looked over at me, then back at Emma. "I ran and got David over here to come help me take you to the hospital. We looked for hours trying to see where you had gone."

She gave out a little chuckle that turned into another coughing fit. It was rough sounding, like hail on a tin roof. After some time of it, she was able to regain her composure. "I don't even know how I got here. Last night was just one big nightmare. I can't think of anything else. Thank you, though, for trying to help me."

I went to dab her face again. "That's alright Emma. That should help us narrow it down. We will leave you alone for now. Please get some rest."

She had already closed her eyes by the time I said that. I watched her as she breathed in spasmodic motions, hoping there was more I could do for her. I eventually motioned to Steven that we should leave so she could get some much-needed rest.

As we walked through the double doors, Steven looked over to me and said, "Does any of that make sense to you?"

I shook my head and said, "I can't make heads or tails of it. How many people did you think were mugging her? Three? Four?"

"I am not sure, to be honest."

I shook my head, "I just wish she got a good look at their faces. Gray shoes and whistling doesn't really give us much to work off of."

"Yeah, I know."

"Do you know of anyone with gray shoes? We might need to go talk to a cordwainer. Maybe they could point us in the right direction."

Steven shrugged as he said, "I think we have more info now than we did fifteen minutes ago, so that's a plus."

I sighed as we walked, unconsciously counting my steps but not knowing the number I had counted to. "Do you remember anything from them? When you ran them off?"

He shrugged and said, "No, I don't. It was too dark for me to see anything, but then again, I was about twelve feet away when I yelled at them."

I shook my head, "Well, either way, there is someone I would like you to meet first. It might help us with the mystery we have on our hands."

Chapter 6
What Has Been Done

Arthur and Gaheris walked anxiously up to the door of the house. The long journey together had been trying and stressful as they talked of what was happening to the kingdom.

"Mother, I am home. Open up," said Gaheris as he hammered on the door impatiently with his fist.

A shrill scream came from beyond the door, cutting through the wood like it wasn't there. He tried the handle, but struggled as it wouldn't budge. Without hesitation, Gaheris started throwing himself at the door to break it down, to get through to help his mother. On the third hit, the door splintered and caved as he fell to the floor with a loud and heavy thud. Arthur rushed in behind him with Excalibur drawn, ready to slay whoever had caused this. He leaned down with his left hand and helped Gaheris up, pulling him to his feet with haste. When he reached his feat, he too pulled a sword and readied for a fight as he surveyed the scene.

"Mother! Are you okay?" he yelled.

The fireplace cast an evil glow, causing the surrounding room to shudder in their eyesight. Wooden chairs were strewn across the floor in all directions. An oak kitchen table was tipped on its side in front of them. There was a late afternoon meal wasted in the mess, rolls and stew inching further from the bowls and plates on the floor.

"Mother!" Gaheris yelled once more. He scanned the room, a look of despair and utter fright growing on his face with every second.

"Help! Gaheris!" his mother screamed.

He panicked as he tried to locate where she had called to him from. She let out a few more cries of help before it was followed by a blood-curdling gurgle. He took off sprinting to the bedroom, the tip of his sword pointing downwards with dread.

"Mother!" he cried as he crashed the door.

What lay on the other side was a horror he wasn't ready for. Something he would never be ready for. His mother lay in a lake of blood, rippling with waves of irreparable pain. Arthur barged in after him, glancing around to find whoever did this. Gaheris fell to his knees near his mother, sword dropping to the ground next to him. The blood began to stretch away from her body as it touched the pommel of his weapon.

With a heavy hand, Arthur squeezed Gaheris's shoulder. It was supposed to comfort him, but they both knew it wouldn't. Time stood still as the pain sunk in, like the blood that seeped into the floorboards.

Gaheris got to his feet as he grabbed his sword. The blood of his Mother stained his hand as his fingers curled around the hilt. His knuckles went white as he spoke. "I swear to you, Arthur, that I will give you my sword and my life to stop this inhuman demon."

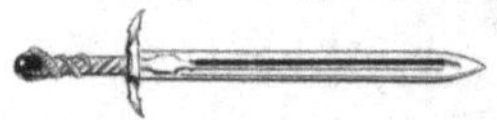

6th April, 1888
Spitalfields Borough, London, England
10:52 a.m.

"Davey, time to get up," a voice echoed in my dream. "The day is leaving without you," Marie whispered in my ear.

As I came to from my dream, I realized she was leaning against my back, her soft and warm skin comforting me. Groggily thinking of the things that the day held, I began to sit up. My eyes protested with frustration as I tried to pry them open.

"Do I really need to get up?" I mumbled.

Without waiting for her response, I started to pull the comforting and loving embrace of both the blanket and Marie's arm off of me. Swinging my feet off the side of the bed, I turned my head to look at Marie. "I suppose you're right." I sighed. "The last couple days have been exhausting. The nightmares keep coming."

I trailed off in my half-awake thoughts as my voice faded to more mumbling.

"What's been keeping you so busy, and what about these nightmares?" she asked as she rubbed my back.

I didn't respond immediately, which caused her to say something else to fill the silence.

"You should know that you haven't told me what it is that's keeping you so busy."

"I don't know where to start. Let me figure some things out first, okay?" I asked.

"I suppose. Should I be worried?" Marie asked.

She took her arm from my back and wrapped them around herself. From what I assumed was concern, she began to shake somewhat, looking small and fragile before my eyes. I reached over to her with my hands, motioning for her to come closer. Embracing her jolting body, I hugged her tightly in my arms. She rested her head in the crook of my neck and nuzzled it.

I whispered in her ear, "Don't you worry. It'll pass. Everything will be okay. I don't want you to be worried about what's been happening, so when I know more I will let you know. Okay?"

"O– Okay." She sniffled. Pulling away, she looked at me and said, "By the way, do you remember the lady named Emma Smith?"

"I do. what happened?"

Marie frowned as she spoke, "She passed away last night. The injuries were just too much to recover from. The internal bleeding never ceased, causing her to lose more blood than she could recuperate."

I sat there quietly and waited for her to finish as I processed the news.

"Whoever did that to her, well, they are just an animal. It was almost like the devil himself walked the streets that night looking for the next victim."

When she finished, my mind started to flood with thoughts and feelings, pushing the calm demeanor I tried to keep off the edge of the cliff. Fury and anger muscled their way to the front and center, ready to orchestrate my moves next, like a music conductor readying to play his last symphony, culminating his life's work that was filled with determination to finish it once and for all.

"I need to go Marie, I need to go see someone," I said in a low, angered tone.

Standing up, I grabbed my trousers and shirt, which were lying on the chair in the corner. Until this day, I never noticed the simple beauty of the chair. The dandelion yellow and the darker yellow floral pattern were more noticeable now than before, just like everything else around me. The mother of pearl inlay caught my eye in a new light. It was like the essence of purity, weaving down the backrest, and the legs, and to the claw feet.

I reached for Excalibur as I turned back to Marie. "I'll tell you soon enough, my love. Please let me know at once if someone else is brought in with similar injuries, alright?"

She nodded in agreement, still holding herself tight in the linen sheet. She called after me as I started out the door. "Please be careful! Whatever you've gotten yourself into, please be safe!"

Finsbury Borough, London, England
12:27 p.m.

I told Steven to meet me at the St. Bartholomew Church today so we could find out if he really was the Steven that The Keepers had been looking for. It took me a little longer than I expected, but I made it there in a decent amount of time. As I came up to the walkway in front of St. Bart's, I noticed the same wireless bulb lamp posts out of the corner of my eye. Even though it was midday, they still cast their bright faces over Steven's as he stood there. He was waiting between the first and second lamps on the rough and worn granite bench.

As I approached Steven, he hailed me with an out-stretched hand. A huge grin spanned his face from ear to ear. "Hey there, Davey, how are you today?

I stopped in front of him and shook his hand for a few seconds. With a grim expression slowly creeping over my face, I began to tell him what I learned that morning. "Well, me wife, Marie, gave me some bad news this morning."

Steven's smile began to falter. "What was the bad news?" As if knowing what I was about to say next, he said, "Please don't say that Emma Smith didn't make it."

Looking around, I tried thinking of a better way to tell him about her. Eventually, realizing that there wasn't one, I continued. "She didn't make it. The injuries weren't healing because they were too bad. I just wish there was more we could've done. I just don't know," I said.

I watched the trace amounts of snow flurries dance around in the wind, circling our heads and around the trees. They raced in and out of archways of the buildings, cushioned by air as they landed softly on shoulders and hats of the passersby.

"Well," I paused for a second or two. Waiting for something else to come to mind. Something to comfort him. Comfort me.

I wish we could have helped. That we would've been quicker last night. If only–.

My thought was interrupted by Steven's clear and calm voice. "That just means we need to find out who did this. Not just for Emma, but so it doesn't happen to anyone else again."

I nodded in agreement.

"What am I meeting you here for anyway?" he asked.

I was about to tell him why, or a form of it when he interrupted me.

"I've never actually been in a church before. I sort of didn't even know it was here, to be honest. Strange, right?" he said.

"I've only been here once, but it was under very strange circumstances. Me shifts as a Sparker have brought me close to the building, but never this close."

Steven nodded and started to talk more. "By the way, when I got done with me shift last night, I talked to my manager Jeoffrey about your sword since I was curious. He informed me that he has no idea why you are carrying one around. Are you going to tell me why?"

"Well," I smiled awkwardly. "It was a gift. I just haven't found the time to leave it at me house."

I really need to come up with something better than that. At least for now, that's the story I'm sticking to.

He shook his head and dismissed the inconsistencies for now. We turned to look at the heavy double wooden doors and decided to get this started. He followed me as we approached them, and upon entering, Steven looked around in awe. All around us were magnificent and plentiful archways that towered above us as they held up the ceiling. Spread throughout were the elegant stained glass windows that let in the flowing, calming light.

The last time I was here I hadn't actually given the windows a good look. Since there was a little less on my mind this time around, I observed the things they depicted. Some of them were wondrous scenes of men in suits of armor, while others were of the men riding horses carrying banners into battle to meet their foes head-on.

We walked down the aisle to stand in the warming embrace of the sun in the nave. The main stained glass window in the middle cast the most light on the ground. There were thirteen knights sitting around a circular table. All the men raised goblets to the air, proposing a toast of a hopeful victory over the wicked and fowl.

After a moment of us taking in all the splendor of the room, I felt a hand rest on my left shoulder. Turning, I saw that it was Father Hubert. I smiled and waited for him to talk.

"Hello Davey, what brings you here today?" he asked.

"We have a few things to catch up on and talk about." I paused and tapped Steven on the shoulder, queuing him to turn too. "This is Steven. I met him a few days ago."

Hubert raised his eyebrows as he spoke, "Really? That's interesting. Quite interesting."

Father Hubert glanced between the both of us before stopping on Steven. He stroked his beard as he cocked his head to the side. After a moment, he extended his hand to Steven. Steven took it, and they shook as Hubert looked him up and down.

"Hello Steven, my name is Father Hubert. I am a clergyman here at St. Bartholomew The Great. Nice to meet you."

"Nice to meet you too, I suppose," said Steven.

After they were done shaking, Hubert turned back to me. "Davey, how did you come to meet him?"

I glanced at Steven and said, "Well, it was the night when you and I first met. I was having a few pints with a friend at me local pub that I usually frequent, The Ten Bells. Without warning, this man bursts through the door yelling about a lady that was mugged, asking for a bobby."

Father Hubert continued stroking his beard as Steven shifted on his feet.

"The friend who was with me is a constable, but he wasn't able to go help her, so I took his place. Upon rushing to her aid, he informed me his name was Steven." I pointed to Steven with my thumb.

Hubert stopped fidgeting with his beard and began to pace in a small circle. "Did you check his hand?"

"I did see something that looked like a scar, but I thought you'd do the honors." I motioned to Steven. "Since you would know what to look for."

"Why would you need to see me hands?" asked Steven as he pursed his lips and cocked an eyebrow.

"There is just something we need to look for," said Father Hubert.

"It's okay," I said as I nodded.

"May I ?" Asked Hubert.

Steven was visibly weary from the question but obliged and put his hand out palm up.

Father Hubert took Steven's hand in his and turned it toward the light to see. I leaned in, and we could clearly see a scar running from one side of the palm to the other, right through the middle.

"Steven, How did you get this scar?" Father Hubert asked.

He shrugged, "I don't know, I've had it for as long as I can remember. Never really thought about it. I just assumed it was from an injury when I was young. Why do you ask?"

Father Hubert let go of Steven's hand and walked off towards an office in the back left corner of the church. While this happened, Steven took a seat in the chair nearest me. It was strange that there was a random chair in a church full of pews but who was I to question such things? We could hear clanging, shuffling, and drawers opening and closing. I assumed he was searching for something, but I wasn't quite sure what.

"Father Hubert? Do you need anything? What exactly are you looking for?" I yelled after him

A few more grunts came before he spoke. "No me boy, I found it."

He came walking back out to us with a small box in his hand. As he approached us, he opened up the brown leather box in his hands. Inside was a red velvet lining with a simple metal ring resting in its center.

Hubert took it out and slid it on his ring finger. He then reached out to Steven. "Shake my hand once more, please."

"Why? What's with the ring?" Steven asked, caution present in his voice.

"Please, my son, just take my hand."

Steven reluctantly took the Father's hand once more. As he did, the ring lit up in a magnificent golden glow.

"I've never actually seen it work before. Very interesting. It seems to only work on contact," he said, stroking his beard some more.

Steven pulled his hand from Hubert's and stared at it.

"I don't know why I didn't ask you before, but it probably is because we haven't had a legacy in quite some time. Davey, give me your hand so we can see what happens." He took my hand and the ring lit up in the same golden, heavenly glow. "Well, isn't that a sight to see? Almost beautiful."

"What's going on here? Why in the bloody hell is that ring glowing when we shake hands?" Steven asked, backing up. "And is anyone going to tell me what exactly is happening?"

"Steven, I'll just be blunt. You're related to a knight of the round table."

Steven shook his head, dumbfounded.

"As in King Arthur, husband to Guinevre and wielder of Excalibur. The ones who fought against evil and keepers of the light?"

"I know who he is," Steven choked out.

"The ring is a test. It only glows in the presence of legacies, descendants, or any way you want to call the relatives of the knights."

Steven's gaze shifted from Father Hubert to me. He laughed and started pacing back and forth in a line. "Are you sure? I mean, it doesn't make much sense."

"I know it doesn't, but trust me," said Hubert.

"Is there any more proof to help me believe?" he asked.

"The scar on the hand is another way to tell," I said.

His pace quickened as he started to shake his head back and forth.

"Oh, and that's not all. There is also an evil sorcerer that has come back to wreak havoc amongst the mortal world to destroy everything good." I raised a finger as I smirked. "And we have to stop him. But no pressure."

I laughed at the last part but stopped when I realized that it wouldn't help the situation much.

"Here, I have something that may be of assistance. I received a letter a while back, and I think it's safe to assume that your father's name was Fredrick?" Father Hubert asked as he looked at Steven.

Before he could get a word out, Hubert turned on his heels back to his office. We heard some rummaging once more and saw him emerge carrying something in his left hand. Father Hubert handed a worn light brown or tan letter to Steven.

He turned it around in his hands a few times looking at the large red wax seal. I saw that it consisted of a phoenix holding a spear in one talon and some arrows in the other. He peeled the wax from the thin paper by wedging his thumb between the two. It popped open, allowing him to unfold it to read to himself. His eyes scanned the letter, darting from left to right before returning to the top. He proceeded to read the letter aloud to the both of us:

> Dear Steven,
>
> I'm sorry about not being there for you, but I tried. By God, did I try in more ways than I'd ever want to tell. I know being a grave robber never amounted to anything and brought disgrace to our name, but alas, I was trying to find what was lost. Our family's artifact. When I was a young boy, my father told me of the magnificent King Arthur and The Knights of the Round Table. At first, they were stories of great triumph, but they soon changed to the perils they faced, including the dreadful Jakobus the Reaper. I hope that Hubert has found you and filled you in on all of this by now because I was not there to do so myself. But I fear that, if you're reading this, I never found what was lost. I have it narrowed down to a few graveyards left near the city's limit. You will have to find it for our family. I love you, son.
>
> Best of luck to you, Frederick

Steven fell to a seat next to me, hands at his sides as he processed what he learned from the letter. I stood up and walked between the two of them.

"It means we need to find the relic of your lineage." I motioned to the sword on my back. "Like this. It's actually the real deal. Excalibur."

I pulled it from the sheath, handing it to Steven so he could take a closer look. He looked up at it as I placed it into his hands. It shimmered and produced a few sparks before settling down.

I turned to Hubert and asked, "Father, do you know where the cemetery might be?"

He cocked an eyebrow and said, "There is one cemetery that I can think of that dates back at least five hundred years. It might be a good choice to start there. It's over on Gracechurch street."

I looked to Steven and asked, "Is there an area where more than a few of your relatives are buried?"

He shook his head and said, "Since I did not know my father, I was raised by me Mother. She did not speak of that side of my family, ever."

I grimaced and turned back to Hubert. "Can we get that ring from you? You never know who we might run into. We might get lucky and find someone else."

"Well, I suppose you can, it's just been sitting in my office for a long time."

He took off the ring and placed it in my hand. It lit up once more and stayed that way while I slid the ring onto my right hand. After a moment the light started to fade away before disappearing completely.

"Hmm that's interesting. Father, shake my hand."

He reached out and took my hand to shake. The ring lit up again in its mesmerizing golden glow. By now, Steven had looked back up at us, color in his face and life visible to the naked eye.

"I think that's so it's not always glowing when it's being transported."

"Quite interesting," said Hubert.

I looked over to Steven. "I guess the cemetery is were we will start."

He looked at me and raised an eyebrow.

"Steven, are you ready to know what the bloody hell is going on here?" I asked sarcastically with a smirk.

He nodded and stood up, determination twinkling in his eye. It seemed he was ready to finally understand what was happening.

"Oh, by the way, can I have my sword back?"

CHAPTER 7

Life After Death

6th April, 1888
Whitechapel Borough, London, England
3:17 p.m.

Field Notes Entry 1

It has been a full day since Marie gave me the news about the passing of Emma. I am trying to juggle the responsibilities of my three jobs and my new found role in the multi-generational crusade of good and evil, right and wrong. Both Steven and I are upset to hear the news, but he took it the hardest. He feels that he let her down by not being there; not being quick enough. But alas that's the story of all our lives, isn't it? Being too late at the right time.

IcheckedbackinwithCommissioner Warren at the station this morning to report on my investigation, which was going very slowly. Some time ago I was tasked with finding proof of any kind to show that Nikola Tesla's New company, TEA, isn't embezzling or stealing money. There are concerns from some of the members of parliament that he, or anyone close, is doing this. Another theory is that someone had bribed the governing body.

The reasons behind this investigation is mostly because of the haste in which he has garnered their support to outfit the entire greater London area with his wireless technology. So far I haven't found a hint of wrongdoing, no matter how hard I look.

But the thing is, the death of Emma concerns me more and more with every second that passes. It has gotten me thinking about how little people care for not only women, but children too. It is horrible that they must do such unspeakable things to make it by in life.

The commissioner agrees with me that I should look into the death somewhat, but keep it quiet and not let anyone know I am doing so. It is also on the condition that I keep looking for any wrongdoing in TEA at the same time. He, of all people, knows that prostitutes are thought to be the scum of the earth, and do not receive the same care as everyone else does.

It's time for me to pay my respects to Emma since I was unable to do anything other than bother her with questions when she was in pain. But, the other thing that comes to mind is that I should also check her body for clues. I will head off towards the hospital again, keeping all of this in mind.

There is going to be a council to decide what they think happened to her, whether it is something we need to fear more of or if it was a one-time occurrence. Regardless, I want to get to the deadhouse of the hospital first before the nurses or coroners interfere with it anymore.

Shadwell Borough, London, England
4:00 p.m.

I reached the hospital by foot in about twenty-five minutes. My TEA badge could get me into quite a few places, as well as the same amount of trouble, but it wouldn't get me into the mortuary. With this in consideration, I showed my police inspector's badge to gain admittance despite trying to keep a low profile. Up to this point, I was never needed in the mortuary, so the nurses at the front reception desk pointed me in the right direction. It took me a few tries to remember the directions they told me,, but it was down a few halls and through a few doorways.

On my way down, I nodded to a few people and tipped my hat to others. Most of the hallways on the main floors had the new Wavergy specific Tesla light bulbs that flickered with the delay of electricity. One problem that TEA was trying to solve was the further you were from the coil substations, the weaker the Wavergy was.

As I approached the staircase for the basement, the sources of light were still the old kerosene-style lamps. The flames danced off the walls as they cast weird shadows on the steps. I descended the staircase in the pulsing light as it changed its mind to shine the way for me or not. After getting to the reception area, I knocked on the desk to get someone's attention.

"Hello?" I yelled while looking around. "Anyone here?"

Looking in the room from behind the counter, I decided to walk back and check for signs of life. My mind was on autopilot as my body did things without me telling it to. I stumbled into the workspace, where I assumed they took care of the autopsies, and looked around for a minute or so. After a few moments that passed, I heard some noise behind me.

"What are you doing back here? This is a restricted area," said the voice.

Jumping, I instinctively reached for Excalibur as I turned. My body flowed to a readied stance, but I stopped myself before doing anything rash.

Standing in front of me was a woman of slight build, only standing at the height of about five feet. Her blazing red hair was pulled back in a tight bun that sat off-center in the back of her head. I could only assume this though, as I saw just the slightest outline of her hair on the right side of her head. She wore a modified version of doctor's clothing that was a mix of both men's and women's, crisp and white. Her face portrayed an annoyed sneer that softened for a moment when she let her face slip. It gave me the impression that it was more of a formality than an actual feeling.

"Oh, sorry, I was looking for the undertaker. I was told to find him back here. No one answered when I yelled a minute ago, so I decided to look around."

"*She* is back and *she* has a name. I am Dr. Penelope Thatcher, but you can call me Dr. Thatcher. I was busy preparing something. Why are you here?" She hissed. Before I could get a word out edgewise, she continued, "What's with the sword? We don't allow weapons in here."

I let go of the hilt and straightened my jacket. "So sorry, ma'am. I meant no disrespect. I am here about someone deceased."

She snorted and said, "Well this is the right place for that kind of thing. You will need to be a little more specific."

I cleared my throat and said, "Emma Smith."

"I can't let just anyone see a body."

"Oh, of course. One moment." I pulled out the leather case that held my police inspector's badge and flashed it to her. "I am here on official business to see what I can find out about her death, and if there are any clues or evidence left over to find who did this."

Dr. Thatcher scrutinized my Inspectors Badge for a moment or so before responding, "I suppose it checks out. You're in luck though. I'm just finishing up with my preliminary tests and observations."

She motioned to the linen-covered table in the back corner of the room. I turned and saw Tesla Bulbs hanging from the ceiling for a source of light, each from their own individual wire. Some were longer than others that provided beams of light that provided larger or smaller swaths of coverage equal to the length of the wires. They swung gently to and fro from a slight breeze running through the room, coming from a source unbeknownst to me. Even with the air circulating, I noticed the smells started to grow in strength. First, the sting of rubbing alcohol filled my nostrils. Then, lingering just below, was a sweet but bitter deceit of perfumes that acted as a candy coating to cover the sharp stench of death.

"This is Emma," said Dr. Thatcher as she reached for the top of the linen. Her fingers curled beneath the unnaturally white fabric and started to pull away to expose her face. "Let me go grab my notes and findings to better point out that I haven't missed anything."

Looking down at her, I reared from the jarring bluntness of it all. I've seen bodies, ones that you wouldn't recognize as human, but nothing hits you more than the death of the innocent. I had seen countless bodies of friends in Sudan during the Mahdist war, but it is completely different when it's a woman.

The time that has elapsed since her passing had made a world of difference in appearance. Her once brown and shining hair was now matted with fluids and dirt while her skin had taken on a milky transparency that seemed preternatural.

As I looked at her, I noticed that her hand was laying off the side of the table, swaying like the bulbs above my head. It was a haunting thing to see, especially if one hadn't known she was dead. Feeling like I could at least help her one last time, I reached down to put it back on the table and underneath the linen. As I took her hand in mine, the ring on my hand lit up in its golden glow. I tilted my head as I noticed that, oddly, it wasn't as vibrant, and the light was slowly fading to nothing.

I turned to see if Dr. Thatcher had seen what happened, fearing I would have to test my luck in another lie. To my relief, her back was still turned to me as it happened. I wiped my brow, turned back to Emma, and stood for a moment.

What does this mean? Was it a coincidence that she happened to be a legacy? This may change everything. It may be a clue in a completely different way from what I was expecting.

Still looking at Emma's hand in mine, I didn't notice Dr. Thatcher as she snuck up behind me. I tried to act as if she didn't startle me, but sadly, like many other things in my life, that was one thing I needed to get better at.

"What's the surprised look for? Aren't you used to this kind of thing?" She asked as she handed her notes to me.

"I– I am," I stammered as I tried to think of what to say. "I'm just not used to seeing the innocence as much, just disconcerting is all."

I took her notes and gazed down at them to look anywhere other than her scrutinizing stare. As I looked, I could tell they were quite detailed, like she thoroughly insisted. It listed a plethora of information like her time of death records, notes on marks found over her body, abrasions, tears and cuts.

"They really did a number on her, whoever it was. I was told it was by a group of people. Monsters, they are. Cowards too. Who would gang up on a helpless woman like that?" she asked, disgust prevalent in her tone.

"Yes, I quite agree with those sentiments. Since you seem to know more than what we've told the general public, who told you about the multiple people theory? I was under the impression that it was still secret since it's an ongoing investigation."

"The damage done to her pointed to more than one person. I had a hunch since I did the preliminary autopsy. But, it was a constable that confirmed my suspicions. His name was Jones? Julian? Jacob?" She trailed off for a minute as she tried to think of the correct name.

I thought for a minute myself, thinking if I knew anyone that worked for the police whose name starts with J. "Jules? Constable Jules?" I asked.

She snapped her fingers, "That's it. At least it really rings a bell."

I mulled that bit of information over as she spoke.

"He was here right away after she passed. Right as they brought her body down here. He was asking a lot of questions. Ones I didn't have answers to because I hadn't been able to perform anything yet. Why does everyone have questions? I'm so sick of questions." She started to mumble, getting quieter by the second.

"My apologies, Dr. Thatcher. I appreciate you taking the time for me so I'll let you get back to it then. I will just have to meet with Constable Jules and compare information. I'll be leaving you to it now, have a nice rest of your day? I said.

I started back out of the autopsy room to the front desk of her department, body moving without instruction as my thoughts raced each other.

I need to go see Father Hubert and talk to him about Emma. It just seems more and more coincidences are piling up, and I want to get to the bottom of it. But first, later tonight, Steven and I are going to check on the tip we received from his father's letter. We need to find his family's artifact so I have someone to talk to that will understand this God-awful mess.

I made it about a foot or so outside of the mortuary when someone struck my shoulder rather hard. Rearing from the unexpected impact, I turned to see who did it.

"Oi, what was that for?" I yelled, turning to confront them.

The man kept going down the hallway without skipping a beat.

"Hey! What's your issue, mate?" I yelled once more.

All I saw was an ivory white shoe rush around the corner.

"Ivory white shoes? Why is that– I feel like those are familiar, where have I–" I murmured aloud.

I tried to shake it off because I knew I had things to get to today. *What time is it, anyway?* I felt around for my pocket watch, fist going toward the pocket I normally kept it in, but it wasn't there. Alarmed, I felt around my other pockets too, patting them down relentlessly, just to be sure, but I quickly realized that my watch was nowhere to be found.

Where is my watch?

I looked back towards the direction the man had gone and squinted my eyes before giving chase.

"Oi! Wait up! You have me pocket watch!" I yelled, running after him.

Turning the corner, I saw that the hallways were beginning to fill with people in front of me. Doctors, nurses and patients slowly milled their way throughout the open doorways and passages to other sections of the hospital. It was thick like flies buzzing and writhing over freshly spoiled refuse. I pushed my way through the crowds of people, looking around frantically, hoping to see the shoes made of alabaster.

My hopes were lifted when I glimpsed one of the shoes sneaking out through the front doors of the building. I tried to scramble past everyone, but it seemed as if they appeared magically in my way. My body cut by them and launched itself through the doors to continue chasing the man.

At first, the sun blinded me as I struggled to get my bearings, so I looked to the left then to the right, unsure where he went. Luckily, I saw the nurse from some days prior walking towards me as she attempted to leave the building. I ran to her before she could get any further, choking out, "Ma'am! Did you see that man? That doctor?"

The lady looked startled and shrieked with confusion as she dropped her bag on the ground. "What? Who?"

"The man, the man with the white shoes!" I shouted.

What was his name again? Dr. Harry? Harvey? Henry! It was Dr. Henry.

"His name is Dr. Henry! Do you know him?!" I asked again.

"I don't know anyone by the name Dr. Henry." She said as she looked around frantically for someone to help.

With all of my incoherent screaming, accompanied by my sword I probably looked like some loon. But, in moments when time is important, the way you look doesn't quite matter.

"He was just through here. He just came out the—"

Just then, I saw a glimpse of the white shoes about fifteen feet or so to the left.

"Never mind, I see him!" I said to the lady, starting to run towards the man.

The icy cold air made it hard to take deep breaths. Each one I attempted sent sharp pains through my throat and lungs. Stumbling past an alleyway, I glanced down and saw something as I skidded past. I halted and backpedaled, seeing the white shoes at the very end about nine feet down.

I ran down yelling, "Hey! You took my watch!"

As I got closer, I heard someone whistling.

That damned whistling, why is it so familiar?

It continued down the alley and felt like the sound coming from all directions. I cupped my hands around my eyes to adjust to the darkness, trying to see better. As I reached the end of the alley, it felt as if the walls had closed around me. It was a dead-end and Dr. Henry was nowhere to be seen, almost like he had just vanished.

My eyes darted frantically around for a door, a window or anything for which he could have escaped through.

Nothing.

There was nowhere he could have gone. Knowing that caused my stomach to drop in my chest. I looked around to see if he could have dropped my watch as I pursued him. My false sense of hope made me think it could be under an old crumpled newspaper or kicked underneath a pile of garbage. I slowed my breath to relax and closed my eyes.

I'll find it. I just have to relax. Stay calm and keep looking.

I opened my eyes and took out my Embyr to aid in the search for my watch. The amber color flooded the alley as I looked near the walls and underneath piles of rotting food. I went as far as to kick over some masses made of God only knows what.

"Damn this!!! WHERE IS IT?!" I yelled aloud.

I stood in silence, and closed my eyes.

If I just stay quiet, I will hear it ticking.

Tick, tick, tick...

I heard it! But it was close.

I opened my eyes again and held my Embyr out in front of me to look around some more.

Tick, tick, tick...

The noise from my watch was loud; Too loud to be on the ground. I reached into the pocket it's usually kept in and pulled it out.

"But how? I checked there... I'm sure of it," I said aloud.

Did Dr. Henry actually run into me? Was it a dream, or did I imagine it? The nurse said she didn't see anyone run past her, and no one tried to stop him. Maybe this is all just a bad hallucination. I haven't been sleeping much, if any, since all this began.

I opened the pocket watch to check the time and read it was 4:12 in the afternoon,

I need to get back home and get some sleep before tonight. I don't need to hallucinate while we are out digging up graves. I already can't tell what's real and what isn't.

Chapter 8

Digging Deeper

Field Notes Entry 2

Yesterday, we made it to the church located near one of the graveyards Steven's dad hadn't checked yet. We were lucky enough to meet with one of the priests to talk about some of the permanent residents that reside there. During the conversation we had, we were informed that some of the graves dated back longer than eight hundred years. To make things easier, I showed him my badge, proving I work for the crown, and that I'm in the public works department of the TEA. A few of the upsides of working for TEA and being a Police Constable means easy access to the graveyards and more information from a multitude of people. After we finished talking, the priest gave us directions to the general area that houses the

> particularly older graves in the graveyard.

7th April, 1888
Nunhead Borough, London, England
11:24 a.m.

The chilled air of early spring bit its way under our sleeves and up our necks, strangling and clawing the warmth away from our skin and chilling us to our bones. We stayed warm by taking the walkways that wound in and around the graves. They collected built-up, leftover snow that hadn't fully melted in the slow thaw. I envied that they were shielded and protected by the markers and the vibrant trees that littered the small and isolated resting place.

As we came upon the small secluded area with five or six crumbling and decrepit headstones, we noticed one with most of the stone intact. Cut onto the front of the stone was an inscription that only showed minimal evidence of erosion from weather and time.

"I'm not sure what language it is. Do you know what it says?" I asked Steven.

Taking off my right glove, I reached into the side pocket of my wool overcoat. It was a motion I was now used to since it was the overcoat I wore during my days in the 21st Regiment of Hussars. Me wife insists that I get a new overcoat. This one may be worn, but it is still worthy of frequent use. Pulling out my Embyr, I held it close to the headstone so he and I could see the words better.

Looking closely for a second or two, Steven said, "I think it's Latin; *Imperfectum*. I haven't read anything in Latin since I was a wee boy. But I think it means something along the lines of *not yet finished*?"

I rubbed at my nose with the back of my hand, hoping the momentary motion would warm my nose icicle.

Steven's eyebrows furrowed for a moment before looking back at me. "What's not finished? What does it mean?"

"If I were a betting man, I'd say it's exactly what we are looking for. We can't do anything about it now though," I said as I stood up.

"I suppose you are right," Steven said.

"We will just be back later tonight when there are no prying eyes to watch us."

8th April, 1888
1:35 a.m.

The ground was surprisingly less dense than I expected, considering it was still only early April. With the late night turning to early morning, the wind caused some snow to blow around in whisps. If I knew one thing it was that we were having a weird spring so far; the weather hadn't warmed up as much as I would have liked.

"Steven, why couldn't your dad just leave something for you with a relative or in a lockbox somewhere? He's got us digging a grave in the middle of the night, in the cemetery. It's definitely not making it easy on us at all." I grunted as we both threw more dirt up over the edge.

"Me old man never did do anything the easy way. Obviously, he didn't believe in honest work either. Being a grave robber was a quick way to make money, but an even quicker way to get caught and sent to jail," strained Steven.

"That can't be the only thing you remember about him. There must be some good memories."

Steven shook his head. "That's about all I remember about him. He left when I was really young, so it feels like I never knew him. I would have never thought he had any sort of honor since I always thought he was just a run-of-the-mill thief. I would have never guessed he was just looking for the artifact of our family's lineage."

We both worked there for a couple more minutes, scooping up dirt and heaving it higher as we went further and further down. Above us, I put my Embyr on the telescopic copper grounding rod, which caused it to sway precariously in the light breeze. I tried to position it to lean over the ledge, hoping it would provide a source of light while keeping it out of the way of our digging. After a while, I noticed we had reached about six feet down, and with two people it had been progressing rather quickly.

"I still don't know if I believe you and that clergyman. You both seem crazy. I mean, King Arthur? That's the stuff of folklore. The things you tell the children for bedtime stories," exhaled Steven.

He pushed his shovel into the dirt as he slowly straightened his back. It popped and cracked like chestnuts at Christmas time as he wiped the sweat from his brow.

Following suit, I took off my hat and fanned my face somewhat. "I didn't believe it either, but for me, things have changed in a very short amount of time. Hopefully your ancestors left something in this grave to help us out, and convince you with what's going on."

Steven shrugged, then twisted from side to side to stretch his core. After he finished, we both grabbed our shovels and got back to work. The hole got deeper as we threw up more dirt, adding to the mountain above us.

Five minutes later, I felt something fall on my neck. Turning up to the light, I saw a silhouette in front of the Embyr.

"What in the —?" I grumbled. Yelling up to the figure, "Oi, you're blocking out the light."

On instinct, I reached back for Excalibur, ready to draw the sword and helplessly swing at the dirt. I paused and turned to Steven and whispered, "Do you know anyone that'd be here at this hour?"

"No I don't," he whispered back.

"Did you tell anyone we'd be here?"

"No, I didn't think to do that. But just stay calm; maybe it's just a watchman or a copper?"

Looking back towards the silhouette, I let go of the sword and cupped my hands around my eyes to see better. I cleared my throat and tried to talk in a calm, level voice. "How are you sir? We are here on official business. I know it doesn't look so, but I assure you, we are."

A couple more seconds passed in a deep-rooted and relatable agonizing silence. It seemed to make the surrounding walls of dirt feel more like our own graves rather than someone else's. Reaching back to Excalibur, I said one more time, "Who goes there?"

A big booming noise came from above our heads. I slowly realized it was a laugh as it gave us a semblance of relief. With that, I eventually put all the pieces together. "Constable Jules? Is that you?"

"How could you tell, my boy?" he yelled down.

He moved out from in front of the light so we could make out his face. In the confusion and worry, I noticed that hat had fallen from my head. I let go of Excalibur and dropped to my knees briefly to pick it up from the mud.

"Well, you seem to have a habit of showing up and trying to startle me. Quite often, I might add."

"What else is there to do? Besides, it's good for you, and it'll help you live longer." He chuckled.

"I suppose," I said as I shook my head. "Isn't this a little far off your normal beat tonight? You're usually more in town, are you not?"

"It is, and I usually am," said Constable Jules. "But alas, the station has been needing me to fill in other places lately. We are spread thin. People just don't want to be in this line of work anymore."

"I guess there is more to do with a killer on the loose," remarked Steven.

I elbowed Steven in the side as we watched Jules hike his pants up to climb down the ladder. He struggled at first as he felt for the first rung with his foot before finding his footing. When Jules reached the bottom of the ladder, he straightened himself as he smoothed down his jacket.

"Steven my boy, how have you been? It only seems like a few hours ago we just met!"

Steven tipped his hat and looked down at his dirt-caked clothing. He then glanced over at the mirrored image on me before talking. "Not all bad, I suppose. It's been a busy day since this morning."

Constable Jules noticed our dirty clothes, looking us up and down. A cold shiver ran down my spine as I started to feel light-headed. I struggled to fight it, but I had to lean over on my shovel as the world around me swirled into darkness.

Scrape, scrape

The world was dark once again. I could hear water.

I've been here. I've heard that water before and felt the same embrace of the sun's rays.

I tried to listen closer this time, taking in new smells and noises I didn't notice before. I could make out rustling from stalks of wheat. I mustn't have had shoes on; all I could feel was sand between my toes. The smell of salty, pungent musk from stagnant leftover seawater filled my nostrils, pooling in puddles on the gritty beach.

"David," said a voice to my left. I felt a hand rest on my shoulder. It was familiar, as if I knew who it belonged to. But it was just far enough out of reach in my mind for me to not remember its owner.

Scrape, scrape

"David?" said a voice to my left.

My eyes struggled to open. Eventually, I prevailed and turned to see a concerned Steven standing next to me. I realized he had put his hand on my shoulder, bracing me as I leaned and teetered over my shovel. I stared down at the mud and grit as I wondered about what I had seen.

Am I going crazy? This is the second time today I've seen this, or something like it for that matter. Is it a daydream or a day night-mare?

I looked at his hand before turning my wandering and unfo-cused gaze to his face.

"How long was I out for?" I asked.

Standing up, I took my hands off the shovel and rubbed my eyes with the heels of my palms. It was partly because it felt as if I hadn't opened them in years, but it was also to make sure they were still there.

"Out? I just looked at you a second or two ago then I looked away. The mud shifted next to me so I looked back, and you were slumped over the shovel. I said your name once or twice, and you looked up at me," said Steven. "What happened? Are you okay?"

I rubbed my eyes once more. I reached back once more to feel the hilt of Excalibur, checking if it was still there. "Yeah," I said, shaking my head and pulling my hand back away from the sword. "I'm okay. I just got a little lightheaded."

I should keep this a secret, especially from Jules. Steven, for that matter, still doesn't fully believe what's going on so it's a no for him as well. I don't know what they would think of all this, especially with something this ridiculous.

"You alright there, my boy? What is going on with you lately?" He questioned with a look of concern plastered across his face.

"I've been preoccupied the last couple of days. It's been a little rough, but I'll make it just fine," I responded. "Don't worry, I am fine. I'll have me wife Marie check me out later. Thank you for your concern."

Looking at me again, Jules continued. "Okay then. Anyway, back to business. What are you two doing here? Why are you at the bottom of a grave at two in the morning?"

He lifted his standard-issue Cynder Box back up to see our faces a little better. The light burned spots into my retinas, making me reel slightly from the brightness flashing back into my face. I looked at Steven to see if he had an explanation ready.

"Um... What are you doing here?" questioned Steven.

Elbowing him in the side, I received a yelp for my actions.

"What he means is, what brought you into the cemetery tonight besides just being stationed in the area for a beat to work?"

He chuckled and shook his head. "Any real policeman would see the light shining in the middle of the night. In fact, anyone could've seen this from the road."

We both shifted uncomfortably as Jules spoke, knowing he was right. I had thought we were being sneaky, but it was now obvious that we weren't.

He continued, saying, "But I will just trust you if it's really official business, since you're a night watchman and all. So I suppose I'll let it slide tonight. Try to be a little more discreet next time. You won't get anyone being as nosy."

Constable Jules started back up the ladder. He struggled as he climbed, shoes slipping from the wet mud on them.

"Maybe he should quit being so nosy," mumbled Steven.

I lifted an arm to elbow him, but he flinched as a response. That in itself was satisfying enough to make me realize he understood what I meant by the gesture.

Jules crested the top of the grave and leaned over as he spoke once more. "Stay out of trouble boys!"

I exchanged looks with Steven. "We need to get to the bottom of this. Pun intended."

He elbowed me in the side as a retort, and I agreed that it was, in fact, justified. Justified but completely worth it.

As we got back to work digging, it only took about four more minutes to uncover the casket. Staring down at it, all I wanted to do was try and pry off the cover. But I wanted to keep a little bit of respect for the deceased, so I waited. My eyes looked for a corner or edge that would work well to pry open. But as soon as I went to start at an uneven part, Steven brought down his shovel right on the center of the casket. It smashed the lid to small splinters and rather large, jagged chunks at our feet.

"Bloody hell, have you no decency? What is wrong with you?" I yelped in surprise.

"What? I'm the son of a grave robber," he said with an innocent look on his face.

I shook my head before we started pulling the slivers and fragments out by hand. We eventually made some headway in uncovering everything, like an archeologist wiping away millennia of dirt on a skeleton. The light that crept through from behind us illuminated more detail inside the casket. Centered near where the head of a body would lay, a small wooden trunk lay on the inside.

We exchanged glances before we both grabbed onto it and heaved it out. There wasn't much room left in the hole to open it, so we started climbing back up the ladder. Steven was in front, holding onto it with his right hand as I pulled up the rear lifting the back side of the trunk. The mud shifted under our weight and the feet of the ladder slid a little into the ground making us both yelp.

"Bollocks," we said in unison.

Regaining balance, we reached the top of the grave and placed the trunk on the ground next to the light cast by the Embyr. We both took a few heavy, long breaths as we recovered from the strain of lifting a trunk up a six-foot ladder.

I strained as I leaned over my knees, opening and closing my eyes as I tried to focus. After a moment of inhaling and exhaling, I took the Embyr off the telescopic grounding rod to bring it closer to the trunk's lid. The top was slightly worn and made of a dark brown wood, probably that of a walnut tree. The bronze hardware consisting of latches, hinges, clasps and handles had accumulated patina with years of oxidation. The main latch on the front that kept the trunk sealed looked very familiar.

"Steven, is that what I think it is?" I asked.

Leaning in closer, bathed in the incandescent glow cast by my Embyr, Steven said, "Is that a Phoenix? With a spear and arrows in its claws?"

I looked closer. "It could be a Golden Eagle? Holding some bread and some sticks?"

Steven elbowed me, making me grunt from the impact.

Rubbing my side, I finished, "But most likely, it's a Phoenix."

He glanced back at me and laughed. "Looks like we're on the right track."

Reaching to the latch, he flipped it open. Inside was a red velvet cushion that lined the walls and bottom of the trunk. On top of a raised bed of the crimson fabric were some gilded pieces of steel.

"What in bloody hell is that? Is it a piece of armor?" asked Steven.

"I think it's a Spaldur. We have an exhibit at the museum that has old sets of armor from the 12th to the 15th centuries on display right now. Most of them aren't full sets. But that looks like part of some jousting armor. See, look at the shield cover that goes over the armpit area."

The metal gleamed as we looked at it. I pointed closer before picking it up. "But it looks like some things have been added on to it. I don't think it was originally used for jousting."

The other plates that made up the armor were a lighter gray color, not unlike polished silver. Part of it was a darker gray, reminding me of the steel used in the newly developed bio-electric firearms, mostly a recent invention. Within the last fifteen years they had become more efficient, and had mostly replaced the normal, black powder rifles. Remnants of gold leaf etched designs followed part of the edges of the Spaldur.

Standing, Steven took it from my hands. I looked up and saw a blank expression on his face. "Steven, are you okay?" I asked, shaking his arm. "What's going on?"

Just then, he snapped back to the here and now.

He turned to me. "Well, Davey... I didn't think I'd ever believe you, but I think I do now. What the hell are we getting into?"

A wave of relief washed over me like an incoming tide to save the sea life.

I finally have someone that knows what is happening.

Looking at him, I said, "I surely don't know, but we better start soon. I don't think it's going to get any better by standing here."

CHAPTER 9
Too Many Questions, Not Enough Time

Field Notes Entry 3

The last week has been a very interesting, complicated, and frustrating mess. I haven't made any headway in anything from the TEA investigation to the newly developing and always changing Emma Smith revelation of who she is and what it means for the Keepers.

Last night was mostly a success because I now have somebody that I can bounce ideas off of. Of course, it's also nice to have someone else that seems just as mad as me now; that's always a plus. We left last night, well actually this morning, around two, agreeing to meet up at St. Bartholomew to talk to Father Hubert.

8th April, 1888
Westminster Borough, London, England
11:17 a.m.

I heard a voice say, "Davey."

I snapped out of my daydream as I focused back on Commissioner Warren. "Sorry, sir, I've had a lot on me mind lately. Not much sleep either," I said.

Commissioner Warren cleared his throat, giving me a concerned look. It quickly changed to a stern stare. "As I was saying, then. In the beginning of May, there will be a series of exhibits in Glasgow to showcase the major technological advances in multiple areas. It will be called The International Exhibition of Science, Art and Industry. You can probably assume that TEA will be there as well to showcase everything it has brought to the great conglomerate known as The United Kingdom."

As he finished talking, he took a pipe from his desk drawer. In a mechanical motion, he placed the pipe on his desk before taking a pouch of loose pipe tobacco from the same drawer. With both things out, he started to pack the bowl of his pipe tightly with the wiry strands. He fished a match from his breast pocket and struck it on the top of his desk, lighting the bowl. He took a long hearty pull and blew it out slowly.

Through the dancing clouds of billowing tobacco smoke, he continued, "Of course this means that you'll be making your way there with TEA to set up and work throughout the event. I need you to see what else you can find out, revolving around the investigation you currently have going. I'm not quite sure how long it will last, but some of my inside sources say the exhibition will last as long as seven months. Not sure what they can all show during that much time, but it will be a great revenue producer and also good for the country."

"What about the Emma Smith investigation? Do you want me to follow up with it?" I asked.

Commissioner Warren looked at me, thinking. "I suppose. Why don't you keep an eye out for anything? Who knows, at night when you are undercover you might see something."

"Will do. When I was at the hospital two days ago, there wasn't much for me to go off of. But the undertaker did inform me that someone had already come by to ask questions. I thought we were keeping it quiet?" I asked as I shifted in my seat slightly.

Commissioner Warren took another long pull from his pipe, "That's right, only you and I were supposed to know about the investigation right now. May have to look into that. Someone is being nosey. Did the undertaker say who it was?"

"Dr. Thatcher is not an undertaker, she is a doctor." I said.

Commissioner Warren raised his hands in defense, "Alright, sorry my boy."

I was starting to get restless, so I decided to get up, and I started to pace. The smoke from his pipe was getting to me, and he knew I didn't like the smell of it.

"She couldn't recall the name, but she was sure it was a constable. I listed some names, and she thought it could've been Constable Christopher Jules. But since she was very unsure, I am not sure how trustworthy her word is. That's about all I got out of the visit and the facts we already knew: that it seemed that monsters did it."

"We might have to meet with Constable Jules; see why he is checking in on her," said Commissioner Warren.

"Actually, to think of it, he's probably checking in on her because he was with me the night she was reported as being attacked. Maybe he just feels a little guilty? I know I did. It felt like there was more we could have done." I shook my head to rid myself of those thoughts. "Anyway, that's probably why he was there," I said.

The constant smoke from the Commissioners pipe started to fill most of the room at this point. The light from the windows broke through sparsely in a few spots. I noticed his office seemed bleak and run down even though it was lit up from the light that came from the incandescent Tesla Bulbs. It was sparsely decorated, and held an old desk with an even older set of chairs. There were a few picture frames hung crooked on the peeling walls that really drove the feeling home.

"Well, keep with it. If you see Constable Jules again just casually talk to him about it," Warren said.

"Okay sir, will do." I said, nodding.

"And as far as I know, the exhibition will be starting in about a month from now. So your task is to just keep a low profile and keep those ears of yours out."

"Alright sir, I'll check back in if I find anything else," I said.

Getting up, I shook his hand and turned to leave this room of depression.

Should probably check with Father Hubert now, too.

8th April 1888
Farringdon Borough, London, England
12:32 p.m.

Pushing open the large wooden doors to the church, I walked through and closed them gingerly. As my eyes adjusted, I heard Steven's voice talking to what I assumed was Father Hubert somewhere in the church. After a moment, I made my way to them, taking in the ever amazing light flowing from the beautiful windows winding around the church. Coming up to them, I noticed that Steven had put on the Spaldur.

What an odd sight this is.

Hubert clapped his hands together and said, "Oh Davey, glad you could make it. I was just informing Steven of The Keepers and all the other exciting, yet depressing, information that goes along with it!"

Steven shook his head at the last small tidbit of information.

"I was also just telling him about the last suspected times that Jakobus returned to wreak havoc."

"When was that?" I asked.

"We think it was most likely during the Crimean War and the Invincibles of the Irish Republic Brotherhood. From what information King Arthur passed down, we figured he usually works from the background and uses influence to cause issues and conflict."

"Hm, well I'm afraid to ask but how many other times throughout the last thirteen hundred years has he shown back up?"

"Honestly," he said, clicking his tongue, "It's unknown. It happens too often to keep track, and the timeframe usually varies. Sometimes we don't even know until after it happens."

"There has to be an easier way of telling," said Steven.

Hubert sighed and said, "I agree. The reasons are unknown and most likely wouldn't make sense to us. Like I was saying, there've been a few instances in my lifetime."

"Kind of makes it difficult, doesn't it?" Steven added.

Changing subjects for the better, I said, "It looks like Steven has shown you his relic. It seems like it'd be much more practical than a sword. Like I was telling him, I think it's been modified over the years."

Hubert nodded as he looked at the design more closely.

I took a seat next to Steven on a pew, "Anyway, I went to take a look at Emma's body a few days ago to see if I could find anything out, and you'll never believe what happened."

Both Steven and Father Hubert leaned in with anxious looks on their faces as Hubert took a seat next to Steven and I on the pews.

"Remember the other day you gave me the ring to hold on to just in case I run into anyone that could be a legacy?" I asked.

"Yes, I do. Did you find someone while you were at the hospital?" Father Hubert asked in retort.

I rubbed my eyes with the palms of my hands. I was exhausted. Since learning all of this I haven't been sleeping much.

"I did but I don't know what it means. The undertaker brought me back to her body, and I noticed that her arm was dangling off the edge. Feeling like she deserved better, I grabbed her hand to put it back onto the table. As I did, the ring lit up with a kind of glow I hadn't seen yet."

"What do you mean?" asked Hubert.

"It was the same gold color as from you or I, but it was dim. As if it was measuring the level of light that was left as it all drained away from her."

I started to feel restless as I finished.

Why do I always feel so restless?

Father Hubert took a seat across from me.

"Why would it measure the life of someone that's dead?" He rubbed at his temples. "That also brings another question to the table: Was this a coincidence like so many others that have happened the last week? Or is it on purpose?"

Steven stood up and started pacing back and forth, small wisps of dust scuffed up off the stone from his dragging shoes. Stopping, he turned to me, "Do you think that Jakobus could have done this? Do you think it's connected to him?"

Father Hubert clicked his tongue again. "Hmmm." He murmured as he rubbed his chin. "That could be a possibility; I wouldn't put it past him. We did hear about some mysterious deaths in the past few hundred years. I think we didn't want to put stock into it because we didn't want to think that it could be related. Or we never thought about it that way. I don't know why it never crossed our minds."

I know I need to keep it quiet but I think I need to tell them that I'm a detective. That I'm investigating the death for them and for the police as well.

I noticed I started to bounce my leg. "I need to tell you gentlemen something. You'll need to know this because of what we are doing together." I sighed, knowing that this might change things. It probably will, a lot. But I can't keep it a secret if I want to get to the bottom of this. "I'm a detective, a police inspector. I've been undercover investigating TEA the last couple years. It wasn't a conflict of interest until now. I was told to look into the death of Emma by the commissioner himself. Now, it wasn't a problem until it became one. The fact that Emma is a legacy throws a wrench into things."

"Well, isn't that something?" Steven chuckled out loud. "Small world it is, isn't it."

I looked back towards Steven. "What is? Why do you say that?"

"I'm an undercover inspector too. Have been for twelve weeks or so."

"Why haven't we run into each other then?" I paused before I realized something, "then why were you looking for a bobby the night we met if you already were one?"

"Different stations, maybe? But I've been watching for illegal importation of shoddy materials used in the manufacturing of the Tesla coils. There were reports of employees buying cheaper materials and pocketing the difference. And as for your second question, I was under strict orders not to blow my cover for any reason whatsoever, no matter how much I disagreed with it."

"Fair enough. As for shoddy materials, have you found anything out? Come across any real evidence?"

"No, but I can tell you I have something to fall back on if I can't find any evidence and lose my job," Steven said.

"What's that?"

"I've gotten really good at repairing the coils and the substations," he said with a smirk.

"That's a way to look at it, I suppose," I said. "But we need to make some headway on not only Jakobus but the man in gray shoes. Emma was afraid to her core of the man with those shoes."

"Didn't you suggest going to a cordwainer?"

"Yes, we should start there." I turned to look at Father Hubert. "Father, do you have a suggestion of who to talk to?" I asked.

Standing back up, he said, "There are quite a few cordwainers in the area, not to mention a cobbler might be able to point you in the right direction. A man that would wear gray shoes seems to me like he'd be eccentric. So, that might make it a little easier to narrow it down. There is one not too far away, and he happens to be a cousin of another clergyman here at the church. Try there first?"

"Well it's still early, let's go down the road and talk to him. Father, what is his name?" I asked.

"Hmm, let me go check with Father Jeremy. He was the man that introduced us to begin with so I would assume he'd know his name," said Father Hubert as he started off towards the office area.

I sat there, thinking about Emma.

This is just like Sudan. No matter how hard I try, I won't be able to save everyone.

"Don't you ever stop moving? You're always pacing or shaking," asked Steven.

"I don't know, I've been like this me whole life. I always just called it reckless leg syndrome," I said as I bounced my leg some more.

Steven looked at me for a moment and then shook his head.

"I don't know, I just don't like staying still is all," I said.

"Anyway…" Said Steven, giving his head one more shake for good measure. We both turned to look at Father Hubert when he returned from talking to Father Jeremy.

"Father Jeremy says that it's actually his cousin; his name is Emmet. The business has been in the family for a few generations, both cordwainers and cobblers. They might be able to help. Father Jeremy informed me they also have a lot of connections, so you never know," said Father Hubert.

"Let's go check then. All this talking is keeping us from walking," I said, looking back at Father Hubert. Steven and I started to walk towards the large double wooden doors. I called back, "We will keep in touch Father, let us know if you see or hear anything."

"Will do. Good luck boys," he said as he waved us off.

Walking down the steps of the church, we both felt a slight chill as the wind picked up. It bit and nibbled without mercy at the bare skin of our faces and hands. Even though it was already April, it was still cold compared to the summer.

"Steven, I think I ran into that doctor again," I said.

"Which one? The odd one with the white shoes? What was his name again? Harry?" asked Steven.

I let out a laugh, "His name was Henry, I believe. It's funny, that's the same issue for me. I couldn't remember his name either. But the weirdest thing is that he was there at the hospital I think. I ran into him at the mortuary,"

"Really? Why?"

"Not sure, but he bumped into me, or at least I thought he did. I even chased after him for a little bit because I thought he took my pocket watch."

We continued walking down the path, passing the worn benches and the trees slowly coming back to life after a long and weary winter.

"So, did he take your watch?" asked Steven.

"No, I was mistaken. I thought he did. I chased after him for a few blocks and saw him go down an alley. I ran after and as I reached the end he was gone."

"That does seem a bit strange," said Steven.

Pulling out my watch from the top breast pocket, I showed it to Steven. "He just disappeared. That's when I found me watch. I actually heard it tick. It ended up being in the pocket I normally keep it in."

"Well that's just odd, you couldn't find it before you started chasing him?" asked Steven.

"No, it was really weird. Just like everything else around that man," I said as we turned the corner to go see Father Jeremy's cousin. "That's not the only thing. I could've sworn I heard some whistling in the alley, I think it was—"

I jumped as I ran into someone. Reeling from the sudden jolt, I reflexively grabbed for Excalibur. But all I noticed was a familiar prickle at the back of my neck.

Scrape, scrape

A cool mist brushed my face, gentle like a painter adding the finishing touches to his lifelong masterpiece. The air was cooler than the last few times I've been here. As if there was a coming storm. One I'll be stuck in the middle of. I noticed the hand on my right shoulder was there again, *maybe the whole time?*

"Hello? Who are you?" I asked nervously. I still couldn't see anything, nor move my arms or legs.

"He is no man, David," said the voice. "He is the devil incarnate. Wanting to watch the world burn."

I could hear the sudden crackle from the skies and feel the sharp electricity course through the air. The charge from the lightning made the hairs on my neck stand up even further.

"He must be stopped. You must open your eyes to the truth," he boomed.

"How am I supposed to do that? I can't open them. They're stuck," I said panicking. "What do you mean by he is no man?"

His voice started to muffle and sink away, turning to just a vibration in the back of my mind. All my senses started to fade again. I felt myself yelling at the man, but nothing came out. Everything was just black again. Deep, dark, lonely and familiar.

Scrape, scrape

"Whoa there son, don't be swinging that around. I need all my appendages," said a voice.

My eyes focused enough to see Constable Jules before me.

"Davey? Are you okay?" he asked.

I blinked a few times and dropped my hand from Excalibur's hilt. Coming to my senses, noticing my surroundings, I cleared my throat and slurred out, "Jules, you really need to stop doing that. You're doing it on purpose now. You must be."

What just happened? What does the man mean?

I turned to look at Steven as he started having a laughing fit. I elbowed him in the arm, followed by a small push to get the point across.

"That's not funny. Do you like getting frightened?" I let out an exasperated breath. "It's all the time," I complained. Angrily, I turned back to the constable and asked, "Jules, why are you over here? Aren't you still on night watches?"

How is Jakobus no man?

"Yes, well, I'm supposed to be. They are short-handed like I said last time, so I'm just helping out," said Jules. Cocking his head he asked, "First you have a sword, now Steven has armor? What are they doing over there at TEA? Getting ready for a war?"

Steven was still laughing about all this, so I elbowed him one more time.

"That? That's nothing, just a fashion statement or something," I said, trying to bring his attention back to me. "Another thing. Why were you at the mortuary?"

My eyes are open; what can't I see?

He cocked an eyebrow and said, "How did you know I was there? Why would it matter if I was there or not?"

"I was there to talk to Dr. Thatcher. Me wife told me Emma had passed away so I went to pay my respects. The doctor told me you were there immediately to ask more questions, so I was just wondering," I said.

Jules shifted as he stood there listening to me in a fluid motion.

"It doesn't matter either way. I was just curious if the police were opening a formal investigation or not," I said.

"Not that I should be sharing this info with you, but yes, we are opening an investigation. We fear this isn't the first and most definitely is not going to be the last."

I looked at Steven to see if he finally gained his professional composure.

"Well that's good that you are," I said. "But it's not good that you think this is going to keep happening. Hopefully we can stop it before it gets worse."

"I agree with you on that, my boy."

I tipped my hat to Constable Jules and said, "We will let you get back to it then, constable. Good luck with all the ne'er-do-wells."

Steven and I made our way past the constable to get to the cordwainer before it was too late. A shiver went down my spine and I wondered if it was because of the deaths, the conversation, or just the weather.

"So, we know he is not telling the truth about something. We are doing an investigation, not him. The commissioner had no idea Jules was involved, so that means there isn't another investigation underway. As far as he is concerned, Jules doesn't need to or have the right to be asking questions," I said.

We picked up our pace a little to get further away from any prying ears.

"Well we will just have to do a little more looking into it. Anyway, are we still going to talk to the cordwainer?" asked Steven. "You think he might have an idea about the gray shoes?"

"Yes, we should do that now so we can get a little more information. I think he will. Father Hubert says the business has been in the family for a while, so hopefully he has a lot of contacts and customers. This might be what we need to come out ahead in this," I said, taking another corner headed towards the cordwainer's shop.

Chapter 10
Need To Know Basis

8th April, 1888
Farringdon Borough, London, England
1:03 p.m.

The wind picked up as we got closer to the cordwainer shop. Not a cool wind, but more like a lukewarm breeze as it brushed against us. The noise of it turned to a roaring that grows from an untamed flame getting larger in size, consuming anything that it touches.

The sun slowly inched its way across the sky in an unforgiving arc, beating down on us as it cut straight through the fog, smog, and soot. The branches on the trees shook and scraped against each other, creating a semblance of strangers shaking hands and meeting for the first time. The streets were sparsely populated compared to the normal days of the same nature, which seemed quite odd to me. The birds and squirrels were missing, along with their normal chitter-chatter, and the familiar clomping from horses pulling carts was strangely absent. Coming upon the store front, the air became still, void of any wind, smell or sound. As I looked around, I noticed the windows of all the surrounding buildings had their shutters pulled.

"Does it seem quiet to you? It seems quiet. Too quiet," said Steven.

Cocking my eyebrow as he finished his sentence, I asked, "Really? What made you think that? The lack of noise? People? Substance in general?

He turned to me and said, "Well, yeah."

"Okay, Sherlock, nice deduction of the evidence provided. Can your skills of reason tell if the shop is open?"

"You don't need to be uppity about it."

I rolled my eyes at him.

He closed his eyes and rubbed his temples. "My brain says yes."

I shook my head and chuckled as I reached for the door handle. As I pulled it open, the sun broke through the crack created by the door and the door jam. It illuminated the dust as it spread into the air and exploded to life. The particles floated to a fro, escaping to the untouched parts of the room that have yet to be given light. As the door opened most of the way, we could make out a few incandescent lamps jittering near the corner at the end of the countertop and another near the wall.

They lit up the rows of shoes on shelves against the back wall and showed a few that lay resting on the worktop of the counter. In the very corner of the room, where the shelves and the counter meet the wall, was a man slumped over what looked to be a pair of boots. As we entered, our footsteps made faint creaks in the uneven wooden floors, adding more dust to the flock floating through the air.

"Sir? Are you okay?" I said as I reached the corner.

There was no reply that could be confused with words. Instead, we heard a faint noise coming from the man as his back rose and fell softly. With another deep breath, a snore started to form in his throat.

Walking past the edge of the counter, we saw a book laying there. The cover was a deep maroon red that made me think of fresh, ripe tomatoes. I picked it up to have a closer look. "Hmph, *Treasure*

Island by Robert Louis Stevenson. You read that one yet, Steven?" I asked.

"No, I haven't." he said as he looked closer at it. "But I hear it's a good one."

I put it down and asked "Should we shake him? Or ring the bell that's on the counter?"

"Probably use the bell. He seems pretty dead to the world right now."

Walking closer to the man, my hand hovered over the bell for a second to give him a chance to wake up on his own.

"Okay," I said.

The bell emitted an ear piercing ring as I slapped my hand down on it. It took me by surprise, but I tried to ignore it. I paused as a second passed, waiting for anything to happen. I went to say something else to Steven but I was caught off guard once more by sudden movement in front of us.

The man's head shot straight up causing the boots he was resting on to fly in different directions. The stool he was sitting on fell to the floor with him still attached to it. Some shuffling noises came from behind the counter as we assumed he was trying to get up.

A small white light illuminated the space he was occupying, casting more all around us. It grew in size and intensity as the familiar crackling from electricity started to fill the air close to us.

More shuffling sounded underneath the steady crackle of visible energy as the man got to his feet. His arms trembled from the power of the gun he raised to his chest, as if he had never had to shoot one in his life. The buzzing leveled out in its intensity and the weapon seemed like it was finished charging as he leveled it in our direction. The pulsing energy lit up his face, skin taut with confusion and fright. He yelled something I couldn't understand because it was blotted out by the deafening buzz that filled the air all around us. The man shook his head in panic as he pulled the trigger to fire the charged ball in our direction.

I shoved Steven out of the way of the shot as we heard the charge go off. Plumes of white and gray smoke erupted from the barrel of the gun. Sparks shot out from the end of the muzzle about twenty centimeters, fading as quickly as they came into this world. The flash etched spidering branches of burning light onto my retinas.

"Oi, what in the bloody hell?!" I yelled as I rubbed my eyes to try and help dissipate the blindness.

I rolled to my feet and looked over at the man. He was bringing his Mason model 1870 back to his chest, blinking furiously in the process to clear the same light from them. I quickly bolted in his direction to stop him from getting another cartridge in, floorboards creaking in disapproval from the motion and weight. He looked back up at me as I got closer, expression changing from confusion and fright to one of terror.

"Just stop! We are here to talk! Why are you trying to shoot us?" I shouted over the consistent crackle.

I yanked the gun out of his hands, causing my skin to burn for a moment while it stayed in contact with the barrel. In the same motion I grabbed Excalibur with the other hand to pull from the sheath. He let go of the rifle without any protest or resistance. Once from his hands, the charge left the mechanism as the electricity dissipated.

"Why are you shooting at us?" I yelled.

We stood there for a moment as we all caught our breath. The man was still shaking in fear from the encounter, lower lip trembling with a nervous quiver.

"I– I was sleeping and you frightened me," he said.

"Do you normally go around shooting anyone that scares you?"

He shook his head in a quick but decisive gesture as he picked the stool off the ground. With his eyes still on me, he placed it on its legs and sat back down.

"Who did you think we were?"

"I– I don't know who you are, I thought you were trying to steal my shoes."

I sighed heavily and waved the rifle in the air as I asked my next question. "What the bloody hell is this?"

He shrugged and pointed at the bell on the counter. "That was really loud. Why didn't you just shake my shoulder?"

"Well I don't know. Why do you have it if people aren't supposed to use it?" I said.

The man shrugged once more.

I turned to look at Steven. "Steven, are you okay?"

"I think so." He stood up and patted himself up and down, seeing if anything broke or felt out of place. He smirked and gave me two thumbs up. "I'm good!"

"Alright, well we have that figured out," I said with a sigh. "I'm Davey, and that over there is Steven."

Steven waved for a second as we both looked at him.

The man that stood before us shifted on unsteady, half-asleep feet. He wore glasses that were as thick as a shot glass, causing his eyes to seem bulbous like a fly. The thick, lush brown hair at the top of his head was cut to be about three inches all around, slicked back tight against his head. He had a clean-shaven face that had a few scars from facial blemishes of his youth, plotted randomly across his cheeks.

"My name is Emmet Kestler," he said with a smile. "How may I help?"

"We are here to talk to you about some shoes. You're a cordwainer right?"

Confusion washed over his face once more, "Why do you ask? What time is it? Isn't it late?" the man asked. "Erm– why do you have a sword?"

Putting Excalibur back in the sheath, I pulled my pocket watch out to check the time.

"I hope I'm not overstepping my boundaries, but It's about thirteen after one in the afternoon. Shouldn't you be open for a few hours or more?" I asked. In reply to the last question, I mumbled out, "It's a new security measure, don't worry about it."

"Hmm, yes, I'm usually open until 5 o'clock or so. I thought it was later than that. I suppose a sorry is in order. Would anyone like some tea?" Emmet asked as he hopped off the seat, nervousness still prevalent on his face.

"I would love some tea," blurted Steven.

I rolled my eyes in annoyance, "You're like a child, you know that don't you, Steven?"

"Why? Because I like tea?" he questioned.

I decided it wasn't worth explaining, so I lifted the rifle up closer to the light given off by a lamp. My eyes took in the details like how I could tell it definitely was a base model Mason 1870 but with a lot of modifications. The stock was a stained walnut with decorative pearl inlay in a flowing floral design. There was a rubber strip fashioned around the outside of the stock from top to bottom in a channel that was chiseled into it. The rubber was mostly flush but stuck out enough to help with the insulation so that the user didn't get shocked. Near the hammer and the breach were fuse tubes to regulate the electricity that channeled from the user to the weapon. Curious, I pulled back the hammer to take a closer look at the mechanism. Upon closer inspection, I saw that the channeling pin had a rubber casing around it to add in insulation as well.

This is beautifully modified. Everything looks as if the gunsmith took great pride and care in creating this.

"Emmet? Where did you get this rifle? They're experimental, are they not?" I yelled to him.

I looked in his direction and saw him walking back towards us with a tray holding three cups and a teapot.

"Oh, that thing? Yes, they are. But that one is of my own design. I've done a lot of additions to it myself. Working on shoes all the time is rather boring. It's good to have a hobby that's not, well, shoes." He said.

As I tinkered with the rifle some more, he set the tray down on the counter. He picked up the teapot and poured an even amount of hot liquid into each cup.

"Tea?" Emmet asked, offering a cup to Steven.

"Please, thank you," said Steven as he smiled. "Do you have sugar or cream by chance?"

Shaking my head, I turned from Steven back to Emmet, "How do you even have the designs? I know that the crown has been working with Nikola Tesla to make these. Do you work for the crown?"

"I may have an acquaintance in the Crown's Bio-Electrical Research Division," he said, the corner of his mouth curling in a smile.

"Hm, and you did this work yourself? That's quite impressive, but why?" I asked while pointing to the rifle.

"Why not? It's better than sleeping all the time," he said while pouring cream into each cup.

"I suppose that is a good reason," I said.

Emmet followed up the cream with a few sugar cubes that made a satisfying plunking noise as he dropped them into the cup. Emmet then handed it to Steven and placed the cream softly on the tray resting on the counter.

"Thank you again," said Steven.

Emmet nodded and started to unbutton his right sleeve, pointing at his wrist as he spoke. "This is how I do it. It's a two stage transfer disk."

Attached to his arm was a device that was connected to a few leather straps. They wrapped around his arm, fastening them tight so as they did not move anywhere.

"It consists of two metal disks with center punched holes in them, steel wire connecting both. It's a single wire from the first disk to the second wrapped around the sides, there is an additional wire coming off of the second to collect the electricity from the body."

He rebuttoned his shirt and grabbed a cup of tea with his left hand, taking a sip for himself.

"Well– Well that's bloody brilliant," I said

"Thank you sir," he said, raising his cup.

"I have to pick your brain about it, but I'll get back to that later. The real reason we are here is because of your profession."

"What, a cordwainer?"

"Precisely. Have you ever made or repaired light gray shoes for anyone?"

Putting his thumb and pointer finger on his chin, Emmet started to hum for about five seconds. Putting his cup of tea back on the tray, he turned on his heels and walked back around the counter.

"Emmet? What are you doing?" I asked, looking over to Steven, then back towards Emmet. I heard some rustling from behind the counter, followed by some thuds.

He shot straight up after a few more seconds. "Aha!"

"Did you find something? I asked.

"No, I realized I can't find it," he said as he chuckled for a second. "But I've had some people come in about brown shoes. Also for regular, generic black and whites."

"So wait, what were you looking for?" I asked in confusion.

"My ledger. But it's missing, so I can't be of much help. It would have the records of what I've worked on in the last year or so. It would be the way to know for sure. I meet a lot of feet."

"Did you just say you meet a lot of feet?" Steven asked.

"Do you smell a lot of shoes?" I asked.

They both looked at me in confusion.

"Get it?" I asked. "It sounds like sell?"

Steven looked at me with a face of slight disgust from my terrible joke. He shook his head and spoke some more. "And you say I'm a child. So you don't think you've sold any gray shoes?"

"Again, I don't remember for sure, but I think I've sold a few pairs of black and white lately." He took another sip of his tea and asked, "Does that help?"

I kicked one of the boots that went flying with Emmets' spasm. "No it doesn't."

"Wait, you said white shoes?" I asked.

"Why yes, a few pairs lately. More than what I am used to making. It is odd, I never really have made them before. Not a commodity people usually look for."

"Do you know anyone by the name Dr. Henry?" I asked.

"Honestly, without my ledger I have no clue. I see so many people it's surprising I remember my own name sometimes."

I kicked the boot some more and said, "Well, when you find it you'll have to let us know okay? It's very important, and it could be a life or death situation. We need all the help and information we can get."

"I will make sure I do that."

Looking back down at the rifle in my hand, I said, "How long did this take you?"

"Not very long at all, why?" he asked.

"I might need something like this made for us," I said with a grin.

Chapter 11
Run Through The Jungle

Field Notes Entry 4

The new spring weather in Glasgow decided to fluctuate drastically when we arrived. At one point, it felt like the winter months, but then switched at the drop of a hat to spring weather. Eventually, it changed from a rainy wet mess to wonderfully pleasant mild days full of sun and budding trees.

The couple of weeks Steven and I have been here have been full of some very interesting issues and concerns. It mostly started with the fact that half of his tools never made their way to Scotland. After that point, it has cascaded into one more thing after another.

All of the components and parts have finally shown up here at the Exhibition Hall. The International Exhibition of Science, Art and Industry started the week of May 8th.

Most of the exhibits were housed in the main building located on the large plot of land, Kelvingrove Park. That same park resided on the west end of Glasgow, nestled against the river Kelvin. The main building consists primarily of wood, with a one-hundred-fifty foot dome composed of galvanized sheet iron atop an iron framework. Surrounding the dome are four brick supporting towers, elegantly crafted marionettes atop.

16th May, 1888
Kelvingrove Park, Glasgow, Scotland
3:45 p.m.

"I miss my tools," Steven whimpered as he looked down at his feet.

"It's okay, we will get you new ones. Let's try and enjoy ourselves while we are here." I said, patting him on his back.

We continued our short walk as Steven pouted. I tried my best to console him, but alas, he chose to be difficult. I was relieved when we reached the main building of the exhibit because that meant we could get Steven's mind off those bloody tools.

I stopped in the archway and looked over at Steven. "Too bad we can't set up the exhibit inside. It would fit in nicely with the steel structure of the dome."

"True, but it would probably be a very, very bad idea. All of the metal would spell danger for all the visitors," said Steven.

Tilting my head to the side, I said, "You're right. We are here to promote Wavergy, not hinder the technology."

TEA received a special area located outside the building in one of the nearby fields, away from anything conductive, or convenient for that matter. Like the others, this building consisted of wood, made to dismantle easily. Scotland was still under development to implement the electrical transformations that London had already completed. Thus the reason for us, TEA, being there. To showcase the elegance and wonders of electricity in hopes of making the transition easy for everyone.

Since Steven and I had more things to do before we could open our exhibit, we cut our stroll short and started back to our own area. The fact his tools were lost on the way over was another reason we had some catching up to do. Most of it was taken care of at this point, but we still had a few more adjustments to do today before we celebrated. About halfway back to our exhibit, Steven started to hum a song aloud.

"Where did you hear that?" I asked.

"It's something me mum used to sing to me," he said between notes.

"That's what it was! That's what I heard!"

"What was what?"

"That song, what was it?"

"I don't quite remember, maybe Ring a Ring o' Rosies?" he said, confused. "Why does it matter?"

Stopping, I turned to Steven, "It's just something I couldn't think of at the time. I think it's what Emma's attackers were whistling."

He furrowed his brow as he tried to remember the encounter.

I rubbed at the back of my neck and turned to continue to our building. "I think I've heard it before that too but I can't quite remember."

"You think it's important? You think it'll help with finding out who did it?"

"I think it will–" I started to say, being interrupted by noise coming from inside the building.

"What was that?"

As I opened the door, light from the sun shone down from the ceiling lights. It orchestrated the dust to dance in abstract shapes, content and free in front of our eyes. I looked around at the Tesla coils that stood erect in front of us, towering over the power cords and tools on the floor.

"And the crowd gasps! The mighty Prince of the Air has done it!" yelled a voice. "Defying gravity once again! The crowd cheers, Ehrich! Ehrich! Ehrich!" Someone chanted from the other side of the room.

Steven and I looked at each other as we listened.

"Who's that? Are you expecting anyone?" I asked.

"I don't know anyone with that name, you? Wait, of course you don't. You wouldn't have asked me if you did. Sorry," chuckled Steven.

Elbowing him unconsciously, we jogged to the other side of the room. Our legs hurdled our bodies over the power cables and tools. It was slightly harder to do than it should have been because the toolboxes lay empty beside them, spread around like a toddler was busy looking for its favorite lost toy.

Steven and I rounded the corner and saw a young boy up in the air walking across one of the Tesla coil wires that stretched across the room.

"World famous, known by all! Fear itself is frightened by me!" yelled the young boy.

"Oi! What are you doing up there?!" I shouted.

The kid's balance faltered a little, causing him to turn towards the side. It caused his perfect form of left foot in front of his right to shift to his feet side by side. He looked in our direction as his arms reeled in large windmills, trying to maintain his equilibrium on the highwire. Regaining his composure, the red in his cheeks grew with every second like poppies in a field, causing him to stutter as he tried to form coherent words.

"I– I–" the boy spat, turning back towards the right. Instead of explaining himself, he ran with nimble grace across the power cable that connected the largest Tesla coil to the wall.

"Hey! Wait!" we both yelled in unison.

We watched as the boy negotiated his way along the various wires connecting all of the Tesla coils with meticulous ease. The speed in which he did this was unfathomable, knowing I certainly could not do the same if I had to. He glanced back in our direction a few times to see what we would do. At first he was frowning, eyes wide in surprise and fright. After the second glance though he now had a confident smile stretched across his face with two or three missing teeth to form a splotchy grin. I narrowed my eyes in his direction as he stuck out his tongue in a gesture of mockery.

"The Prince of the Air, up in the clouds. Oh look, what's down there? Geese in the sky? Silly geese, I am too high for you!" He beamed.

"Kid! Get down from there. It's dangerous.," Steven yelled. "What are you doing in here?"

Steven and I clamored over each other trying to keep up with the kid's grace, tripping on things we already knew were there. It felt like we made three or four passes around the room before he leaped to the ground from one of the lower wires, performing a perfect backflip and landing without injury. Dashing out the doorway, we followed behind, trying to get the young boy to stop once again.

"Why won't you stop?" I yelled, panting.

Ehrich, assuming that was his name, sprinted off across the field of dew covered grass. Clouds cast patchwork shadows moving along with him as he put distance between us and him. The wind picked up around us that swept a cacophony of smells into the air. The mixture consisted of spring flowers and fresh meat pies sitting on vendor carts to be sold and enjoyed. Ehrich made it to the gate of the circus, cutting off vacationers in the process of running through the entrance. Steven and I got to the front gate, chests heaving from being out of breath and apparently out of shape too.

"Lad, do ye got a ticket?" asked a man as he stopped us in our tracks.

I looked up at the person that halted our pursuit of the child ne'er-do-well. He was a burly fellow with a thick Glaswegian accent that towered over us. The rising moonlight reflected off the top of his bald head, giving him a crown of angelic light. Behind him in the sky were stars that started to twinkle and wink into existence that mesmerized me temporarily.

"Ticket? What ticket?" I asked, jolting to a stop.

"Ye canne come in without a ticket. This ain't free," he gruffed.

"I don't need one," reaching into my pocket for my TEA badge and showed off my skeleton key.

"See here. Ticket is what youse need. It don't matter who you're 'ere with there, laddie," he said, shaking his head.

"Bollocks, how much?" He reached into his pocket before the man could respond and pulled out two shillings. "Take this, we just need to get through."

Steven dropped the money into the beast's hand and pushed past him. We looked around frantically at the bustling stalls that held goods for sale that sat between the food vendors and sideshows. Sadly, it seemed that the boy was nowhere to be seen.

"Where is he?" I asked Steven, looking at him, then at the sea of people.

"I don't know, keep looking?" he asked.

"We need to see how he got in there. He was lucky that the power wasn't active."

"I'm sure he just snuck in through the front."

How did he do that? He was so graceful.

Walking around, we looked for the boy a little while longer. The paths that weaved around the tents on the circus grounds had deep ruts from the hundreds of people before us carved into the ground. They created fissures for water to fill and form miniature bodies of water full of wonder and mystery. Performers littered the grounds on their mountain tops, separated from the onlookers by the well-worn paths. My eyes glanced around as I looked at sword swallowers defying logic and fire breathers lighting up the sky.

The early spring sun began its slow descent inviting the glow-worms on the verge of friendly and familiar spring dusk. They happily faded in and out, overcome with the joy of simply just being alive. Still looking around, I bumped into a man standing near the entrance to one of the larger circus tents, knocking off his hat.

"Sorry, mate," I said, leaning down to grab his hat. Standing back up, I reached out to give it back to him, "Didn't see you there. I was looking around for someone."

The man took his hat back from me and turned it around in his hands a few times. Dusting off the top of his hat, he placed it back on his head and said, "It's quite alright, no harm done. Did you come for the show?"

This man looked very familiar. Why is that happening so much lately?

"What show?" I asked as I leaned around the man. A few signs hung next to the entrance that advertised a young trapeze artist.

"No, we didn't. We were looking for a kid," Steven said. He peeked around the both of us to look at the sign himself.

With the sun setting, the gas lamps and torches were ignited to help keep the evening alive. The fire from some of the closer ones danced off the front of the signs as we read them. The front read, *Ehrich, The Prince of the Air* in thick, black lettering.

"*The Prince of the Air.* Wasn't what that kid was yelling?" I asked, looking back at Steven.

Steven shrugged.

"Are you here for the show?" I asked the man.

Steven pushed past us and entered the tent, drawn in by the clamoring commotion. I looked at the man one last time before following Steven in as well.

In the center of the tent stood a man talking to the crowd with a booming voice. "And now for the next act! A high-flying adventure of thrills and excitement."

He gestured to the high wire stretched from one end to the other.

"Wandering the streets of New York after he was brought here from the barbaric land of Hungary, climbing the trees and balancing on branches of his native land." Motioning to the band in the corner to queue the drumroll, he continued, "Without further ado, Ehrich, the Prince of the Air!"

Light came from different angles centering on the far end of the tent, twenty feet in the air. Eyes still trained on the boy, I heard the man from outside the tent talk again.

"How has the quest been going?" he asked.

Realizing who it was, I turned in surprise. "Gregory?"

He looks less haggard. He looks more well kept than the last time we met, when I received the sword.

Gregory nodded. "He has a dim glow about him. But he will do great things."

"Who?" I asked.

"The kid," he said, pointing at the ring on my hand. "It will also show you if someone is a distant relative, blood muddled over decades. They will still have a glow when you touch them with the ring, but their memories are lost to time."

"Even if they find their artifact?" I asked.

"Yes, it will stay dormant for them. The artifacts only show the memories to true bloods." Coughing, he asked, "Have you found him yet?"

"Who? Jakobus?" I asked.

"Yes, you know him by that name. He has gone by many more over the ages. I tried to help King Arthur and his knights when we were still at the height of our strength. But alas, we couldn't complete it," he said, sorrow in his voice.

"We've been trying to find him, but I can't make sense of these visions I've been having. What do they mean?" I asked.

I didn't hear him respond, so I looked back only to see he was gone.

"Steven, he's gone," I said.

"No, he's not. He's still up on the tightropes," Steven said with confusion.

"You mean you didn't see the man I ran into?"

"Um. No, you ran into someone?"

Why could I only see him? He must've been there... right?

"Steven, I have to tell you something. I don't know what it all means, but I've put it off long enough."

Steven stopped watching the show and turned to me. "What do you mean? What have you put off?"

I shook my head gently. "I have been having visions, daydreams or whatever they are called. So far I didn't know what to think of them. Maybe I thought I was looney."

"What have they been about?"

"No weird looks? No saying *you're just crazy*? You're gonna believe me just like that?"

"Davey, I have followed you through this rabbit hole of a journey for a while now. There really isn't much I wouldn't believe at this point," he reassured. "So, what are they about?"

I glanced at Ehrich, his figure brightly lit up with a multitude of lights. My eyes glazed over as I thought, looking through him instead of at him.

"They are of me on a beach. To begin with, I can't see or hear anything. They always seem to happen at the worst moments," I said, still focusing on the memories.

"Why do they happen at the worst moments? Like when?"

"Once was when we were at the bottom of the grave. That's why I zoned out or whatever. I'm not sure what happens when I get them," I said. "The last time I had one, a man told me about Jakobus; how he is a monster. That he isn't a man and wants to watch the world burn."

A look of concern started on Steven's face. "Looks like whatever it is, it's trying to warn you. Hopefully you understand before it's too late."

Chapter 12

Literally Anyone

Field Notes Entry 5

The frequent trips to Scotland with Steven have been very taxing on my other duties. It has been a slight godsend that I had the forethought to quit me job as a night watchman some time ago. I try my best to keep up with the other tasks included with my job as a police inspector.

What seems worse is the fact that we haven't made any more progress with finding Emma's assailants. If there were more than one, that is. Frankly, we are still trying to find what Jakobus' place is in all of this. We know that he ultimately wants to end all lines of heritage to each of the knights of the round table, but what else are we missing?

Since I found some downtime in between one of the trips to showcase Wavergy at the expo, Father Hubert

thought it would be best I learn how
to use Excalibur. Some basic training
would do me some good, apparently. He
said to me, 'Just running around with
a pointy stick isn't enough to scare
them, you need to learn how to hold
your own'. Or something close to that.
I was too busy looking at my pointy
stick.

2nd July, 1888
Farringdon Borough, London, England
7:45 a.m.

"Remind me again why I decided to come here this early again, Father?" I asked, dragging my feet.

"Because my son, all descendants, especially ones of Arthur, should know how to wield such a weapon the correct way," he said.

Probably good I quit me job as a watchman then. Gives me more time to play knight.

Hubert led me outside to a small area right outside the back-door of the Church that was separated from the rest of the lot by a weathered fence. It stood guard as best it could like a loyal and faithful hound, warding off the evils in the night. The paint was chipping and peeling, creating a design reminiscent of the dried lake beds in Egypt.

I followed him through the rickety gate that sat off-center in the fence. It creaked in anger of being disturbed as I pushed it open, snapping back into place as we both passed through. On the other side of the fence was a small graveyard that extended back further by about thirty feet, filled with six rows of headstones. The sides of the graveyard were separated by eighteen feet of headstones at three-foot intervals.

"My parents are buried here," Hubert said, pointing to the left side two rows back. "My mother passed when I was twelve. She was loved by many, always putting people first." He stopped for a second, looking at the grave marker he pointed out. "My father raised me alone. At the age of fourteen, I was told of the stories and the legends based on our family's truth, as well as the knights of the round. It stayed that way for many years," he said, sighing.

"It must have been a lot to take in at that age," I said.

"It was, but I eventually trained in swordplay and hand-to-hand combat, among other things."

"How do you know everything that happened," I asked. "Did the knowledge just get passed down? Or did Taliesin have an artifact prepared by Merlin as well?"

"Both. He scribed Arthur's adventures and had this blessed." Hubert held up his wrist, pulling back his sleeve to show a plain gold bracelet. "Not quite as bold as your sword, but it does the trick."

I looked at the bracelet resting gently around his wrist, watching the early morning sunrise glint slightly off of it.

"What about the sword training? Was that your father that taught you?"

"Yes and No. Some from my father, but mostly from a descendent of Sir Gaheris. His name was Edward. Not only was he a great swordsman, but he was also Steven's grandfather. Steven's father, Frederick, trained with me as well."

We continued on, walking past the rest of the headstones. Some were simple crosses, while others were large and opulently designed to reflect the wealth of their owners.

Past the last row of graves, the area opened into a worn patch of ground. Tufts of bleached and thinning grass were dotted at the edges while the middle was rubbed bare by years upon years of trampling. This area was about twenty-four feet long by eighteen feet wide.

"Back here is where The Keepers used to train when the order was far greater," he said, gesturing. "At its height in the late 1500's our numbers crested the three hundred mark. Some were true full heirs, or Brighters, while others were partials; Dimmers. In fact, I trained many late nights and early mornings in this very spot," Hubert said.

Stopping him for a moment, I sighed. "Father, I haven't been honest with you about everything."

"What do you mean, my boy?"

"I have been having visions. At least that's what I think they are."

"What are they about?"

"Honestly, I am not sure. I am on a beach somewhere. There is a man, he is telling me something. Warning me about Jakobus, but the vision always fades out before I can get much more than that out of him," I said. "And it usually happens at the worst possible moments. Like in the middle of a conversation."

He began to rub his chin. "That is odd. Like you said, it's a warning of some kind. Have you learned anything from it?"

I kicked up some dust. "No, not really. I wish I could understand it,"

"Have you had any strange dreams?"

"Not too many, a few right as I took the sword months ago. Why, what do they mean?"

He shrugged. "What happens in them?"

"Well, I believe they are about King Arthur. One is of him as a child, but others are as a young adult."

"Those could just be memories of King Arthur. It might be your mind's way of processing them."

I nodded and thought about them for a moment.

Father Hubert clapped his hands together and said, "Let me know if you learn something or if it comes to you later. Usually, those kinds of things are hard to understand."

Nodding, I motioned to the dust-covered clearing. "Father, I don't see the need to train, though. You really think I will come into contact with anyone else carrying a sword and actually needing this training?"

"Why don't I show you then. If you don't think you'll need any training, I can just prove it to you." He smiled, starting to undo his robe. "Here, take Excalibur out of its sheath."

I slid Excalibur from its sheath and held it in my right hand as I watched what he did. Father Hubert then took his robe off, folding it gently while walking over to a wooden barrel next to the fence. Setting it down on the top, I could see he was wearing a set of leather armor. It was composed of a chest plate, bracers, and pauldrons, all worn from years of use. At his waist hung a sword about three feet long.

"Okay, now what?" I asked, puzzled.

"I will show you something," he said.

Without warning, Hubert sprinted at me. His sword centered at my chest, ready to pierce my stomach.

"What are you doing?" I yelled.

I didn't even see him draw his sword!

Getting close, my elbow pulled into my chest, forearm and hand swinging Excalibur into an upward arc. Effortlessly swiping his sword away from his readied assault, performing a perfect parry.

I looked at Excalibur in my hand, "How did I–?"

Before I could finish my sentence, he was already bringing his sword down in an arc, attempting to cleave into my skull. My right arm brought the sword above my head, upper arm bracing underneath my chin. My wrist and forearm tightened to absorb the impact of his blade.

"How am I doing this? I have never swung a sword in my life!" I yelled with excitement and confusion.

Hubert's sword clashed off mine, sending him backwards.

"See Davey, this is what I mean," Hubert said, straining to regain balance from his sword glancing off mine. "Excalibur will do a lot of the work for you if you are inexperienced. It is a very powerful weapon."

He came at me again, pressing me further and further, making me trip back as he advanced.

He's so fast, I can barely see what he's doing.

I tried to bring up Excalibur on the offensive, sneaking in a jab myself. It got past his defenses, and he slid to the side fast enough to make the jab scrape across his leather chest plate. I stood there in shock.

I almost killed him. I could've killed him. But I got him! I actually got him!

In the excitement of actually landing a hit, I forgot all about the fight, giving him a chance to land a hit for himself. Instead of a slice or stab, he punched me square in the face with his free hand.

My face exploded in pain, and warm, coppery liquid filled my mouth. My hands flew to my nose to staunch the bleeding. I dropped Excalibur, and it fell to the ground with a heavy clang and clattered to rest.

"You punched me in the face!" I mumbled through my fingers. "Who does that?" Anger swelled in my gut, igniting as quick as flames to kerosene.

"Anyone would do that. Literally anyone. I am trying to prove a point, Davey," he said, leaning down to pick up Excalibur. "Now I would like to show you something else." He walked back over to the barrel, leaning Excalibur up to it. Then, grabbing a sword on the opposite side of it, he hefted it up to the light. I could see the blade was rusty in some spots, definitely nothing as magnificent as mine. Walking back over to me, he said, "Take this," handing it to me.

I let go of my nose with my right hand, switching to the left. I looked down at the blood-stained skin, covered in already congealing globs. "What about the blood on my hand?" I asked.

"It won't hurt it any. Just take it." He reassured me.

I took it as he placed it in my hand. Turning it over, I noticed how ordinary and plain it looked. It was heavier than Excalibur as well.

"That's another thing you need to learn. As I said, Excalibur is a great weapon, and as you noticed, with little training, it helps the user defend. That doesn't make up for a total lack of knowledge, though. You need to learn how to attack as well as defend. How to keep your enemy on the defensive, not the other way around. Now ready yourself again. This time I will go easier, I promise," he said with a wink.

Left hand still holding my nostrils together, I readied my right hand. The blade seemed to sway, my wrist having a hard time keeping it upright. I gritted my teeth and waited for the impact, planning out what I would try to do.

"Ready?" he asked, smiling.

I nodded my head. "Yes, do your worst."

In the matter of one single second, the sword was flying through the air, hilt over tip. Crashing to the ground about six feet away. The tip of Father Hubert's sword was pressed against my throat.

"*THAT* is what I am trying to tell you, Davey," he cautioned. "You won't have a second chance when you find Jakobus. He will take you down without remorse or feeling. In fact, he will probably enjoy it. He might kill you slowly, making it last as long as possible. Especially knowing he is killing off one of the true descendants."

"Okay," I swallowed hard, worrying about my adam's apple turning to apple slices. "You're right. I need to train, I need to learn. This is serious."

He lowered the sword from my throat, depositing it back in its sheath before I could blink.

By God, is he fast.

"How are you that quick, Father?" I asked in bewilderment.

He explained, while taking out a handkerchief, "Like I said earlier, many years of training. You'll have to promise me one thing, Davey. Come here to train whenever you can, please."

Taking the handkerchief from him, I held it up to my nose. Blotting at my face, I realized it was mostly dry at this point. "Okay, I promise, Father. I will whenever possible," I said, muffled by the cloth.

"Davey! Davey!" yelled a voice from behind us.

Turning, Steven came trotting up past the headstones, trying to hop from empty spot to spot. "What are you doing Steven?" I asked.

"I don't want to step on a grave; that's bad luck." he said, watching the ground intently.

I rubbed my temples. "Steven, we dug up a grave. Pretty sure that's more bad luck than what you're worried about."

Holding held foot in the air mid-step. "Huh, you're probably right. Either way, I don't need more." He walked past the last row of graves, stopping next to me, "What happened, Davey? Why are you covered in blood?" he asked.

I stayed silent, peering over at Father Hubert.

"That was my fault. I got caught up in the moment. I was trying to prove a point," he said.

"What point? That he bleeds?" Steven asked, confused, looking at my hands and face.

"He punched me in the face. He was trying to teach me that everyone is a jerk. That at any moment I could be hit in the face," I rebuked.

Before Steven could ask another question about my face, or being punched, I asked, "What do you need Steven? Why are you up this early?"

"Early?" he asked, "It's almost ten in the morning."

"Really? Huh, that's odd." I said, taking out my pocket watch. Clicking open the lid to check the time. It read about ten in the morning."

"What time did you think it was?" He shook his head. "It doesn't matter, there's a strike forming uptown. All police personnel are being called to the scene for crowd and riot control."

"What for? What's happening?" I asked.

"There is some unrest at the Bryant & May match factory. It's about an employee getting fired," he said. "I know her personally, she's a friend."

"Why did she get fired?" I asked.

"You know about the unfair working conditions there, right?"

I nodded in agreement, "Mostly, it's pretty bad for them."

"Yeah, poor pay, excessive fines and fourteen-hour shifts. It's bad. I know a lot of people are trying to find good work, but some of the jobs out there are horrible," he said.

"Aren't employees getting diseases from the chemicals they use?" Father Hubert asked, putting his robe back on after offering Excalibur back to me.

Taking her, I put her back in the sheath on my waist. "Isn't it called phossy jaw? I have a few friends that suffer from it." I shook my head. "Awful stuff, it is. Up there with tuberculosis and such."

"Exactly, that's why they need us there. We may agree with the people going on strike, but we need to do our jobs too," he said.

I handed the handkerchief back to the Father. "Alright, let's get going then. I promise I'll keep coming back for training. I see that this is important now. God, I am horrible at this."

Chapter Thirteen
Thicker Than Water

6th August, 1888
Whitechapel Borough, London, England
10:47 p.m.

A sweet summer breeze wafted around me as I stood on the ladder. I finished the grounding process of the Tesla bulb before climbing down to rejoin Steven on the street.

"Steven, you know you didn't need to tag along. I would have met you at the pub in a few hours," I said as I picked up the ladder, sliding it underneath my arm.

"I don't mind. It keeps me out of trouble," he said with a smirk. "But only till we start it together, that is."

I chuckled at his joke, appreciating the lightheartedness he could always find in life.

"But really, I don't mind. I have a pint with my name on it waiting until we get there," he said.

We both made our way to the next lamppost, trying to expedite the process to allow for us to enjoy a few rounds quicker. I kept an eye on the world around me as a few people walked about, making it from one pub to another. Some of them could magically stay upright without impairment, while others seem to be walking sideways. The dancing shadows that bounced about while the owners mumbled things to themselves reminded me that everything is different than what it seems.

I shivered as I tried to rid myself of the thought.

"How has your wife been lately? It's been a little while since we've been home," asked Steven.

"We've kept in touch for the most part. Some letters back and forth, but it's been a little rough. What about you? Anyone special I don't know about?" I asked.

I leaned the ladder up against the next post, giving it a light shake to ensure it was relatively stable. Putting one foot on the first rung, I climbed up it while listening for Steven to say something.

"No, sadly. I haven't been very lucky in that regard. But I do have a lady that I am very fond of. She's the one that works at the match factory, you remember?"

I shook my head no. "Sorry, I don't"

"Ah, that's okay. I'm not sure it will even work out. You almost done here?"

"A few more to go. It's monotonous, I know. But someone has to do it," I said as I got to the top rung of the ladder.

I strained as I reached for the bulb, turning it to the right to engage the amplifying process. This caused the lamp to spark to life right before our eyes, burning the lightning-shaped filament into my eyes. Stepping down from the ladder, Steven and I heard footsteps shuffle and scuff against the cobblestone off behind us. Hearing people in conversation, we turned to see if they were coming or going and if we needed to worry or not.

We made out about four people in the dark alley coming from the part of the street I hadn't gotten to yet. Their faces emerged from dark voids of wonder and uncertainty into the luminescent reflections of the light. Steven and I could hear broken clumps of laughter and conversation that got clearer as they got closer to us.

"How's the night been for you, love?" The lady on the left asked.

She was hanging off the arm of a stout man in a guardsman outfit. Unlike the stern-looking man, she had a smile of what I assumed was joy stretched across her face.

"It's been mighty fine there, poppet. But maybe the night could be a whole lot better," the stout man slurred.

The woman giggled and took his hand as she tugged lightly. "Call me Martha, love."

I could make out a lady on the far right, taking in the fact that she was slightly older and a bit more corpulent. The man she had in her grasp was taller than the first with a strange, lanky gait about him. As the men drew closer to Steven and I, I could tell they were stumbling, evidence that they had something to drink that night.

"What about you, love? Have you been happy with the evening?" the older woman asked as she pulled the taller man along.

"I think it's been more than enjoyable, Polly. But I need some other kind of enjoyment," the beanstalk said, reaching for her bosom.

She slapped at his hand. "Not yet, love. Soon." She giggled as they made their way further down the alleyway.

The group was past us now, starting their way around a corner. Their voices faded, and the giggles lost their potency as they drifted down other corridors and alleyways further from us. It made me wonder if I should have been concerned or not, but we decided that it was best to leave it alone; no sense in bothering them.

"With what happened at the match factory, you'd think that more women would be trying to get professional jobs," Steven said.

"I know. I agree. They have come leaps and bounds in the last few months," I added.

"A consistent stream of money and better working conditions? Yeah, it has to be better than meeting men at night for a few pence," Steven said, looking at me. "Either way, too much for us to think about tonight. Shall we go to the pub?"

Looking at him with a grin, I said, "Time to get lushy."

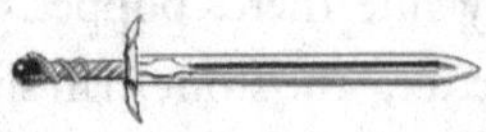

7th, August, 1888
Whitechapel Borough, London, England
3:30 a.m.

Leaving the pub with another few drinks in hand, Mary giggled with a happy buzz from all of the alcohol. Tripping over her own feet, she yelled out to her friend, "Martha love, how's your joe?"

The air stayed silent, devoid of any laughter or chatter. Mary thought this was odd; she just left her friend for a moment to go get something for them to drink. Even though she was alone with some joes, Martha could usually handle herself very well.

Mary decided to call out to Martha once more. "Martha? Are you there?"

With no response, she walked to the corner of the decrepit brick and mortar building, wondering where her friend was. She heard someone talking beyond her sight, so she peeked around the corner. Upon doing so, she saw the two men she and Martha were with that evening talking amongst themselves. They had another person with them that was standing in the shadows, making it difficult to see them. A faint yellow glow in the shape of a small stone came from the shape of the man at waist height.

"We need to get this one right; he told us that she is one of them," said the beanstalk.

"We both thought the first one was taken care of," said the stout man.

"He needs her blood. If we don't make this one work, he will have ours instead," said the beanstalk.

The two bickered with each other while the third man stood without speaking. Martha lay on the ground in a heap, motionless with her extremities at odd angles.

The dancing light from the sparsely spaced lamplight reflected off the small pool of blood that had started to collect at the men's feet.

"We should probably move her from here. This is way too out in the open. I saw a courtyard a little while back that would do," said the beanstalk, crouching down to Martha. He took a lock of her hair in his hands and lifted it to his nose. As if the smell was intoxicating, he breathed in heavily, still rubbing the strands of hair between his nose and fingers.

"Well, come on then. Let's go take care of this," said the stout man.

Standing back up, both men reached down to lift up her still form. The stout man grabbed her shoulders as the beanstalk grabbed her feet.

"Hey! Put her down!" Mary yelled. She threw the drinks in the men's direction. "Leave her alone! What are you doing to her?"

The men looked at Martha with surprise and frustration.

"Go grab her. We don't need anyone screaming to no copper about this," said the man in the shadows.

The stout man dropped Martha's shoulders without hesitation, causing her head to make an audible thud as it hit the ground.

"Why would you do that?" asked the beanstalk.

"What? You want me to go get her or?" the stout man asked.

Mary started to turn and run to get help. Scared, she tried to stay upright, but the buzz of alcohol came back with a vengeance.

"Just go get her, you numbskull," said the beanstalk. "Hurry up, we don't have all night."

Mary had a few hundred feet on the stout man when she tripped and hit the ground. Grit and small stones dug their way into the skin on her palms, elbows, and knees. Panicking, Mary tried to get up, grabbing onto the nearest lamp post to aid in her struggle.

Mary turned her head to see behind her only to realize the stout man was nowhere to be seen. She began to panic as uncertainty welled up inside her.

"Please! Leave me alone!" she yelled. It was followed by a wave of crying as she choked out "Someone help!"

Mary slowly got to her feet as she looked around frantically for the stout man. Silence strangled all hope from the air, leaving room for other things like fear and dread.

Mary's breathing wouldn't let up, so she began to hyperventilate, chest heaving violently where she stood. The world blurred with tears that filled her eyesight, causing everything to become unrecognizable.

"Come here, Polly," echoed the stout man's voice. It boomed from what seemed to be all directions. "Where are you going, love? We can still have so much fun together!"

Mary tried to start running again to no avail. As soon as she rounded another corner, she ran right into the stout man's arms. She struggled and kicked, screaming for help, for anyone. Her lungs were being crushed with a tremendous weight, like an avalanche brought on by a whisper.

The squeezing caused darkness to creep in around her eyesight. She couldn't take in any more air, and the strength began to leave her muscles.

The man in the shadows came closer to them, tapping followed with every step. The glow grew in size as he approached, shining atop a jagged black cane. Everything around her got fuzzier by the second except for a smile on his face. It glinted in the light from the lampposts, almost as luminous as the man's cane.

"Don't you worry, Polly. It'll all be just a dream," the stout man whispered in her ear.

With her last breath, the world went black.

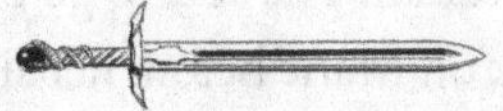

7th, August, 1888
Spitalfields Borough, London, England
5:32 a.m.

I shot forward in my bed, causing the whole frame to skid underneath me. My body was frozen to its core from the cold sweat plaguing me.

Looking around, I could see that nothing was out of place even though for a moment, I felt like *I* did. Nothing was missing that I could see in the early morning dusk. I moved my arms to check them, realizing they were good. The next thing I tried was my legs, followed by my wiggling my toes.

I really don't like when I wake up at home without knowing how I got there. I don't remember leaving the pub last night, nor do I remember what happened during that time.

The fading moonlight sprinkled through the flowing and flapping window curtains. With each new gust of wind, the light danced on the worn wooden floorboards. It reflected off the hilt of Excalibur leaning against the chair in the corner of the room.

Reaching over to the bedside table, I blindly pawed in the dark for my pocket watch. After a second or two of knocking things over and making more of a mess, I found what I was looking for. I clutched the watch in my hands and crawled towards the light to tell the time.

Only five in the morning. Well, that's a bit of a let down. I was hoping for at least two or three; then I would have been able to sleep longer.

Knowing that I wouldn't be able to go back to sleep, I decided to get up and go check on Marie before her shift was up at the hospital. I rolled off the bed, padded over to the chair, and threw on my clothes from the night before. I followed this up with putting on my sheath, jacket, and hat.

I went to grab for the front door when a feeling of paranoia washed over me. Almost like something, or someone, was watching, and I was unaware of it. Out of the corner of my eye, I saw movement, causing me to spin on my heels toward the source. As I looked around, I saw there was nothing, so I ran towards the window to look. I peeked my head out to around some more, still feeling that same sense of paranoia.

The late August air was muggy and thick, hitting me like a brick wall as it made it hard to take deep breaths. A small gust of wind swept up dust and sand into my eyes, temporarily blinding me. I rubbed them, struggling to open my eyelids when I heard a cough and heavy breathing come from around the corner.

My mind went foggy, filling up with the same heaviness that I felt in the air all around me.

Scrape, scrape

The smell. The now familiar acrid, salty smell. It hung in the air like dust swept up in a storm.

I don't quite think I could get used to this; this uneasy feeling of helplessness.

But something was different, something was wrong. Like usual, I couldn't move my limbs, but the difference was that I felt like I was sinking. Like I slipped off the safety of the nearest moss-covered rock while crossing a stream, sinking deep into the muck of semi solidified silt. I shook, trying to get out, trying to scream, but nothing worked. I tried opening my eyes and was rewarded for my continued efforts. I could see, and that was all that mattered.

It wasn't much, just a haze of shapes and colors, mostly grays. My vision started to go dark once more. Panicking, I tried yelling again, to no avail; all I heard was silence. The darkness took over once more.

Scrape, scrape

I faded back to the here and now, feeling disoriented and stuck.

I wish my visions could actually tell me something useful. No, I would even just settle for something direct rather than all of this mysterious stuff.

"Hello? Who's there?" I strained while rubbing my eyes, hearing no one answer.

With my head still leaning out the window, I finished blinking to get the rest of the debris out. While Glancing down the road to the left, I heard scrapes on the cobblestone coming from the right, followed by a familiar whistle. Snapping my head towards the noise, I could see someone turn the corner about twenty-five feet down where the lane came to a crossroads.

"Oi! What are you up to?" I yelled. "Who are you?!"

I groaned from the awkward pressure on my midsection as I pulled myself out the windowsill. The whistle's tune was familiar and gave me cause for concern. I made a split-second decision and took off down the street after the person.

This is all so suspicious. I hope no one breaks in while I'm gone.

The footfalls of the stranger became fainter as I ran, so I decided to pick up the pace. I rounded the corner and saw the person about forty-five feet away, with more people filling in the gaps between us. Some were coming home from a rough night out, while others were just starting their day by heading to work.

I tried to keep up with the person, but I kept losing ground. My eyes seemed to be playing tricks on me because, at this point, it almost looked like two people rather than one.

If they were trying to rob me, one could have been a lookout.

"Hey, you! Stop!" I yelled, getting more and more winded the further he, or they, ran.

I could see them duck underneath the archway that leads into George Yard. Following them, I ran headlong into the empty void, but to my surprise, there were other people there.

I skidded to a halt and saw four of them standing in a circle off in the corner near the set of stairs leading up to some of the apartments.

One was a taller man dressed in a constable uniform that seemed to just come upon the scene. Another looked like he was a day laborer in simple layman's attire. There was a woman in a beautiful flowing dress, cowering behind what I assumed was her husband, who was dressed better than the day laborer. The fourth man was turned towards whatever they were standing around, head tilted to the ground. I couldn't make out his face, but he was wearing a bowler hat, a cane, and nicer black clothing.

Everyone but the constable began to back away, gasps of fright and confusion coming from them.

"Blood! There's blood everywhere!" the woman screamed.

It was a bloodcurdling noise. One that struck fear in the heart. One that made dogs tuck tail and run. Backing up further than the rest, the woman tripped on her dress as she tried to turn and run off. Her husband reached down and helped her up before they both took off out of the courtyard.

The day laborer talked to the constable while all this was happening, motioning to whatever was on the ground between them.

"Lord in heaven, who did this?" asked the constable.

He moved closer to the mystery lying at their feet as they spoke. I heard the man next to the constable retch from the sight, liquid slapping the cobblestone beneath their feet. He mumbled something that sounded like he could've lived his whole life without seeing what he saw today.

"I was heading off to work." The man stopped to gag some more before spitting. "I thought she was alive at first. I thought she was okay."

He retched again as he turned away from the gore.

I got closer to have a look at the source of distress myself. "Sir? Is everything okay?" I asked.

To get his attention, I placed a hand on the constable's shoulder, my dry skin clung to the wool uncomfortably. It had the desired effect and then some, causing him to jump and knock my hand off him.

"Who are you?" he asked as he turned in my direction. The man gathered his composure, flattening his ruffled clothing.

Without saying anything, I pulled out my ID badge to show the constable, hoping it would be enough of an explanation.

He took it out of my hand for a moment to look it over. After a moment or two, he gave it back and said, "Nice to meet you, David, my name is Thomas Barrett. It's good to have another lawman here."

I nodded and asked, "What's going on?"

"John Reeves brought me here," Thomas said as he motioned to the gentlemen, who was still dry heaving next to us. "He was leaving for work and saw her laying here."

"I thought she was okay. I thought she was fine," he stammered as he dazed off into his thoughts.

Searching for the right words, Thomas spoke again. "John thought she was just a vagrant, sleeping off a night's stupor. But then he realized it was a woman, savagely killed. That's when he came and got me."

I thought about his words as I took out my Embyr to get a closer, more clear look. My knees popped as I crouched to look at the mess on the ground.

Constable Barrett patted John on the shoulder to get him out of his trance. "John, we need you to go get someone. Would you go and fetch a doctor?"

"Yes– yes, I can do that," John said.

He turned away, heaving some more, jogging out of the courtyard.

I couldn't believe what I was looking at. There is a difference between what lay here before me and what I saw at the coroner's. When Emma was on Dr. Thatcher's table, she looked peaceful, elegant almost. Skin of porcelain, smooth and flawless, devoid of anguish and pain.

But this, this was madness, this was senseless. The blood and viscera painted a picture of pain and suffering. Her face, whoever she was— she wasn't here anymore. Whatever lay in front of us was no longer human, stolen away from the world in the deep endless dark hiding from the moonlight.

Moving my Embyr up and down, I could see she was in shambles, pieces almost. Blood was everywhere as it spread out from the center of all the nonsense. The smell started to get to my nostrils, sparking a sense of urgency for me to evacuate the latest meal from my stomach.

"Do you know who she is?" I asked, still soaking in the nightmare at our feet.

Constable Barrett kneeled down for a moment while I held my Embyr near her face. Taking out a pencil from my pocket, I used it to move a few hairs from her face.

You seem so familiar. Why are you familiar?

I wanted to help in a way I could, so I put my pencil down for a moment and reached up to close her eyes. Those cold, hopeless, distant eyes.

"She looks familiar. Meredith? Martha? I don't quite remember. What I do know is that she's a prosti– was, I mean," he stopped himself.

Probably to help preserve what little humanity; dignity she might have left.

"She normally ran with the more unmentionable crowd," he finished.

I stood up in hopes it would hold my dinner down. My hopes were dashed rather quickly, so I turned to walk for a moment to get some fresh air.

"Who would do this?" asked Constable Barrett. "What kind of monster could do this to someone else?"

"I don't know–" I said with concern.

"I got one! Here she is!" John yelled, coming back from fetching a doctor.

"She?" I asked, turning around.

Walking behind John was Dr. Thatcher. She had a brown leather bag slung over her shoulder, dressed in a white overcoat, dark pants, and shoes.

"Doctor Thatcher? I thought you just dealt with dead bodies in the morgue."

"Of course you would assume I am only capable of one thing," she said with a tone of defiance. "I am also a practitioner. I saw John running around yelling for someone, so I decided to come help."

"It's great of you to come help, Doctor Thatcher. Sorry, I didn't mean to make it sound condescending. Of course you are capable of other things," I said in defense.

Dr. Thatcher bent down to have a closer look at the woman on the ground, or at least what was left of her.

"It's only been a few hours," she said.

"A few hours?" I asked.

Looking up at me, rolling her eyes, "Yes. A few hours."

"Whoever did this certainly didn't have control. We need to get her to the mortuary. I can tell you more information about what happened here after a closer examination."

"Alright, Constable Barrett? Can you handle this from here?" I asked.

Looking over my shoulder, I checked to see if he was successful in keeping his dinner down as well. The constable looked as if he was fairing.

"I can," he said.

I nodded and looked around for the last man, the one wearing the bowler hat. After a moment I realized he was nowhere to be seen, so I turned back to the constable. "Wasn't there someone else? He had a hat and cane I thought."

He looked around for the other man, "I don't see anyone else, sir. Did he run off with everyone else?"

"I don't know. You should probably find everyone that was here to get statements for the investigation."

Who could have done this? Why?

I returned my Embyr to my right side pocket as I stood up, deciding that I needed to go and see Marie. I took my hand out of my pocket and rubbed my temples with my eyes closed. As I did this, I noticed something bright beyond my eyelids. I opened them to the warm radiant glow of the ring.

What? When did this start glowing?

Stopping in my tracks, I turned immediately to take another look at the group of people hovering over the body.

I didn't shake the Doctor's hand, nor did I shake Constable Barrett's. Could it be from the woman on the ground? I did touch her eyelids to shut them, so maybe. I need to see Father Hubert and find out what's going on. If the glow is from the woman, then this could mean it was Jakobus hunting after yet another descendant.

Chapter 14

Second Hand

7th August, 1888
Shadwell Borough, London, England
6:30 a.m.

I walked through the double doors that led to the infirmary. Without paying much attention to my surroundings, I turned the corner fast and ran into someone. It threw me off balance, causing me to fall to the floor in a heavy thud. As I hit the ground, I rolled to the side and sprung up to my feet, sword ready to be pulled. Before I could start hacking and slashing, I noticed who I had bumped into.

"Dammit, Jules. Why? Can I get through one day without seeing your sorry face?" I asked.

"Can I get through one day without seeing you run into people, me included?" he retorted.

"I feel like we both have issues that need to be worked on; regardless, why are you here?"

"I heard about an incident last night, and I was going to check on one of the people involved. But since you're here, I'll let you handle it, considering it's your wife in there," he said, motioning to the hallway to the sectioned-off patient quarters.

"I appreciate the concern and trust; I'll inform you of what I learn. See you around then," I said, departing towards the quarters.

Why do I always run into him?

I entered the room and immediately heard Marie's voice near a bed sectioned off with a privacy curtain. Satisfied with the quick deduction of where she was, I walked over to her and peeked around the curtain.

In the bed next to where Marie stood was a woman sitting propped up. She was an unremarkable woman with features that would blend in with a crowd.

"Hold this on your head. It will help with the swelling," said Marie.

"What's this?" she asked.

"It's just ice. Now, stop fussing and put it on that awful bump."

The woman took the rag filled with ice and brought it up to her forehead, staring off into the distance.

As I got closer to Marie, she glanced over her shoulder at me. "Give me a moment, would you dear?"

I nodded and whispered, "Sure."

She smiled before turning to the patient, giving her a warm, hope-filled smile. "I'll be right back. Just keep holding that on your forehead."

The woman on the bed made an unintelligible comment as she continued her stare at nothing. Marie put her hand softly on the woman's shoulder and gave it a gentle, reassuring squeeze. She let go and stood up as she led me back around the privacy curtain.

"Davey, what are you doing up so early?" she asked.

Before I could reply, Marie gave me a quick but warm peck on the cheek. She rested her arms around my neck for a moment with her face on my chest. I put my hands around her and squeezed.

"I missed you. I know it's only been half a day, but I missed you," Marie said as she let out a long, slow breath.

"I have too," I said as I dropped my arms down around her waist. "I woke up and couldn't get back to it. But that's okay. What happened here?"

"Oh," she said, looking back at the privacy curtain. "She came in an hour or two ago. Talking about a man beating on her."

"What's her name? Did you get one yet?"

Marie wiggled out of my grasp and grabbed the chart hanging off the edge of the metal frame of the curtain. She peeled back the first few pages to check for the woman's name.

"Her name is Mary Ann Connolly, but she goes by Polly," Marie said as she put Polly's chart back on the small, loose, crooked hook. It teetered back and forth on the metal supporting rod after she let go of it.

I watched Marie as she rubbed her hands together, warming them from the cold that seemed to never leave her alone.

"Like I said, she came in not too long ago. Her injuries aren't very serious. She was bashed on the head with a blunt object. Would you like to talk to her? Maybe she could tell you something import-ant."

"Sure. Of course I can," I said.

Marie muttered a thank you and gave me another peck on the cheek.

I walked around the curtain and saw Polly holding the rag to her forehead still. "Mary? Are you doing okay?"

She shook herself out of a dazed state and croaked out, "Huh? Yeah. Yeah— I think— I think so."

"Mary, can you tell me what happened? Why were you roughed up?"

"Are you a peeler?"

"Yes, I am. Is that a problem?"

"I have nothing to say to no peeler," Polly sneered as she shifted her gaze off to the right, ignoring me for a moment.

Marie came back around the privacy curtain and muttered something under her breath that I couldn't quite make out. She reached for Polly at the same time, one hand to her shoulder for an embrace and the other to the ice on her forehead.

"You need to keep this on your forehead, Polly. It'll help. Please," said Marie.

Mary nodded in understanding.

"Why won't you talk to him? He just wants to help," Marie gestured.

"It's true, I am only here to help. Please tell me what happened," I said.

Mary put the rag back up to her forehead, followed by a wince and an exclamation of pain. She shifted on the bed and said, "I'm not talking to no peeler."

I looked over at Marie, "Just let me know, okay? And there is another thing I'll need you to let me know about something else."

"What might that be?" Marie asked.

"On my way here, I ran into another one," I said.

"Another what?" she asked.

I motioned for us to go behind the curtain again. We walked back around it, and I murmured, "Another murder. I stumbled upon another murder."

Marie gasped, covering her mouth with her hand. "What happened? Do you know who it was?"

"She was stabbed. At least that's what it looked like. Blood was everywhere..." I trailed off as I saw it again in my mind's eye.

"I can't believe this keeps happening. Are we even safe?"

I pulled her close into my arms again. "Of course we are; please don't worry."

Marie mumbled into my chest, "What can I do?"

Pulling her back away from my chest, I said, "I need you to tell me if anyone comes in; if any more women come in injured. Anything may help."

Both of our heads jerked around to the sound of metal screeching on the worn wooden floor. Polly had gotten up from the bed and leaned against the privacy curtain, peeking around the corner looking at us.

"What was her name?" she asked, tears flowing like a flood, carving through the dust and makeup on her face.

"Whose?" I asked.

"The woman! The one you just mentioned to her!" Polly yelled as she jabbed a crooked finger at Marie.

Marie walked over to Polly and put her arm around her shoulders. "Please, Mary, have a seat. Getting this worked up isn't good for you."

Mary struggled slightly, trying to shake off her arm. She eventually gave in, and they walked back around the curtain.

As they sat, I started to explain. "I'm not really supposed to tell you this, but we think her name was Martha or Meredith. The constable on the scene wasn't sure."

"That's my friend. Her name is Martha," Polly said as she dropped to the bed, seemingly defeated. She started to cry again, soft sobs turning violent as she tried to talk more.

That's her friend? That can't be. Wait, her name is Polly. Could it be the same Polly I saw last night?

"What were you doing last night, Polly?"

"Why do you need to know about last night?" she choked out, blowing her nose into a muckender. The noise reminded me of the elephants trumpeting in the traveling circuses that came through town.

"I was with— I was with a friend last night," Polly said as she looked at my wife for support. "We were with clients. They took us to a couple pubs around eleven last night, for a few hours at least."

She shifted uncomfortably again on the bed, switching hands holding the rag to her forehead. Her body heat started melting the ice, causing water to trail down her arm and splash softly onto her dress.

"Can you tell me more about last night? Anything at all? Whatever little detail you might remember could help," I said.

"I don't know what happened," she said with a sigh. "Near the end of the night, before we dealt with business, we stopped so I could get Martha and I another drink. After leaving the pub, I came back to—" Polly choked up for a second.

Marie patted her on the shoulder and said, "Go on, it's okay."

"They were standing over her, just talking. Saying something about needing her blood," Polly gasped.

Marie and I exchanged quick glances while we listened to her talk.

"She was bleeding, and I ran, but they were chasing me, and I didn't know where to go. I'm next. I'm next," Polly said. She started to get more agitated again, shrugging off Marie's hands.

"It's okay, please, relax. You are okay," I said.

"I'm next! I can't be here. They'll come for me. I'm not safe," she yelled.

Marie grabbed onto her arms once again. Trying to put her back on the bed, she looked to me for help.

"I don't know their names. I don't know who *HE* is. How did I survive? Why did they let me live?" she said hysterically, not letting us get any words.

Polly was inconsolable at this point, crying and looking around frantically. Marie grabbed my arm and started to pull me away, saying, "You should leave. I will try and get more information about what happened to her after she calms down a bit."

"Wait, what do you mean by *he*? Who is he?" I asked, trying to stay calm as Marie tried to push me away.

Polly choked out the words between gasps of air. "The man with the glowing cane."

"Please, honey. Just leave," Marie said.

A few other nurses came flooding over to help with the now thrashing Polly. They were able to get her under control and calm her down with the aid of a drug. She stopped moving so frantically and became limp on the cot. Marie was able to peel herself away from the mess of a situation and walk with me away from the other nurses.

Looking back over Marie's shoulder, I saw what this was doing to Polly. I would probably be the same. Not knowing why your friend was dead. Not knowing why you were alive. Not knowing why it was even happening, and wondering if you were even safe to go back outside at night.

"Okay, you're right. I have to go check with Dr. Thatcher to see what she found out about Martha. She was nearby when it all happened," I whispered to Marie so as not to get Polly worked up any more than I needed to.

"I'll see you at home then, Davey? Will you be long? Or Will I just see you tomorrow morning?" Marie asked.

"I'm not sure, sweetpea. I don't know what's going on around here, and I don't want to sleep if I can help with any of it," I said defiantly.

"Don't be daft; you need your sleep. You won't be any help if you're falling over, dead to the world, every other minute," she said, throwing her arms around me once more.

I need to do what I can. I can't leave all this to chance. It's all connected. Martha must have been a descendant. Maybe the men she was with could be Harvesters, the ones Father Hubert talked to me about before.

"Davey? Did you hear me?" Marie asked.

"Sorry, no I didn't. What was that again, love?" I said sheepishly.

"See, you already are dead to the world. It hasn't even been three hours since you've been up," she said, giving me a judgmental look.

"Okay— Okay. I will make sure not to run meself into the ground. I just need to see a few people."

"Alright," Marie said, pursing her lips, giving me the look that can only mean one thing: *You better listen to me.* "Please just be careful. I don't want to be on me shift and see you hobble in." Her eyes started to tear up. "Or be dragged in."

Taking her hand in mine. I said, "It's okay, Marie, I'll be fine, I swear. Remember? I have the luck of the Irish."

She turned from Polly and said, "But aren't you always saying it's bad luck?"

I smiled as I tried to choke down a chuckle. "It's actually supposed to be good luck. Like I said, don't worry so much. I'll leave you to it then. I don't want her to be without your amazing, calming presence any longer."

Marie reached up and rested a hand on the side of my face as she spoke. "You always knew what to say to make me forget why I'm upset, or why I'm worried. Just be safe."

Shadwell Borough, London, England
7:11 a.m.

I arrived at the hospital and immediately went downstairs to the basement. Normally I wouldn't go to such a dreary place, but it was where Dr. Thatcher's office was located. The further down I went, the more I was filled with a sense of dread. It crossed my mind that the reason I felt this way was because of all the dead this place housed before they were carted off to their final destination. But I arrived just in time so that I didn't get lost in the rabbit hole of my psyche.

"Hello? Anyone here?" I shouted as I looked around. Deciding I didn't want to get yelled at again, I waited in the front near the entryway. "Hello?"

"Will you stop yelling? Honestly, it's annoying. I know you're here," she said, walking towards me.

"Sorry, I don't mean to annoy you. How did you know?"

"Look to your left," she said, pointing over my shoulder.

I turned and followed her finger to where she was pointing. In the corner of the room, I saw a large circular mirror hanging from the ceiling. The tin-mercury amalgam foil that coated the back surface of the glass was peeling in some spots, causing a darkened spider webbing effect in certain areas.

"Is that a mirror?" I asked.

"He can use his eyes. But can he use his common sense?" she asked sarcastically.

I frowned and turned back to her.

Dr. Thatcher sighed. "Maybe we didn't start off on the right foot. We can be more professional about this if that is okay with you?"

Looking at her, I laughed. "Of course. I'm right-handed anyway."

She glowered at my response, huffing out some air in the process.

"Okay, you're right, sorry. I would prefer this to be a more pleasant ordeal. I came by to check and see what you could figure out? If anything stood out to you?" I asked.

"I haven't been able to tell much, especially with what was left. I ran into someone on my way back here, and he happened to know the victim. He offered to help since he is currently going to school to be a doctor, so I accepted." Dr. Thatcher held her hand out, motioning to her left.

A pair of white shoes walked in front the darkness of the doorway, stopping next to Dr. Thatcher.

"This is Mr. Edward. He told me he is a family friend of the victim."

White shoes?

I looked the man up and down as he took a bow.

Isn't this Dr. Henry? I met him when I was helping with the other murder, Emma's. I saw him at the hospital right after it happened.

His features seemed more sinister and dark, with sharper lines and pointed edges. His cheekbones and nose came to more of a point, skin blotted with pot marks from smallpox or scarred pimple tissue. An unnatural curve to his smile lines slashed their way into the deepest parts of my mind, causing my body to want to involuntarily cower in fear.

I reached my hand out to his. "Me names David, but I usually go by Davey."

Before he could take it, I felt the world around me go blurry, and the light drained from my sight.

Scrape, scrape.

Everything was bright. The clouds in the sky flowed like first thaw in the early creeping stages of spring as the water hastily made its way to its final destination. The sun breaking through in streams felt warm and new, making the hairs on my arms stand on end. The smell of salt caused goose flesh, accompanied by the uncomfortable yet welcomed tingling feeling.

What is the purpose of this? Why does it keep happening?

"If I am to learn something, I need to know what it may be!" I yelled. "This certainly doesn't—"

Wait a minute, I can see!

Looking down at my feet, I wiggled my toes and dug them into the soft, coarse sand. Surrounding me were a few rolling hills that formed from crashing violent waves throughout the years. Ammophila grass swayed quietly back and forth in the cool ocean breeze, waving to whoever stood near. Slowly, darkness crept in and closed the gaps that were letting in the light. The sweet breeze turned sour with a violent force that thrashed the reeds in fits of anger.

"Davey, time is running out," said the voice that was accompanied by a hand on my right shoulder.

"What am I to do? I can't find him. There is no direct proof of who he is," I said as I turned to see who was speaking to me.

I took in the man's features, taking note of everything in case I needed to remember this. His face was soft but stern, weathered but understanding. Curly black hair flowed from underneath a magnificent gold and jewel encrusted crown. He had a full mustache and beard that matched his flowing locks, all while dressed head to toe in armor beautifully etched in gold.

"He's been in front of you the whole time. You've met him, more than once," said the man.

"But who is he? I can't do this on my own!" I yelled in frustration. "Who are you?"

"You know who I am," he said.

Just like the light around us that was fading away, so did he, disappearing from my sight. Thunder rolled in again as it branched through the sky, etching in my eyes. As like last time, the wind picked up and threw sand into the air as the world around me grew as thick as a foggy night at sea.

Scrape, scrape

Why does that keep happening? It's a warning, but what is it pointing towards? Who is it pointing towards?

"Davey, you okay?" asked Dr. Thatcher.

"Um, yes. Sorry," I said, shaking the vision from my mind.

"Okay... Anyways, like I said. Here is Mr. Edward," Dr. Thatcher said, motioning to Mr. Edward.

"Hello." He nodded, shaking my hand. "You can call me Edward. No need for formalities," Edward said.

"Are you– Your name isn't Dr. Henry? I asked, confused.

He looks an awful lot like Dr. Henry. He even has the white shoes.

Edward chuckled, patting up and down his body. "Last time I checked, I was still Edward. But I'll let you know if I notice a difference," he said, winking. "Anyway, back to business. From what I could gather, she was alive as it happened. At least to begin with."

Edward motioned to have me follow him as he led me back to the table in the examination room. As before, the table was held in the back room of the lab in the middle of the space.

A single Tesla bulb swung back and forth, light cascading in alternating waves over the white linen sheet laying over the body. The splotchy blood stains were a stark contrast to the pristinely white linen. Mr. Edward and Dr. Thatcher grabbed a few leather aprons off some hooks from the wall and put them on over their heads. Edward took an edge of the sheet and pulled it free to expose what lay beneath.

"There was severe damage done to the lower abdomen all the way up to the neck of the body. I believe from the preliminary investigation, we determined the wounds consist of about thirty-nine stab wounds."

I looked at her again and noticed she was clean. Edward or Dr. Thatcher must have washed her while they did their autopsy. They either did this to look at the wounds to count them all or to help with her decency. Either way, I had the strange feeling that Edward was treating her more like a specimen than a human. If that was the case, then something told me that the latter, being decent, wasn't the first thing on his mind.

I get a really bad feeling about him, and seeing all these wounds clean is really messing with my head.

"I also think it was done with two different sharp objects." Edward pointed to the lower abdomen area. "One, which was smaller, could have been a pocket knife." Moving his hand up to her bosom, he said, "And the larger one was most likely a dagger, sword, bayonet."

"Why?" Dr. Thatcher asked, hand covering her mouth. "I've seen quite a few things, more than I'd like to admit. But why?"

"Only God knows," I said. I paused for a second, looking at her face.

I may be able to know why her if I check, maybe...

"After I did my autopsy, I found that she was missing an organ," Dr. Thatcher said.

"An organ? What organ was that? I asked as my eyes darted from Martha's body to the doctor's face.

Dr. Thatcher met my gaze. "Her liver was missing."

"Why a liver?" I asked.

What would Jakobus want with a liver? If he did this, why?

"A liver is a good source of many different nutrients. I have seen people using it for a large array of things," said Mr. Edward. "But anything is possible."

"May I have a moment? Just to say some prayers for her?" I asked.

"Uh, sure. Just come check with us when you are done. We will be in front going over some other notes," Dr. Thatcher said, eager to find something else to do.

I covertly watched them as they left the dim room in haste, trying to seem occupied. As they left, I turned back to look a little closer at Martha.

I wonder if she was another descendent, or maybe she was just collateral damage. I also have to take into account that there may be more than just Jakobus to worry about. He wouldn't be the only one that's ever killed someone around here. Maybe she might give off another glow like Emma did, and I would know for sure.

Deciding it would be easier to do this without seeing her, I carefully covered her back up with the linen. I reached to her hand gently, trying to be cautious and keep the noise down. They already probably think I am crazy, so I didn't need Mr. Edward or Dr. Thatcher to see what I was doing to solidify their hunches.

My eyes closed as I reached underneath and grabbed a finger on her right hand. It was an involuntary gesture, maybe to help me from feeling horrible about the situation. Soon though, I realized it would be hard to see what the ring would tell me with my eyes shut, so I opened them and looked.

The light glow showed through the thin white linen, confirming my suspicions that I was mulling over this whole time. A surge of images flashed in my mind's eye as I saw a man walk from the deep dark depths of the night's shadows. There was an amber light that was accompanied by a haunting, chilling click. I let go of her hand in confusion as I fell to the ground from surprise.

What was that? More random things in my head? Why? Who is that man? Is it the one Polly was warning me about? Could they be The Harvesters that Father Hubert warned me about?

"David?" asked Mr. Edward. "You alright?"

I looked up at him as he entered the room. My eyes peeked around him to see if Dr. Thatcher was following but realized she wasn't. When I shifted my gaze back to Mr. Edward, I saw him hold out his hand to help me up. I almost did but stopped myself as I remembered the ring was still likely glowing.

"I'm fine. Thank you, I'm fine," I said as I got to my feet without help.

"What was that? Why were you on the ground?" he asked.

"I uh– I slipped. I think there was a little water on the floor or something. Maybe it was on my boots from outside. I have a bad habit of falling and running into people," I said, feeling my face grow warm with embarrassment.

"Hmph, okay," he said, pausing. "Why is it like that?"

"Why is what like what?" I asked.

It dawned on me that he may have seen the ring on my hand, so I put them behind my back. I saw his gaze look past me so I turned to see what he was looking at. Martha's hand dangled over the edge of the dissection table. It was most likely caused by me as I fell to the ground.

Mr. Edward scooted by me as he invaded my personal space a great deal more than I felt comfortable with. He reached down to her arm and gently lifted it up and over onto the tabletop. I observed his actions as he did this, noticing he tucked the linen underneath her forearm in a fashion that reminded me of someone mourning.

"There, that's better," he said.

His voice contained a strange tone of care and regret. A sense of shame and pride lingered in his inaudible whispers. He cleared his throat after a moment. Standing up, he said, "I uh– I think you should probably leave."

10th August, 1888
Farringdon Borough, London, England

"Father, how are you?" I asked.

"Well, my boy, I am doing okay. What of you?" Hubert asked, reaching out his hand to shake.

Returning his gesture, I took it. "Not the worst, I suppose. But I am not here for pleasure Father. I have been meaning to make it by to talk to you again."

"It is nice to see you nonetheless. What can I do for you today?"

"There was an actual murder this time. I basically stumbled upon her this morning."

Father Hubert gestured to the chairs next to us. "Have a seat, Davey. Now, tell me what happened."

Taking a seat, I started. "I woke up early this morning. I thought I should just go give my wife a visit. I started to get ready When I heard a noise outside my window."

"Do you know what it was that made the noise?"

"No, I wasn't at first. I leaned out the window to have a look when I saw a man, or men, jogging down the alleyway. With everything going on lately, I decided to run after them. Especially because they were spying on me outside me window."

"Probably a good choice. Did you catch him?"

I shifted on the seat beneath me, feeling as if it was more unbearable than it usually was.

"No. He, or they, were too quick. I then stumbled upon the scene, where a group of people were looking at the body," I said.

"Do you think he blended in with any of them?" Hubert asked.

"I thought that at first, but I couldn't find out who. The undertaker I have been keeping in contact with happened along with a constable. I ended up going to talk to her later about the victim."

"I'm assuming that is what you want to tell me then."

"Correct. Doctor Thatcher found out that whoever did this also took something." I paused, mustering the stomach to tell him what else was on my mind. "Whoever did this took her liver."

I looked over at Hubert to see what he thought, to gauge what his response might be. At first, confusion was present on his face then along came dread that was muddled with anger. He shook his head and stood up, beginning to pace back and forth.

"Father, what is it? What does it mean?" I asked.

"Not sure. I have heard stories of everything they believed in back then. Who's to say that Jakobus uses his Harvesters to gather ingredients for barbaric rituals and offerings to prolong many things, including himself," he said.

"Maybe it isn't what we think. Maybe we are getting ahead of ourselves," I said. "I don't want to put all of our focus on one thing, and it turns out not to be correct."

"You're right, my boy. Let us see what comes our way next. But we need to be careful and watch what happens around us," he said.

Chapter 15

Too Little, Too Late

30th August, 1888
Whitechapel Borough, London, England
11:25 p.m.

The night set into the city streets like a low flowing fog. A sickness, something contagious that followed people closely during their nighttime endeavors.

The Tesla bulb street lamps flickering, giving light to a patchwork of alleys and archways. It illuminated the women on the corners, working for their wages for the next night's lodgings. One would not need to look hard to see men wandering about, looking for something to fill the loneliness in their hearts instead of going home to their beloved families.

A man in black walked quietly and elegantly down the cobblestone to the next pub. It was with a sense of knowing where he could get what he wanted that he made his way past each of the darkened doors. The clicking of his tongue to the tune of a simple little rhyme echoed along in step with his footfalls. As the man stopped three or four paces past one pub in particular, he heard a woman talking, giving him pause. He sank into the shadows just beyond their sight, allowing him to see everything that was going on.

"Well come on, love, let's have it. We had our fun, now I need me money," said the woman. She adjusted her skirt back down to her knees, fixing her hair. "Unless, you want to pay for more than one?"

Off to the corner, still on the ground, a man mumbled something inherently. Lifting a bottle to his lips, he took another healthy pull from it before lowering it once more. He let out a massive sigh of relaxation as the bottle clinked on the ground.

"C'mon Mary, can this one be on the house?" The man questioned in the form of a garbled mess.

"No, I can't be doing that. I need to make doss money somehow. If I don't get charity I won't be giving any either," Mary said.

Stumbling to his feet, the man swayed back and forth for a moment. Reaching into his pocket, he pulled out some coin, putting it in Mary's outstretched hand. "Here you go love, I'll be seeing you soon," The man stuttered out. He turned to walk out of the small courtyard. Slurring, he said, "See you around, Mary."

Watching the man continue away, she called out, "Hopefully sooner than later. I'm okay with you letting me have your money, love."

A smile touched her lips as she looked at the coin in her hand. After a moment of admiring it, she started off towards the closest pub. The man watched her as she departed, slowly following behind her. He made sure he kept his distance, but stayed close enough to hear her as she started to sing aloud:

Swept away but never gone,
I'll go my way but won't be long,
Someday soon I will return,
Knowing more from what's to learn,
All the wounds time will mend,
No matter what I'll see you again.

She sang aloud happily and let the words bounce off the walls, filling the air all around her. It felt almost as if it cut through the thick hopeless smog that sat in the streets of the city. After she finished up the last verse, she arrived at the door of another pub with the sign above the door reading, 'The Frying Pan'.

Stepping through the doorway in his search of Mary, the man's nostrils were assaulted with the pungent odor of pipe tobacco. The stench of sweat from men and women that hadn't bathed days combined in the air with vomit from those who had too much to drink. Keeping his distance, the man watched as Mary squeezed between patrons to get a footing at the bar.

"A pint?" asked the grungy bartender.

"Oh Thomas, you know me too well," she said, tucking a few locks of hair behind her ear.

"Well there, Mary, it seems to me that a lot of people know you too well," Thomas smirked, his gaze visibly settling on her barely contained bosom.

"Oh quit it. I have *some* modesty," Mary said, sitting up straight, mocking offense. Her breasts spilled over her corset even more so than what was thought possible, adding to the sarcasm she was trying to convey.

A few more men at the bar stopped their fuzzy conversations to look at Mary and her friends that came in with her earlier in the night. They all drooled over them, acting more and more like heathens than men.

"Now boys, I'm here for a drink. Come find me later on if you need some release," she said, winking. She plucked the hat off the closest day laborer and put it on her head as she turned and swayed away from the bar.

Vermin. Pests. The lot of them. A waste of God's energy and a waste of space. I need to correct what should have been done long ago.

The man sat down at a table near the back, sneering over an ale left over from the man before him.

I think she is a good choice. She won't be missed much.

Picking up the ale, he drank from it and threw it on the ground after he finished. The noise and commotion from the other pub-goers covered up the racket the mug produced, causing the man to get just a little bit angrier. He thought, *of course they hadn't noticed, they all were too busy sinning the night away.*

As the night drew on, he stayed for a few hours, watching her through thirsty eyes. After a while, she finished the last few drops of her drink and left The Frying Pan. The man was pleased with this, falling into step behind her as she left the pub.

31st August, 1888
Whitechapel Borough, London, England
1:15 a.m.

After all, me mother stayed strong,
Me father left, he said so long,

Mary sang, walking down the street as she swayed back and forth. She continued her song after a few short, shallow breaths.

Down to the pub, he'll be back,
I remember, and never lost track,
Counting the days till he's here,
Losing track of all the tears.

The man in black crept behind, hearing the pain and sorrow creep into her voice with each verse.

I'm doing them a favor, letting them drift from this life full of pain and misery.

He himself recoiled in pain, keeling over from the sharp jabbing in the stomach. Something in him reasoned and said that he would not do this. That this wasn't the right thing to do.

The man shook himself from his momentary confusion and jogged to catch up with Mary. Silently, as he got so close, he could smell her perfume float behind her. He took in the aroma into his nostrils and held it for a moment.

Mary stopped at the entrance to a lodging house on the corner, talking to someone invisible to the man. He listened as they spoke, intent on not missing any small detail.

"Mary, you don't have any money. You can't stay here tonight," a man behind the cover of the doorway said.

She frowned at his response.

"Why can't I? I can make the money up. I can make it tomorrow," Mary said, anger crystallizing in her words.

"If you don't have the doss money now, I can't help. Sorry, Mary."

Mary batted her eyebrows and flattened down the bunches that had formed in the front of her dress. Plumping up her breasts, she teased by pulling her sleeve down and showing some bare skin. "Anything I can do?"

The man snuck closer to them, making the other voice's face visible. He heard the other man turn her down once more, expressing a mixture of pity and regret. With a few more choice words of anger and resentment, Mary turned from the man and walked off in an undetermined direction.

The man began to get restless, frustration stirring and growing as he followed Mary for hours. It began in his feet, boiling, hot and molten like bubbling magma. The longer he watched her, the quicker it spread to his legs and chest, finally spilling over as it reached his head. A throbbing feeling that forced him to frequently rub his temples.

The constant following and watching was wearing his patience thin, fraying like a violin bow of an undervalued orchestra member. Doing his part but unable to feel the release that appreciation brings.

The time is now. NOW!

His eyes bore imaginary holes in the back of Mary's head, burning hot with hatred and disgust. The night, early morning now, brought all of the events from the evening before crashing to a halt.

"Emily!" Mary squealed, running to embrace her.

The two hugged, wrapping arms around each other.

"Mary! What have you been up to this fine evening?" Emily said, audibly inebriated.

Make your move.

"Just doing what a girl needs to do," she smirked.

"You know, we– we are here for each other," Emily spilled, hiccupping.

What are you waiting for? What are you doing? WHAT ARE YOU DOING?

The two girls giggled. It was a contagious kind of giggle that threatened to change any kind of mood a person was in. The kind that would grate on the nerves of anyone who was seemingly immune to it.

Shaking off the infectious humor, he followed them into another pub. The laughter did, in fact, cause him to become more furious as it pounded like a drum against his temples.

Too late, going to have to wait. Now we have to wait.

The door opened to a long wooden bar top along the right side of the wall. Behind it were rows upon rows of shelves housing bottles of alcohol that consisted of gin, rye whisky, bourbon, and

Madeira wine. Stools lined the worn bar top, a few empty but most of them filled.

In the middle of the room were a few small round tables spaced ten feet apart with four chairs surrounding each. Attached to the far left wall were partially cushioned booths with leather torn and splitting from time and wear. Some of the pub occupants started to hum and merrily sing with each other without rhyme or reason.

"Where are you staying tonight?" asked Emily, now twirling in circles, dancing to the music.

"I was going to stay at the lodge house on Thrawl," she said, starting to go along with what Emily was doing. "But I spent all me doss money on drinks earlier. They turned me away."

He sat in a booth furthest from the door and watched them more, waiting for the right moment. *Now we wait. We wait to take. Take care of the mess. It's just a test, the test to clean the mess.* He started to carve grooves into the wooden tabletop with his fingertips, chips forming in his nails.

He stared nervously for long periods of time but turned his gaze away in fear of alerting the women. The back and forth of conflicting intentions wore him down to the last string. Shrill ringing in his ears began to get louder, drowning the music down to a faint hum.

"I think that is enough for the night," said Mary.

"Where are you going to stay?" Emily asked.

"Not sure, but I'll be fine," Mary said, turning towards the door.

Step step, watch your step. Time to follow the chosen one. Now we need to start the fun.

He followed with a renewed determination, small amounts of the frustration seeping out of him through each step of his feet. Mary started humming once more, something off-key and less intelligible than earlier in the evening. It was more just noises and sounds of happiness and content than any actual words. She walked slowly down the sidewalk, somehow staying upright. Mary stopped a few feet ahead and began muttering to herself.

She won't be able to fight. He tells me this is right, I believe it is. I see it with the sight.

"I think right here. Yes, right here will do. Right here is the place to be," she said.

Mary started to lean against the wall, starting the awkward descent to the cold cobblestone that seemed cozier by the second. Off in the corner of her eyesight, Mary saw a man walk along the sidewalk.

"Why hello there, love, fancy a four-penny knee trembler?" hiccuped Mary, trying to stand upright again.

"Why, little birdie, why are you out here all alone?" asked the man.

"For a good time, can you help me with that? What's your name, love?" she asked, now leaning against the wall.

"Well, I go by a few. Yes, yes I do. But for you, I think Jack will do."

"Will you help me then, Jack?"

She stood from the wall and walked in a half sultry, half-drunk saunter toward Jack. He was suddenly on her, grabbing her by the neck, arm stretched out tight. Mary let out a small yelp, still unsure of what was happening. Jack's grip tightened as she started to scream, cutting it off with each squeeze. Her arms began to flail, struggling to gather the strength and coordination.

"I will help you, yes I will. Just be quiet now, please be still," he said.

His face was now illuminated by the small amount of light given off by the lamppost. Mary tried to scream again but was rewarded with another squeeze of her throat. A smile pulled tight across Jack's face, teeth crooked and yellow like a crescent moon haunting the night. Jack knew that being close to one like this was jeopardizing his control. His mind shuffled back and forth, causing him to struggle with even simple thinking. He let go of her neck, causing her body to drop to the ground.

"You don't need to worry now, no you don't," Jack said, pulling out a knife. He spun it for a moment, letting the light reflect off it. His smile somehow grew bigger as each second passed.

Mary gasped, breathing in lungfuls of air as she struggled to keep the darkness from creeping into her sight. Feeling around on the ground for something to pull herself up, she began to panic when she noticed there was nothing there to help. Everything finally sank in as she struggled, hitting her like a runaway freight train. Jack lifted her back up by the fabric of her dress, pushing her against the wall.

"Now, Mary, where are you going?"

"Please. Please don't," she cried, tears trailing down her face.

"Sorry Mary, it's too late. Too late, but you just wait. It'll all be over soon," he said.

He held her firmly against the wall and raised the knife into the air. The moonlight glinted off the perfectly polished metal of the blade, reflecting the beauty of the night into Mary's eyes. In one strong swipe, the knife came down, slashing deep into her throat. In the seconds that passed, beads of blood formed from ear to ear in a long thin line where the knife had sliced through her flesh. As her body fell limp to the ground, blood flowed heavily from her neck as it formed rivers in the cracks of the cobblestone.

With her quick death, clarity washed over Jack. Clearing away the impulsive urge to kill, the frustration and anger draining from him just as the blood did from Mary. The ringing ceased, allowing the silence in the night to seep back in.

"This is how it's supposed to be," he said as he took a few steps back, looking at his work. His art. "But not quite done. One more thing I need. There is one last thing you can do for me, Mary."

CHAPTER 16

And Then There Were Four

31st August, 1888
Whitechapel Borough, London, England
4:00 a.m.

The air was muggy and thick, relentlessly choking the sweat from people that were unfortunate enough to be out at this time. Silence was the only thing fighting to be most prominent in the early hours against the darkness that was receding quickly.

"Steven, how often do you have to do maintenance on these things?" I said, straining as I held a few large wires in my hands.

I peered up at the towering mass of copper, steel, and wires in awe. Tesla coils were quite a sight with their large hulking shaft that extended ten yards into the sky. The entire device was surrounded by row upon row of metal tubing and atop all of that rested a metal sphere.

"This one is always breaking on me," he said, straining to wrap the cords with the patch. "Okay, you can put them back down. Let's take a few steps back this way. Got your rubber grounding boots on still?"

Looking down, I shook my right foot in his direction. "Yup, still on."

"Alright, let's see if I actually know what I'm doing," he laughed. He leaned down to check the reception rods and a few more things on the Tesla coil to make sure everything was back in place. He reached for the switch and asked, "You ready?"

I nodded. "Yes sir, let's see if she lives."

With a loud clang and a hum, the machine fired up and began to produce the sparks. They arced from the top of the device to the reception rods, zapping in random rhythmic bursts.

"It's alive! It's alive!" Steven yelled, faking a maniacal laugh.

I elbowed him in the side and shook my head. "Really? Frankenstein's Monster?"

He recoiled in pain, hissing.

"You'd think you'd stop being stupid. You know I'm just gonna keep elbowing you."

"But it's so ingrained in my personality, can't you accept me for me?" he said as he feigned a hurt expression.

Rolling my eyes, I looked to my right. Someone was running up the road towards us. "Oi! What's going on?" I asked.

Panting, the man gasped for air. "There's someone hurt!" he said, pointing down the road, "A woman, she's hurt!"

"Who? Who's hurt?" I asked, looking at Steven, then back at the man.

"Don't know her name. The other constable sent me to get help. I'm on me way back now. The doctor wasn't there for me to alert," he coughed out, trying to catch his breath some more.

"Let's go then, we'll come help. Come on Steven," I said, starting to jog after the man.

4:15 a.m.

A few minutes later, we got to the woman. She was against a wall, somewhat lit by the lamppost about six feet from her. There were two people talking with their backs to us, presumably about the woman. Getting closer, I recognized one of the voices as that of Dr. Thatcher.

"Dr. Thatcher! What's going on here?" I asked, coming to a stop next to her.

Steven and the man fell in line behind me, halting on either side.

"Oh good, it's Tweedledee and Tweedledum," she said before sighing. "Sorry, I forgot. We are trying to be nicer and a tad more professional."

I shrugged off the comment, knowing she was actually trying.

Gesturing to the ground with her head, she began again. "Constable John Neil flagged me down because he thought she was badly injured. I just got here. Do you mind if I continue with my questions, Davey?"

"Sorry Doctor. This man... Erhm. What's your name, sir?"

John Neil looked at me. "That's John Thain," He looked back at John. "Thanks for trying to get help. Luckily, the Doctor here showed up right after you ran off for help."

"Alright, we're all on the same page. So what happened, then?" Dr. Thatcher asked as she crouched down to look more closely at the woman's neck.

"I was just walking me beat. I had made me rounds about an hour before now and saw nothing. Nothing of this sort," said Constable Neil. "I was just minding me own business."

"What exactly urged you to stop?" asked Dr. Thatcher, continuing the examination.

"I saw something on the ground," I said, motioning to the original spot where she was leaning against the wall. "I took me Cynder Box and decided to take a closer look," he said, shivering.

"It's okay. Go on, Neil. You know every bit of information is important," she said.

Neil rubbed his neck, looking at the ground for a moment. "When I got me Cynder Box closer, I saw she was hurt. Bad. Blood was everywhere on the ground, and the front of her dress was covered with it."

Dr. Thatcher leaned in closer, noticing the starting point for some of the blood coming from the abdomen. "Neil, bring that Cynder Box a little closer. I need to see this," she said. With more light, Dr. Thatcher lifted up the part of her dress that covered her stomach. The cloth was torn to shreds revealing a deep gash in the lower abdomen. "What a monster," she choked out. The doctor stood back up, taking a step back. "From what I can tell without a close examination is that she was disemboweled. But obviously, the entrails were taken. Either to another location to be disposed of, or something else." She shuddered at the last part. "The odd part is that her legs are still warm, so this must have happened within the last half hour. He, or she, could very well still be around here," she said, looking at every one of us.

I don't think I'll ever get used to this.

Crouching, I decided to take a better look at her myself. Like Neil did, I took out my Embyr to get a better look. As I held it in front of me, light glistened off the semi-solidified blood that caked her and the ground in front of her. Her ice white dress turned pink and thirteen shades of red with the ever-staining blood oozing and spreading.

Wait, the ring is glowing. Was she a–?

"Steven, come here. Tell me what you think," I asked. Crouching next to me, I whispered, "Look, the ring."

His eyes turned from me, to the body, then to my hand.

"This can't be a coincidence anymore. We should probably talk to Father Hubert again," he whispered.

I looked back at the woman's face, expression of terror frozen onto it. Feeling like I needed to, I reached out to close her eyelids. Upon contact with her skin, a flash of memories flooded into my mind.

Shaking it off, I stood up. I said, "Steven and I will have a look around. Maybe we can find who did this."

"While you do that, I'm going to have the body transported to the morgue so I can do a better examination on it," Dr. Thatcher said.

"Like always, Doctor, let us know if you find anything odd. We'll be in touch," I said. "Come on Steven, let's see what we can, well, see."

Farringdon Borough, London, England
10:15 a.m.

"Ah gentlemen, come in, come in. Have you made any headway in finding Jakobus?" Hubert asked, holding the door open for us.

"Hello, Father," I said. "Some, we believe. Not particularly the best, but some nonetheless."

We walked to the main part of the church, becoming more familiar with the place each visit. But even so, it is still just as impressive as the last. We both took a seat in the worn chairs off to the left.

"I just had a first-hand experience with the memory transplant, or whatever you want to call it," I said. "Actually, it was the second one I had."

Father Hubert took a seat next to me and said, "Really? I've never experienced it myself. How did it feel? What did you see?"

"It was weird, a mixture of a dream and a memory. Like deja vu, it felt like I've lived it before, but new for the first time. Hazy and distant but familiar," I said.

He raised an eyebrow as he listened intently.

"I saw who did it, or at least parts. The memory was shrouded in darkness. The man that did this, his face was fuzzy and darkened with shadows. I couldn't make out many features except his mouth."

"What made it so memorable?" asked Hubert.

"Crooked yellow teeth, in a smile could chill to the bone." I paused before continuing. "I saw a series of events; they flashed through my mind. I think it was the man that killed her. He was stalking the woman all night."

"Anything else?" Hubert asked.

"Not really sure. It was all out of order, I think. Flashes of seconds here and there. That really was about it. I think it was from the woman that was murdered. But this means she was another descendent. That makes two women that are, so far," I said.

"And she was disemboweled as well," added Steven.

"Did you check if she was missing any organs? A liver, perhaps?" Father Hubert asked.

"I couldn't tell from where she lay, but I will be seeing Dr. Thatcher later to check," I said.

"If so, then Jakobus is using them for something. Maybe like we talked about before," Hubert said. He rubbed his chin and spoke again. "You said this was your second?"

"Yes, and I think we may be dealing with The Harvesters. Or at least for one of the killings."

"Quite an issue, dealing with not only the evil one himself but his followers too," Father Hubert mumbled.

Shaking my head, I stood up in anger and said, "We are always two steps behind him."

Steven put his hand on my shoulder, trying to calm me down. "Of course we are. For all we know, he knows us, and knows that he is being chased. But we just need to catch up is all."

Father Hubert chimed in. "I think the first thing you two can do is follow up with any friends of hers. Maybe they know something. Maybe they've seen something. At this point, he may just keep killing for the fun of it. Who knows, if anyone has seen anything, they might be in danger as well."

"I'm just tired of these things happening. Me whole life has been uprooted because of this thing." I strained, rubbing my temples.

"It's okay, Davey, we'll get him. We'll put a stop to all of this. Let's go back and talk to some friends. Maybe talk to the person running the boarding house she stayed at. See if anyone at the pubs in the area remembers seeing her last night," Steven said soothingly.

8th September, 1888
Farringdon Borough, London, England
8:23 a.m.

The newspapers had been circulating information about someone named "Leather Apron". The nickname was somewhat of a reference to the rumors people had of the killer that had been making the rounds, killing at what seemed to be random to the general public.

Of course, this is causing some people to worry about their own safety. But most everyone still stays out late in the evenings and early mornings, thinking that nothing will happen to them. The police, Steven and I included, have been hard at work trying to flesh out all the possibilities and investigating everything we can. Interviewing everyone that's talked to the victims before their deaths. We received word from Emmet Kestler, the cordwainer, that he needed to speak to us.

So that early morning, we made our way to his shop for the second time. Surprisingly, this time it was open with some people milling about inside.

"Emmet!" I said, entering his shop.

Emmet hopped off his chair and walked around the counter. He stopped at the end and said, "Davey, Steven! Nice to see you again. I was just thinking about the both of you," Emmet said.

"Really?" I asked. "What for?"

"Firstly, I did some more tinkering with my bio-electric rifle. I wanted to actually give it to you, Steven," he said.

"How come?" Steven asked.

"It seems your investigation is heating up, so I thought it would be more useful to you than me."

Emmet leaned over and picked up the rifle from the underside of the counter and handed it over to him. As Steven took it from him, it was promptly followed by the focusing pack.

"You have any instructions for this thing?" Steven asked, looking gracious but bewildered. He turned the rifle over in his hands as he examined the carved wood.

"No! But you can figure it out. You work on Tesla coils, don't you?" he asked.

"Yes, I do," Steven stammered.

Smiling, he said, "Good. Now, the next item of business. I found my ledger! It was right where I thought it was."

"Where was that?" Steven asked, cocking an eyebrow.

"Underneath another book, actually. I forgot I was reading the book over there and put it back on the counter the last time I saw you two." He pointed at the edge in front of him. "It's ironic because of what the name of it is. *Treasure Island*."

Emmet paused momentarily, staring at us expectantly. With his hands, he made air quotations. "Get it, because it's hidden 'treasure'?"

I rolled my eyes. "Did you find a name for gray shoes?"

"No, I forgot to look. But I can now!" he beamed.

Not thinking my eyes could go back any further, I decided on just looking at him. "Well then, let's get to it."

Grabbing the ledger from underneath the other book, he walked back to his chair and sat down. The cover of the ledger was brown, worn, and decorated with water rings all about it. There were gold corner protectors with a Celtic knot design. Next to the bottom right corner was a scratch that, upon observation, seemed to grow in size with each use.

Emmet flipped about three-quarters of the way through and stopped on a page filled halfway to the bottom. The writing consisted of names, addresses, and the kind of service or repair he did for them. Putting his finger at the top, he trailed down the page, reading each name out. Stopping at the tenth name down, he looked over at the service section of the entry. "Hmm, hmm," he sounded, rubbing his chin.

"What?" I asked.

"It doesn't say anything about any gray shoes. But it does contain the information about white ones I have worked on," he said. "Yes, I remember him. Odd fellow, he was. The first time I met him was normal, nothing special. But after finishing the work on his shoes, he came back to pick them up about a day or two late."

"Steven, could it have been white shoes this whole time?" I asked.

"Maybe, it has always been at dusk or at night when they were seen. Maybe the darkness cast on them made them seem gray instead," Steven said.

I rubbed at my temples and asked, "Anything else about him?"

"He seemed like a completely different person the next time I saw him. But I do have a name; do you want it?" he asked.

"Yes, what is it?" Steven jumped in, wanting to feel involved.

"His name is Mr. Edward Hyde." He cocked an eyebrow and shrugged. "Well that's weird. The address is smudged. Isn't that odd. Well, at least you have a name."

Thinking, I blurted out, "Of course! Steven, we've met him before!"

Looking at me, he exclaimed, "At the hospital. He was with Dr. Thatcher!"

"You think that means he did it? That he was the one that hurt her?" I asked, looking at Steven.

Steven furrowed his brow. "I'm not sure. Possibly. We may be jumping to conclusions."

"What about Dr. Henry? It can't just be a coincidence that they look exactly like each other," I said. "Are you sure you don't have an address, Emmet?"

"Yes, sorry. You may need to access your police records, no? Maybe go check with the London hospital. I remember him saying something about working there the last time he was here."

"A good place to start. That's where we've seen him both times before," I said. "Steven, let's go."

"Wait, I didn't have a chance to offer you tea!" Emmet shouted to us.

Steven and I were already halfway out the door before Emmet could finish his sentence.

"Thanks again!" we yelled back in unison.

Whatever happens after this point is beyond our control. To think that everything else that will happen will somehow be worse; that we were in the calm of the storm. God help us all.

Chapter 17
Heads Or Tails

Field Notes Entry 6

The city is spread thin in a state of panic. I have made frequent visits and left urgent notes to Dr. Thatcher at the hospital. But it seems that whenever I stop by, she is out on a call, either to help with the investigation or help out at the universities. I need to see her to ask about the latest victim and pick her brain about what is happening lately. It seems she may be the only person that knows Mr. Edward, or whomever he is.

2nd September, 1888
Shadwell Borough, London, England
8:37 a.m.

"Dr. Thatcher? Hello?" I called out, walking into the morgue.

Silence came in response as I looked up at the domed mirror in the corner. The dark hallway behind the front counter was reflected off the spidered surface as I scanned it for any kind of movement.

I turned to peer down the hallway, hoping to see something more clearly without the stained surface hindering my eyesight.

So far, I hadn't seen anything amounting to life, but instead of leaving, I decided to go check the back room. Maybe she was busy and hadn't heard me from back there. Since the wireless light fixtures were all turned off, I reached for the switch to add some light to the situation. Trying to turn them on, I flipped the switch, but nothing happened.

That's weird. I wonder if the coils have some issues upstairs. I hope they have someone to check into that.

"Hello," I yelled once more.

Again, no response. Deciding I didn't want to walk down the hallway without light, I reached into my pocket to take out my Embyr. Upon contact, the Embyr lit up the hallway with its incandescent glow.

That rules out that the Coil Substations are out of order. Maybe the issue is with the fixtures themselves. I'll let someone know about that when I leave here.

Holding it out in front, I continued down the hallway. The weight of my feet caused the worn floor to creak.

Good thing I'm not trying to sneak up on anyone.

Halfway down the hallway, I began to hear a few voices arguing with each other.

"I can't keep doing this," said the soft voice.

"But we need to, yes we do," said the harsher voice.

"I don't want to. I want you to go away," said the soft voice again.

Those voices are familiar. It almost sounds like—

I crouched and quietly inched my way to the doorway at the end of the hallway, trying to catch a glimpse of the voices' owners.

"Soon, there won't be a *we*. Soon it will just be *me*," said the harsh voice.

I peeked around the corner and saw the room still had some power. The swinging Tesla Bulbs in the middle of the room gave off enough light to reveal the shadow of a man behind the privacy curtain.

Should I just ask them who they are? Or should I wait till they walk around the curtain?

"Just stay out of my head! I want you gone!" said the softer voice.

The shadow started to pace, staying hidden by the curtain. After a few back and forths, it came around the right side, walking towards the doorway.

"Hello? Have you seen Dr. Tha–" I began to ask. The surprise took me off guard and caused me to stop in mid-sentence. "Edward?"

The shadow looked up from the ground. "Yes?" he asked, focusing on me. "Oh, it's just you, Davey. How are you?"

"Okay, I suppose. Have you seen Dr. Thatcher around?" I asked.

"No, I haven't seen her. I think she left an hour ago. Why? Did you need her for something?"

"Yes, actually, but I can wait around for her. Wait, where's the other person that was here?"

"What other person?"

"You were arguing with someone, weren't you?"

"Oh, Henry? You know him," he said, smiling. Moments after, Edward's head twitched, neck spasming backwards and to the sides, abruptly stopping at unnatural angles.

"Help me," he croaked.

They are the same person. Edward and Henry are one. How can this be?

"Oh, stop. You're being dramatic," Edward said.

"What was that?" I asked in terror, hoping what I was seeing wasn't actually real.

"That was Henry, don't worry. He's not feeling well right now," Edward said.

Henry's head kept twitching back and forth. A few cracks from his neck filled the air, crisp and to the point like a ringmaster's whip.

"Davey, please listen. I don't have—" Henry attempted to force out, but was cut off.

"Sorry about that. He gets a little riled up sometimes. What were you saying?" Edward asked.

"Wait, I thought you said you weren't Henry. I asked last time I was here," I said.

"Oh, I'm not. I'm Edward. This is Henry."

For a split second, Edward's face flashed from calm and collected to strained and in pain. He collapsed to his knees, fingers laced around his neck. Worried, I took a step closer to help but then stopped myself.

Be careful. You don't know what in the bloody hell is going on.

"Davey, please listen. It was me. I can't control him anymore," Henry said.

"Who?" I asked.

"Edward. I can't control him. He isn't just a part of me. He is a part of him," he whispered in pain. "He has plans for more. He was doing it for a reason. But now it's just for fun."

"More what? More killings? Who is planning these things?" I cried.

"Jakobus! He won't stop! He is just toying with you. He wants you dead. Your blood must end!" Henry bellowed.

A scream came from his form on the ground, causing me to throw my hands to my ears. With my eyes fixed on him, his mouth shut as he stood up once more. Henry's face returned to a calm expression, and he motioned to me to lower my hands.

"Sorry about that," he chuckled. "He doesn't know when to shut up, I suppose. Where were we?" he asked.

His face switched back to one of anguish. "Please, I can't kill anymore. I don't want to."

"Let me help you then, just come with me, Henry. I can help. I have others that can too," I said, trying to coax him.

Within a split second, Edward was front and center again and laughed. "Tsk, tsk, tsk. You can't stop us. We will get you all."

"What's going on here?" asked a voice from behind me. I whirled around to see who it was. Dr. Thatcher stood in the doorway, looking at us with anger.

Before I could give her an explanation, Edward ran past us, pushing me into Dr. Thatcher. Off balance, I saw him run off down the hall.

"Sorry doctor," I shouted as I took off after him.

He ran down the corridor that spilled out of a service entrance in the back of the hospital. I could see him about thirty feet ahead of me.

"Wait, Edward! Or Henry!" I yelled.

He turned a corner and kept running. Rounding it myself, I was clotheslined to the ground. Looking up at the sky, I tried to shake the fogginess that filled my head from the impact on the cobblestone without any luck. My eyelids became heavy, and my mind swam in confusion as everything went dark.

Scrape, scrape

I opened my eyes to a spacious, open ceiling room. A reassuring breeze rubbed against my arms and legs, like a childhood dog, protective and loving. The all-knowing night spread far and wide, blanketing the sky like a comforting lullaby.

I looked around and took in the tranquility in all its splendor. The bright stars lit up the night like a million candles, alive and free. A calm fire crackled and spit forth sparks telling a tale of woe to anyone who would listen.

In the center of the spacious room stood an ornate table surrounded by twelve large wooden chairs with a throne at one end. On the table was a spread of food meant for kings and queens. Goblets were filled to the brim with tart red wine next to plates covered with a variety of plump grapes, ripe apples, freshly baked rolls and many kinds of meat.

Only one seat was filled besides the throne, leaving the others cold and vacant. The shadows cast from the fire competed against the overhead starlight, creating a tranquil dance of life and death on the tabletop. A man wearing a set of gold-gilded armor and a jewel-encrusted crown sat at the center as a man wearing a simple brown robe sat next to him.

"Arthur, it is okay," said the man. "We all have followed you for a very long time. Through many harsh battles and unreasonable odds. And so we will continue to follow no matter the odds."

The fire spat and snapped more, voicing its concern.

Sighing, Arthur shook his head. "And for that, I thank you, Merlin. For that, I thank all of the loyal knights that have followed me down this dark and never-ending path."

"We will follow you to the end, till we stop him, or till he succeeds," Merlin said.

Arthur leaned forward momentarily, lighting up his face in a warm orange glow. The expression that lay upon it was one of sorrow, one of pain. The long years etched crooked lines and deep ravines, swallowing the bright hope of youth.

"Are you sure this will work, old friend?" Arthur asked.

"I am. It has to. It needs to. We can't leave this fragile world to fend for itself against an evil like this," Merlin pleaded.

A few long moments passed, both sitting in an eerie silence. King Arthur pushed his throne out abruptly as he stood up. He pulled Excalibur slowly from the sheath at his side, as if it could set off a chain reaction at any moment. Arthur held it up in the starlight as he turned the blade, reflections adding to the dance on the table. He placed it down gently in front of Merlin.

"Let us try then," he said, removing his hand from the hilt.

Merlin nodded and closed his eyes as he spoke. "To connect thoughts through blood, we need an offering of blood."

Arthur reached his hand to Merlin, holding it outstretched over Excalibur. Merlin opened his eyes and pulled a sharp dagger from underneath his plain robe. Merlin then placed Arthur's hand above the sword. He closed his eyes once more, chanting in Latin, and said a few words. With a flash, he shallowly cut Arthur's palm horizontally from side to side.

Arthur tightly squeezed his hand, fingers curling inward into the cut. It caused the blood to fall in droplets to the blade of Excalibur. "With this blood I give, by blood we may live. Connected through all time, by memories we will prevail."

A vibration grew from Excalibur, causing the room to shake. The sword lit up with a dull glow, slowly fading seconds later.

"Merlin, please retrieve who is left. We need to ensure our triumph," said Arthur.

Scrape, scrape

10:30 a.m.

"You alright there, Davey?" asked a voice.

"Ugh, what did I hit?" I mumbled.

Rolling to my side, I started to rub the back of my head.

"You really like running into people, don't you," said the voice again.

Looking up, I opened my eyes to try and decipher which direction the voice came from. They strained to adjust to the bright light above my head.

"Wha– who?" I strained. Trying to lean up in the saggy cot, I was met with resistance, causing my body to jerk back down.

"Whoa there. You took a nasty hit to the head, Davey. What were you doing to make the ground so angry with you?" the voice asked.

My eyes finally adjusted to the searing light, allowing me to make out the source of the voice. It was coming from Steven, who was standing closely over me to my left. At the foot of the bed stood Marie, leaning into Father Hubert's arms on my right.

"Where am I?" I murmured.

"In the hospital. You're lucky I found you, Davey. Some rapscallions knocked you out," Steven said, patting me on the shoulder.

"Did you– Did you catch him?" I asked, struggling to talk with the dryness of my mouth.

"Who?" asked Father Hubert.

"Henry. Edward. Whatever the bloody hell his name is," I said.

I looked at the bedside table, checking if there was anything to quench my thirst. Not seeing anything, my mouth decided it wasn't dry enough, so it kicked up a dust storm to help with that.

"You saw him?" asked Steven.

"Yes. He was in the morgue." I coughed from my dry throat. "Marie, can I have some water?"

"Yes, of course, Davey," she said, breaking Father Hubert's embrace. She walked around Steven to gently peck my cheek. Placing her hand on my face, she gave a few more kisses. "I'll be right back."

I looked back at Steven and Hubert as Marie briskly walked away. "I was looking for Dr. Thatcher to ask if she had seen him in a while. Guess I learned right from the source."

"So what happened after that?" Steven asked. "Was she there? Was he?"

"Dr. Thatcher was not in the morgue. It was odd. Scary even." I looked at Hubert as I continued. "I walked in on Henry arguing with someone. They were behind a curtain. But he eventually turned and walked towards the exit as I confronted him, and that's when I realized there was no one else in the room, besides us two."

I shuddered, thinking of the nightmare that had unfolded in front of me.

"What happened next? Why were you on the ground unconscious?" asked Father Hubert.

"He started to have a fit, and I was not quite sure what was happening. But he switched, changed from Henry to Edward. It just kept going back and forth. One second it was Henry asking for help, saying it was him that hurt Emma. Then he proceeded to change back to Edward, saying that Henry was weak; that he was just overreacting."

Steven and Hubert looked at each other in shock. Looks of confusion and concern mixed on their faces. As I finished, Marie came out from behind Father Hubert toward me.

"Dear lord, that sounds like something we've run into before. It's a very dangerous thing to deal with."

"Really?" Steven asked.

"Mhm, very, very unpredictable. I have heard of doctors and physicians doing tests on this kind of thing. I think it's called dissociation disorder. In fact, I have heard of a Doctor that is doing a class in Oxford soon, and I think I remember hearing he specializes in that kind of thing," Marie said.

Father Hubert rubbed his chin as Steven paced a few times.

Marie reached down and handed me a glass of water as I leaned forward. Steven walked over to me and braced my back with his arms as I tried to take a drink. The water was refreshing and cool as I took careful, measured sips. It soothed my writhing stomach, bringing it back from the brink of expelling anything left in it.

"I also had another memory, or vision. One from a past descendant," I said in between sips. "At this point, I can't really keep them straight. It felt as if I was there, which would make me believe it was a vision, but it was more like a memory."

"What was this one about?" asked Hubert.

"It was about how they attached the memories through the artifacts. It explains how the scar on the hand is a giveaway. The process involved a blood offering," I said.

Marie stood back up, giving me a quizzical look. "What do you mean by memories, by descendants, and blood offerings?"

"Wait, you haven't told her?" asked Father Hubert.

"Tell me what? Davey, what is he talking about?" asked Marie.

Steven and Father Hubert looked at me. Marie looked at them, and their eyes switched to the ceiling and floor, keeping occupied to avoid the awkward situation we all are in now.

"Marie, love. I haven't told you what has been happening these past months. Let alone what I, we, have been dealing with." I gestured to Steven and Hubert. "We are all related to knights of the round table. We are a part of a group called The Keepers."

She stared at me for a moment. "Obviously, that head injury is worse than we thought. I think all the running into people is taking its toll on you."

"No ma'am, it's actually all true. Well, maybe all the hits to the head are taking some sort of toll," Steven interjected.

Conveniently Steven was still holding me up, so like usual, I rewarded his humor with an elbow to the side.

"Ow, why?" he asked.

I gave Steven a quick glare before I continued. "It's a lot to take in. It's why I'm always running everywhere and why I jump out of bed without a good reason. I just wanted to protect you and don't want you involved because I would never forgive myself if you were injured because of me. The letter I showed you wasn't rubbish or blank. It was the truth."

"Davey, I think we will just leave you two alone. Maybe some catching up to do is in order. Good luck," Father Hubert said as he grabbed onto Steven's arm and pulled him out of the room.

12:30 p.m.

My mind was drifting in and out. The talk Marie and I had gone relatively well, all things considered. She took most of it in stride, but still maintained the illusion that because I ran into so many people, I hurt my head, and that is the real reason I believed all of this. It will take some time, but I think she will reluctantly believe too.

After she left, I also started thinking of the days of old, when King Arthur was alive, busy trying to stop the menace we are facing today. My thoughts were interrupted when a rustle from the curtain brought my attention away from myself.

"Davey, are you doing okay?" asked Dr. Thatcher.

I sat up in the cot, trying to look more presentable. "For the most part. I really have to be more careful."

"Yeah, maybe a little less running into people might help too," she said. Dr. Thatcher took a few more steps closer to my bed. "By the way, what did you need to talk to me about?"

"How did you know I needed to talk to you?"

"I saw Steven outside the hospital, and he told me you were in here."

"Ah, right. I did have a few questions about the last women we saw. I needed to know what you found out from the autopsy."

"Hmm, I did the autopsy. It is sad to say that the killings are getting more gruesome."

"Worse than before? Why, what happened to her?"

"Upon taking a closer look, I realized she was gutted." She paused, visibly disgusted. "She was cut from her sternum to her hips, deep, really deep."

"Was she missing a liver?" I asked, inching further on the cot.

"Yes she was, among other things too," she said.

5th September, 1888
Farringdon Borough, London, England
7:45 p.m.

I took in a huge breath, struggling to catch it. The sweat poured off my skin like a melting glacier.

"Would you like to quit Davey?" Father Hubert asked. "We've been at it for hours."

"No," I said, breathing heavily. "Not until I can knock your blade from your hand."

The sun started to set, casting the training field in partial shadows. It threatened us with the ghosts of the past, creeping ever closer with each passing minute.

"Are you sure? You're exhausted, and I am getting a little tired myself. Let's call it quits," Hubert taunted playfully.

I stood straight, rolling my shoulders and cracking my neck from side to side. "You may be right there, old man."

Before he could respond, I used all my strength to launch off my right foot, sprinting in his direction. Hubert brought his sword up for defense. I jumped up about three feet away, bringing my sword down on him in the same motion. My weight caused his block to falter slightly, both of us breaking contact and sliding off to the side.

"Looks like you have some energy left," he said. "But not for long."

I advanced again, determination overtaking my frustration and anger, readying my sword one last time.

I have one last chance. After this, I don't know if I have enough energy to try again.

I pointed Excalibur to the sky, left forearm close to my chest and right forearm elbow level with my shoulder. I charged, kicking up dust as I seemingly felt lighter than air. Hubert decided to take a swing at me instead of going on the defensive, which would prove to be a wrong move on his part.

I tilted Excalibur towards the ground, digging the tip slightly into the dirt. Bringing it back forward in an uppercut, I caught Father Hubert's sword in the middle. A vibration formed at the point of contact, causing his grip to loosen on his hilt. In an instant, the sword flew from his hands, coasting through the air and landing a good distance away. As the clang from the sword sounded, I had my blade at Hubert's neck.

With a hard swallow, he said, "Well done, Davey. That was impressive."

Dropping the point to the ground, I sighed heavily. "What was that? Why did Excalibur shake like that?"

"Honestly, I don't know," he said, rubbing his neck. "That sword holds many secrets. Not quite sure what else it could do but a good job nonetheless. You are now ready to face Jakobus in a sword fight, Davey."

Chapter 18
Friends At First Sight

Field Notes Entry 7

At this point in time, Steven has been brought to work at the same station I am a part of, mainly for convenience. Steven's inquiry of shoddy materials used in the production of the Tesla coils and my probe of any embezzlement by TEA employees have been formally combined for ease of investigation as well. So far, the findings, or lack thereof, have turned up no evidence of either. After a long day of tedious groundwork, amounting to a whole lot of nothing, we have received word that the Commissioner has requested our presence to speak in private of said inquisitions.

9th September, 1888
Westminster Borough, London, England
7:00 p.m.

"Davey, Steven, please take a seat," said Commissioner Warren, motioning to the oak chairs placed on the opposite side of his large desk.

"Ladies first," said Steven, snickering.

I squeezed through the doorway past Steven, elbowing him in the stomach as I passed. The wooden frame creaked from the added stress of our bodies pinching between it.

"Worth it," he strained, smirking and clutching his abdomen when I was through.

The commissioner's office was the biggest in the station's building, taking the same amount of space as the bullpen. The room was tasteful but sparsely decorated. On the right wall hung a painting of Commissioner Warren and his family. In said painting stood the ever stoic Warren on the left side, to the right sat his radiant wife Miriam and in between sat his beautiful daughter, Jessica.

I looked around and saw a bewitching oil painting about five feet tall by eight feet wide on the left wall. It depicted a woman with the skin of porcelain with hair of red that rivaled any fire. She lay upon what seemed to be a simple fishing boat guided along by a man in mourning of her presumed death.

"Commissioner, what is that painting of?" I asked, taking a seat.

"That?" he asked, pointing to the wall. "That is by an artist named Sophie Anderson titled 'The Lily Maid of Astolat'. My wife knew her from a while back. It is based on an old poem, I think."

"What is the poem about?" I asked.

"It is about a maiden that falls in love with Sir Lancelot, but he rejects her love in favor of Lady Guinevere. The story tells that the maiden died from unreciprocated love. To help atone for his sins, Lancelot embarked on a voyage to take the maiden's body to Camelot," said the commissioner.

I stared intently at the painting for a moment, wondering about the tale told by the poet, and thinking about what parts of the story were true and what were a fantastical tale of love. How many of the King Arthur stories were based on actual events? Which are facts and which are fiction?

"Davey?" Asked Steven.

"Huh? What?" I asked, shaking my head.

"Commissioner Warren was just talking to us. Were you listening at all?" he asked.

Looking at the commissioner, I said, "No, sorry, sir. Have had a lot on me mind lately. Please continue."

Like many times before, habitually, he pulled his pipe from the top drawer of his desk. He then grabbed a small leather pouch of loose tobacco to pack the bowl with.

"Davey, Steven. I have received word from the powers above me to select my two best men for a particularly special mission." He paused for a moment. As he did this, he grabbed some more of the tobacco from its pouch and packed the bowl of his pipe. "Yes, that's what we will call it. A mission. The reason for the escort is that Nikola Tesla needs a few bodyguards that have some familiarity with his technology. Tesla informed parliament he needed to go to America to retrieve some equipment he left in storage. Another reason is to try and pitch some of his technologies to the Americans, hoping to recuperate some of the money the Crown has invested in him and his inventions."

Steven and I looked at each other momentarily, then back at the commissioner. A second passed, and Steven let out a booming laugh. In response to this, Warren gave him a lazy stare laced with impatience. Warren then took a match from a box on his desk and brought both the pipe and the match up to his lips.

"Why us?" I asked.

We can't leave now. We have an investigation to attend to. It would be a bad thing to leave now.

Commissioner Warren took in a deep, extensive pull from his pipe, tobacco and match glowing red-orange. He then exhaled a rolling cloud that swelled and crashed over itself, spreading out ever further into the air.

"Yes. You two not only investigate him and his company, but are interwoven into it too," he said.

"But we can't. People are dying. They are getting murdered and killed for no reason. We can't just leave in the middle of it," I yelled.

"Now calm down, please," the commissioner said. "We will have many men on this while you two are gone. I simply can't do anything else about it. What the Crown wants, the Crown gets."

"Should we continue our look into him on our journey?" Steven asked.

"You're detectives aren't you?" he retorted.

"True, we will keep at that then. It'll keep our minds off it for a little while," I said, still furious.

"Also boys, remember, the Crown wants to make sure you are protecting an asset who is not only important, but worth quite a bit of money. So keep a good eye on him," Warren said. "Anyways, he has a driver ready outside to take you to meet him, so please, no more questions. I expect results and professionalism from you two. See you in a month."

As he finished, he took another hearty pull from his pipe. Exhaling with the force of a locomotive, he reached over to his waste bin and tapped his pipe on the rim. Orange and red glowing shreds of tobacco fell in force from the bowl, pulsing with the rush of oxygen, fueling their life.

"I still think we need to keep up with investigating all of the murders going on around here lately instead of being glorified babysitters to some spoiled Jolter," I said.

The Commissioner pulled the drawer out and placed the tobacco pouch gently inside, followed by the pipe. Sliding it shut, he cracked his neck, rolling his head from side to side.

"I have that covered. Please, don't be concerned. The women are getting the justice they deserve," Warren said. "Do you have any leads we could follow while you two are gone?"

I thought for a moment, deciding it was okay to tell him. "Yes, we have a person of interest. His name Is Dr. Henry Jekyll, or maybe Mr. Edward Hyde. We think one is an alias; not sure which, though. He seems like a good suspect overall."

Commissioner Warren mulled it over for a moment. "Okay, I will have some people tail him."

Hopefully, he is telling the truth. We can't afford to stop watching out for him.

My focus shifted from them, thinking about everyone that has been killed up to this point. Emma, Martha, Mary and Annie.

What is going on with this world?

Warren's and Steven's bickering crept back into my consciousness, momentarily causing me to forget about my misery.

"What is he retrieving?" Steven interjected.

The commissioner looked up at us with renewed frustration.

"Steven, I don't know. Maybe you should ask him yourself. Now get going!" he barked, cuing our departure.

I turned to say one last thing. "Mark my words Warren, he will strike again. You need your men to stop him before he can do that."

Steven put a hand on my shoulder. "Davey, it should be fine. The other men on the force should be able to take care of it while we are gone."

Leaving the room, Steven asked, "Why do you think he requested bodyguards?"

"Like the commissioner said, to make sure our asset is safe and doesn't veer off the decided path, I suppose," I said, walking down the hallway that led outside.

The sun peeked between the brick buildings and slate rooftops, reaching its grasp ever further into the sky as we walked out of The Great Scotland Yard. A friendly breeze welcomed us as we descended the stairs one at a time. Off to the right, a man of medium build was waiting for us. He was very pale, short, and had a head full of skin. On his face lay a beast of a mustache, an imperial, most likely made of all the hair that was missing from his scalp. He stood in front of a horse-drawn carriage while holding an old-fashioned oil-burning lamp.

"Davey? Steven?" asked the man, holding the lamp up to see our faces.

"Why are you using an oil lamp? It's not that dark out yet," I asked, pointing at it.

"Oh this?" the man asked. "I have a hard time seeing. Not much left in the way of eyesight, I'm afraid."

"Ah, okay, I suppose." I reached out to shake his hand. "I'm Davey and that's Steven."

I nodded in the direction of Steven.

"Nice to make your acquaintance, my name is Rick Cormac," Rick said, shaking Steven's hand after mine. "I am here to escort you to Mr. Tesla. Please, step aboard."

He ushered us to the carriage and opened the door, holding it for us. Upon entering, we both realized the windows were covered with immovable black curtains.

I wonder why we can't move the curtains.

"Ready mates? Okay, let's get going." He said, slapping the side of the carriage.

"Wait, you're driving? I thought you said you can't see very well," I stammered.

"Oh don't you worry. Ol' Jimmy does most of that," said Rick, patting the horse on the back with his left hand.

"Wait, why are the windows blacked out?" Steven asked, concern growing on his face.

Smiling, Rick turned and reached around the front to hang the lamp upon a hook near the coachman's seat. "Mr. Tesla is one for theatrics, so we indulge him as much as possible. Trust me, you'll see what I mean."

Before Steven or I could get another word out, Rick slammed the door shut. Deciding I didn't want to ride in the dark, I pulled my Embyr from my front breast pocket. In the minimally illuminated darkness, we could make out the scrape of boots on cobblestone. With a few grunts, Rick pulled himself up onto the driver's seat. Taking a few short breaths, he let out a brief and sharp whistle. In response, the horse drawing the carriage let out a few snorts and whinnies followed by the start of hard clomping on the cobblestone.

Richmond Borough, London, England
9:15 p.m.

The ride from the Great Scotland Yard to our destination lasted about forty-five minutes. Steven and I tried to keep up small talk, going over some of the investigation details and other things like the local weather. We realized we could pull the middle parts of the curtains inward to peek outside as we rode along. The night crept into the sky, spreading far and wide, reminiscent of an ink splotch coalescing in a glass of water.

The carriage slowed in momentum, eventually coming to a stop. I took this as us now being at our destination. A few obnoxious chuffs escaped Jimmy's mouth, breaking the momentary silence.

"Alright, we're here!" said Rick. Seconds after the announcement, he jumped off the coachman's seat, feet stomping to the ground with a thump. Rick leaned over to the oil-burning lamp and took it off the hook. "Now, come boys. Mr. Tesla is waiting for us!"

He opened the door to the carriage, letting us both out. A source of pulsing light off to the left streaked across the fields and trees that extended for a mile or so on our right-hand side. It lit up expansive sections of the grass, reflecting off the fresh dew that collected on the individual blades. Branches and leaves shook in the continuing light breeze, showing their underbellies like a submissive King Charles Spaniel.

Shutting the door, Rick did an about-face, leading Steven and I around the back in the direction of the light. Rounding the back of the carriage, our eyes landed upon a magnificent sight.

"This, my friends, is the Temperate house!" he shouted, gesturing to the building with his hands.

Presented in front of us stood a magnificent iron structure of thousands of windowpanes. The light radiated from each, breaking through the early night's darkness.

"What is this place?" Steven asked, glancing at Rick.

"The Temperate House was built and designed in 1862 by Decimus Burton and Richard Turner. It houses the larger plants here at the Kew Royal Botanic Gardens," said Rick, smirking.

"It's magnificent. How have I never heard of this before?" Steven asked.

I looked at him, puzzled. "You've never been here?"

A sheepish look danced across Steven's face. "No, I don't get out much."

Shaking my head at his ignorance, I looked back at Rick. "Why are we here?"

Rick let out a hearty chuckle. "Like I said, Mr. Tesla loves theatrics. Come, follow me."

Without any more warning, Rick started to walk up the steps in front of the greenhouse. Shrugging, we both followed Rick, interested to see what he meant by that. The steps were carved from a stone as white as alabaster, almost glowing from the light cast upon them from ahead. Feeling compelled to do so, I counted how many steps it took to the top. Taking each one, I counted my footfalls to a total of nine.

Why did I count them? Weird.

"One thing I need to tell you is Mr. Tesla has a bizarre effect on some people. He also has a few eccentricities of his own. Please try not to stare at him for too long or ask questions pertaining to said eccentricities. It would be the best thing to do. Also, he doesn't shake hands, so don't be offended if he doesn't offer," said Rick, reaching the top step.

"Why doesn't he shake hands?" I asked.

"Well, the easiest way to put it is that he likes to stay clean. Nothing on you; he just thinks it is a very dirty world," replied Rick.

As Steven and I reached the top of the steps ourselves, we took in the view a little closer. The light coming from the greenhouse was emitted from thousands of lightbulbs. Rick held open the door to the inside, bowing as he said, "Please, he is waiting just inside. Stay on the path to the center of the greenhouse."

Before we could go any further, Rick stopped me. "David, why do you have a sword?"

"Umm, it's actually a cane. See?" I said as I took the sword and scabbard from my back. I made a show of walking around with it for a moment, trying to sell the ruse.

Rick squinted his eyes, scrutinizing me for a moment. "Ah, okay then. I thought it was a sword, my mistake." He let out a few laughs. "Please, like I said, he is waiting for you."

We took a few more steps when we heard Rick clear his throat.

"Um, Steven, lad. Is that a gun?" he asked.

Steven looked at me for a moment, and I knew he thought about trying what I did. A few seconds ticked by, but eventually, he decided against it.

"Yes, here," he said, hanging his head as he gave it to Rick.

"Alright, in you two go now," Rick said, motioning to us.

Guarding the doors stood statues of the Roman gods Flora and Silvanus. Flora looked off into the distance while Silvanus stared intently at anyone who entered, making one second guess whether the statue was alive or not. Upon walking through the open door, we both immediately felt the difference between the inside and out. The temperature abruptly changed from the comfortable and cool September night to a balmy and humid mid-summer heatwave. Lush green vegetation grew in dense sections on either side of the walking path, guarding like an ever-watching army.

"What do you think he means?" asked Steven.

"Not sure, but we should probably listen to him. Wouldn't be good if Mr. Tesla requested someone else after meeting us," I said.

Steven let out a chuckle. "And what was that? Saying it was a cane. You're lucky the man can't see very well."

I let out a few laughs myself. "Probably won't work again."

We continued down the center path, looking above at the pitched roof with Tesla Bulbs spaced at random intervals, all of which hung at the same length, about two yards above our heads. It was a sight to behold. A magnificent display of the wonder known as electricity. It made one believe that no matter how dark the world felt, it would never be without light again. The possibilities of the future were endless. A grim and bleak tomorrow was no longer the promised outcome.

The flora housed inside the greenhouse consisted of many we had never seen, lining the cobblestone paths that spread further throughout. Trees from multiple continents were starting to grow and flowers began to bud into beautiful masterpieces. Three or four yards ahead stood a man in the center of the crossroads of the cobblestone path. Surrounding him were more bulbs in a circular pattern. But instead of them at the same length as the others, they hung between four inches to three feet from the ground.

He held two light bulbs, one in each hand, arms outstretched at shoulder length. As we walked closer, we took in the awe-inspiring spectacle. The dazzling gilded glow brightened him in a warm grand light, showing off the light brown tweed suit he wore. His hair was parted down the middle, combed in waves to the sides. His face bore a respectable but rather small mustache, clean-shaven besides. His ears were a very prominent and noticeable feature, along with his very slender stature. Upon stopping about three feet from him, he opened his eyes, looking deep into ours. It felt as if he was scrutinizing every wrinkle and hair we had on our bodies.

"Hello, hello, hello! I presume you two are David and Steven?" asked Tesla.

He dropped the two bulbs he held, causing them to fall momentarily. They abruptly stopped two inches from the ground and began to swing back and forth.

In awe, I stammered out, "Y–yes. But please Mr. Tesla, call me Davey."

Steven tried to play it cool as well but failed miserably. "Sorry sir, there isn't really a shorter way to say Steven."

Tesla chuckled, "Oh, oh, oh. It's okay Steven, I can call you that. What do you two think?" he asked, gesturing with his hands. He put them to the heavens, palms up as if he was beckoning the angels to come down and take his soul to keep, here and now.

"It's magnificent," we both said in unison.

"Isn't it? Electricity is a thing of beauty. You know it is a growing theory that all humans, in a simple way of explaining, run off of electrical impulses," Tesla said, looking up at the bulbs still.

"Are they hanging from wires?" I asked, knowing what they were truly powered by.

Time to be a bit of a suck-up.

"No, no, no, my friends. They are fueled by Wavergy!" Tesla said, smiling extensively.

"Powered by a substation located nearby, correct?" asked Steven.

Tesla cocked an eyebrow. "Why yes there Steven. Acute observation. They are just hanging from a non-conductive string. Wouldn't want the whole structure to be charged, would we?"

"Sorry to interrupt, sir, but we were brought here under the notion you needed to see us?" I asked, trying to stay respectful.

"Ah, yes, yes, yes. You two work for TEA, don't you?" he asked.

"Yes, we do sir. I work in the coil repair division. Davey works in the lamplighter division," Steven said.

"Of course. Aren't there some creative names the employees like to go by?" Snapping his finger, three times to be exact, he continued, "Sparkers and Buzzers right?" he asked.

"Yes. we do. Kind of a status for some, but for others, they feel as if it's a derogatory term. For the most part, I think it's kind of creative," I said.

"They certainly are imaginative. Regardless, I thank both of you for the diligent service you have provided the company, but I am calling on you for another reason tonight." Tesla began pacing in short bursts back and forth.

Three steps left, three steps right. He stopped in the same spot he started in.

"We are to be your escorts to the United States?" Steven asked.

"Yes! You are also going to help me prove that old pigeon-livered foozler wrong, among other things," Tesla exclaimed, growing red in the face with anger. "You English lads use those terms, right?" he asked.

"Um, yes sir. Yes, we do." I replied, knowing that was a ridiculous way to talk.

"Anyways, please gentlemen, my assistant Rick will help you two back to your homes. He will be by tomorrow morning to take all of us to the docks. Then it's a short voyage to the United States!" Tesla yelled in excitement.

"Tomorrow already?" Steven asked.

"Why yes, of course. Just like time, progression in electrical engineering waits for no one!" replied Tesla. "Now off you two. Sleep well, my friends!"

Chapter 19

Early Mornings and Sea Sickness

A sunset cast its last promises of the new day, slowly drifting beyond the horizon. It sank ever deeper as it came to the realization that even though anything is possible, it too must come to an end.

"Sir Gaheris, Sir Lancelot, thank you for coming," said Arthur. "Is everyone else on their way?"

Gaheris and Lancelot bowed momentarily. "Yes sir. Well–" Gaheris paused, looking for the right words. "Everyone that is left, my lord."

A grim expression washed over Arthur's face. He leaned back in his seat, bringing his hands up in a steeple around his nose. "Who has fallen?"

Lancelot came forward, lowering to one knee.

"No, please, rise, Sir Lancelot. No need for that." Arthur said.

Lancelot rose from the ground, expression still one of sorrow and loss. "Some have fallen, my lord. Sir Bors the Younger, Lamorak, Kay Sir Gareth and Geraint. The battle against Jakobus is taking its toll on us. We are unsure what to do next."

Arthur stood, pacing back and forth on the rough stone floor, boots scraping with each heavy step. The weak fire in the old hearth cracked sympathetically, growing smaller with each shortened passing day. The years began to take their toll on not only King Arthur but his faithful knights as well, on the ones that were left.

"Sir Gaheris, please go fetch Merlin. The time has come for the ones that are left to pledge to the cause. Sir Lancelot, please go rally the last of the knights and the first able-bodied family member of the fallen. We need to assemble one last time," said Arthur.

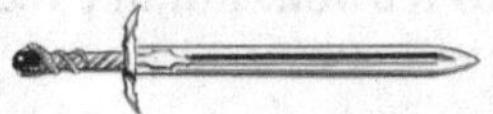

10th September, 1888
Spitalfields Borough, London, England
5:33 a.m.

"Honey, where are you going?" asked Marie, changing into her nightgown. It clung to her form like a fresh blanket of snow in early winter.

There really isn't a better way to say this, so just get it over with.

"Steven and I were chosen to escort Nikola Tesla to the United States of America," I said.

I turned as I finished my sentence, trying to shield myself from the onslaught of questions. A handful of seconds ticked away, silence growing louder with each one passed. I continued to button my shirt, readying myself for the anger and frustration.

"Is this for The Keepers?" Marie asked, her voice cold and distant.

"No, no, it isn't." I whispered, turning towards her.

The Tesla bulb lamp in the corner of the room surged from an influx of power momentarily. It quickly faded back to normal, returning the shadows to prominence, relinquishing power back to them. The added light lit up Marie's face, revealing a river of tears gently rolling down her cheeks.

"How long will you be gone?" she asked, sniffling.

"I am unsure, my love. It may be a month or so." I stopped what I was doing and walked over to Marie. I took a long look at her, thinking of how beautiful she was. Even with the tears tainting her face, she radiated brighter than any Tesla bulb I've ever seen. "Marie, I'm so sorry I waited to tell you. I didn't want you involved. I was worried."

More tears fell from her eyes, heavy like hail. Her body shook and shuddered from a losing battle of fierce emotions. "I don't know what to think. I don't know what to believe. All of it seems like nonsense. How can any of it be real?" she cried. The dam broke, crumbling to pieces that washed away with the roaring river, causing all of her anger, fear and sadness to explode forth.

I embraced her in my arms as the heaving and sobs rattled both our bodies. "Shh. It's okay, Marie. It'll all be okay. I know it doesn't make sense. But I will be okay, I promise," I said, hoping it was one I could keep.

Marie's head still lay in the crook of my neck, heavy breathing and coughs filling my right ear. She shuddered and whispered, "I'm pregnant."

What did she say?

I gently pulled her from my chest, looking into her eyes. "What did you say?"

Her face was as red as the rising morning sun, flashing memories from Sudan surged through my head. The surprise left me speechless, and I struggled to kickstart my brain to take it all in.

"I can't do this without you. So whatever you need to do, just do it. Complete your quest or whatever you need to call it; finish the missions they give you. But please, if there is one thing you need to do, it's to come home safe," she cried. More tears welled in her eyes. Before I could get a word out about this revelation, a knock sounded on the door.

"Hello? Davey? It's time. Are you ready?" asked a familiar voice. It was Rick, who was earlier than I thought he'd be.

"Marie– I can't believe it." I said, struggling to say anything else.

She cut me off before I could.

"Just go, my love, please make it home safely. I believe in you," she said. Her cold, distant expression changed to one of love, pure and simple. It turned to belief. Belief in the fact I would return unharmed. Belief that I would be able to overcome anything that unfolds in front of me.

"Can you get word to Father Hubert, then?" I asked. "He needs to know how long we will be gone."

More banging on the door interrupted Marie once more.

"Hello? Davey? Mr. Tesla is waiting for us downstairs. Please, we must be going," said Rick.

"Yes, I will. Please just make it home." she said, kissing me and holding me tight one last time.

It would be a while before I felt this again, so we held each other in that moment, which felt like forever, enjoying every second.

"Hello?" said Rick, this time banging on the door.

"Alright, I'm coming, I'm coming," I yelled. "Give me a moment to get dressed."

With all of my gear and belongings put away and tidied up, I reached for the front door and opened it. On the opposite side stood a flustered and frustrated Rick. He patted at his forehead with a handkerchief while he shook his head.

"Sorry Rick, I wasn't expecting you this soon," I said.

"All is well. It is just Mr. Tesla. He likes to be on a tight schedule," Rick replied.

I bit my bottom lip before I spoke again. "By chance, can we make a stop? I need to speak to someone before we leave."

He sighed heavily but nodded his head in agreement. "I think that should work."

"Thank you Rick, I appreciate it."

Farringdon Borough, London, England
7:33 a.m.

"Father, can I ask a favor?" I said, taking my usual seat off to the left in the church.

"Why yes, of course, my son," Hubert said.

"Steven and I have been tasked with escorting Nikola Tesla to America, specifically New York. Would you be able to keep an eye on Marie for me while I am gone?"

He nodded. "Of course. But I have to say, the timing couldn't be better."

I raised my eyebrows. "What do you mean?"

He held up a finger and departed to his office. After a moment, he returned with a newspaper clutched in his right hand.

As he handed it to me, I asked, "What is this?"

"It is a newspaper from New York."

"And?"

He pointed out the headline on what I presumed was the back of the newspaper. "There is an auction this month."

"Why is that important?"

"I believe there may be an artifact there. One of the artifacts for a knight of the round."

I raised my eyebrows further. "Do you know what it is?"

"Uh, no."

"Seems about right. So we need to try and catch the auction and guess what the artifact may be?"

"You are a very clever young man," he said with a smile. "Unless you can get your hands on the item for the ring to tell you it is one, you'll be on your own."

"Alright, Father, I will see what I can accomplish."

10th September, 1888
Liverpool, England
11:15 a.m.

It has been the longest four days of my life. To get to Liverpool in a decent amount of time, Rick has only stopped for a few hours nap each night. Meaning, I have spent the last eighty hours imprisoned in a small box with Steven, an annoying dunder-head and with Tesla, a germaphobe. Upon arrival here, I stepped forth from my cage and fell to the ground, loving it more than I thought possible.

"You know we haven't even left England yet," said Steven, stepping out of the carriage behind me.

"It felt as if I would never feel the dirt underneath my feet again. I thought I would never know silence or peace, both now a distant memory of better times!" I exclaimed dramatically.

"Well, well, well, Davey. I'm glad you are enthusiastic about theater! I love it too! But come along, we must make it to the ship for boarding." Tesla tipped his hat to Rick. "Thank you, my loyal friend! Please be safe and sleep well tonight; you have earned it!"

Tesla waved off to Rick once more. Turning, he trudged through the muck to the large timbered dock. Steven and I scrambled to grab what little luggage we brought, hoisting it over our shoulders. Rick then proceeded to point out that we needed to carry Tesla's luggage as well.

"Bollocks," I said, growling as Steven and I grabbed his three bursting bags.

We struggled through the mud, feet sinking with each step. I tried not to overthink and kept my mind busy by counting to thirteen, looking around with a small amount of interest. Finally making it to the wooden log dock, we tossed Tesla's bags down, which landed with a reverberating thud. Our relief was rewarded with a frustrated slew of Serbian words I could only assume were, "Your mother is the most beautiful flower I have ever laid my eyes upon." You know, something poetic like that.

"Please, be careful, friends. This is full of very fragile materials," Tesla said, shaking his finger at us three times. He walked over and picked up one of the bags. Turning, he asked, "Please grab the other two, my friends?"

Steven and I both fished one up off the planking. I looked back and saw Tesla was already walking off towards a massive boat. I rushed off after him and said, "Come on, let's keep up."

The hulking mass of a ship towered high, casting a vacant shadow over the ground in front of us. A Wavergy lamppost stood solemnly near the end of the dock, adjacent to the furthermost part of the ship. The light cut through the shadow of the sun, illuminating the name stretched across the barnacle and seaweed-covered hull of the bow.

"S.S. Britannic. Isn't it a beauty?" said Steven.

"It is actually." I smiled, taking it all in. "Tesla, do you know anything about this ship?"

Tesla turned around to look at me, smiling. He then clapped his hands three times. "Why yes, I have done a bit of research on it!"

"Oh yeah? like what?" Steven asked.

"Well, my friends, the S.S. Britannic was built in 1874 for the White Star Line. The sister of the S.S. Germanic," said Tesla.

"How many people can it transport?" I asked.

Tesla made a show of thinking for a moment. "I think I remember hearing it holds around 1,700 people."

"How many–" I began to ask. Before I could finish the question, Tesla walked off again to presumably board the ship.

"I guess he has a short attention span too. Hopefully he stops doing that" Steven said.

Shrugging, we scooped up the bags once more and followed after him.

15th September, 1888
The Atlantic Ocean
7:33 a.m.

During the previous four or so days we had been aboard the ship, both Steven and I had gotten to know Tesla a little better. He was, in fact, a very odd fellow, and I tried to steer clear of the little things Rick mentioned. But, that didn't mean I can't pay attention to them, especially since Steven and I were housed in a room located across from Tesla's.

His room number was eighteen, presumably on purpose. Like clockwork, he requested the delivery of eighteen towels to his room every morning. The number eighteen came up a lot so far in this voyage, and I soon understood why: it is divisible by three. We had eaten in the extravagant dining saloon every meal since boarding. As I now have guessed, for each of said meals, Tesla requested eighteen napkins as well.

Like each day before, Nikola and I made our way above deck to take a walk, hoping it would wake us up. The chilled Atlantic air swept over us as the sun rose off in the east, turning the horizon a beautiful shade of pinks, oranges, and reds.

It's probably morning now for Marie too. I do miss her so.

"Hey, Mr. Tesla, I had a question." I paused. "Or, rather, a few if you don't mind me asking."

He turned to me, smiling. "Be my guest, but please, call me Nikola."

"Okay, I will." I pursed my lips before speaking again. "I know you came to England from America originally, but I never knew why. Is it okay if I ask why?"

I turned to look at Nikola, waiting for a response. He did not give one right away, which made me concerned that I hit a nerve or offended him.

He finally shifted on his feet and looked at me. "I thought America would have been the place I was looking for. It was, to begin with, at least."

"What happened?"

"I started to work for Thomas Edison at his company, The Edison Machine Works Company. After some time there, I noticed I, I, I, could improve upon his inventions."

"What did you do about it then? Did you just tell Edison that?"

Nikola nodded. "I did, but I also offered to improve them for him for better pay."

"Did he accept the offer?"

"Yes, so that is what I did. When I was done with it and informed him, all he did was laugh."

I raised an eyebrow.

"He laughed me away all while telling me that he would not pay me more and that I did not understand American humor."

I shook my head. "That is not right. He should have held his end of the bargain."

Steven came running up next to us, interrupting the conversation. He leaned over the edge of the railing and expelled his previous night's meal violently overboard.

"How much longer do we have? I am wasting away!" he yelled.

I walked over to him and started to pat him on the back. "Not sure, it's been quite a few days. It's too bad you get seasick. Have you ever been sailing before?"

Steven looked at me with a pale and pained face. Unrecognizable paste clung to his chin like a fresh coat of paint that the hull of this ship needed quite a bit. He reached up to wipe it away with his sleeve, only to be rewarded with another taste of the meal.

"No, I've never been before. Land legs, these are," he moaned through his misery.

"By my, my, my calculations, we are only four more days away!" Tesla interjected, leaning on the railing opposite side of me, away from the awful mess Steven was making.

"Four days?" Steven wailed inconsolably.

I patted him on the back as I tried to hold back my laughter. "There, there, Steven. By the end of all of this, you'll be begging to ride on a boat again."

The wailing continued on for a few minutes, and at this point, I felt as if he was doing it on purpose now. Nikola Tesla added to the noise by talking up a storm, making me yearn for the silence of the lonely nights I used to have as a simple Sparker.

Deciding I had heard enough of the insistent noise, I cut both of them off. "Either of you two want to get some breakfast?" I looked at Steven as he wiped his face once more. "Steven, I know you need to eat something." A cacophony of rumbles and gurgles from both of their stomachs agreed with my offer. "See. Obviously, you two agree."

Chapter 20

Home of the Free

19th September, 1888
New York, New York
10:12 a.m.

The hustle and bustle of the morning made the docks of the city feel alive. Each man, woman and child created a living hive of worker bees completing their own tasks at hand.

Nikola, Steven, and I stood in front of the Astor House, looking at the city around us. Free of luggage, and other things of that nature, we decided to start the morning following Nikola around. It didn't bug me very much because that's what we were here for. As long as the beds at the Astor House were comfortable, I could deal with babysitting for a few days.

"It smells like refuse," Steven said, scrunching his nose at the awful stench. He coughed once, trying to hold down a few gags.

"Reminds me of home," Tesla said, rubbing his hands together three times. "Come, friends. We have things to do."

"It smells like rotting food and matter in The Austrian Empire?" Steven asked.

Like always, Tesla began to walk off in a random direction, completely disregarding Steven's question.

"I suppose he knows what he is doing; let's just keep up," I said, turning to follow Nikola.

The sun began to slowly rise in the cloud-covered east. The rooftops of the buildings cast extensive obsidian shadows jaggedly breaking up the surrounding ground. Bustling, dirty streets were filled with horse-drawn carts navigating the droves of people on foot as we navigated them cautiously.

"Come and try Iceland Bros! Brand new Delicatessen on the corner of Ludlow and East Hudson! Great food and great atmosphere!" yelled a kid walking past. "Only a twenty-minute walk from here! Come try our Jewish delicacies!"

"You hear that, friends? A delicatessen!" exclaimed Nikola. "Let us go try it. Maybe it is like back home in London!"

Steven smiled and said, "Maybe they have tins of beans. I could go for a taste of home right about now."

"Oh, you mean the ones from Fortnum & Mason? I absolutely adore those!" Nikola replied.

That's odd. Usually, I can't get those two to agree on anything. America is a very different place.

The short walk was brisk. Keeping up with Nikola was a chore in itself. The man always walked with a sense of urgency, mostly towards a direction or goal unknown to anyone else. The crowds flowed in fluctuations, thicker in some areas and sparse in others, depending on the direction we traveled.

With his stride leading the way, the walk only lasted about fifteen minutes, give or take. The closer we got to Iceland Brothers, the heavier the congestion was compared to most of the walk. I pulled out my pocket watch to check the time. I paused momentarily to look at it, thinking of Marie in the process.

I can't believe what I am coming home to and what is in store for us. I pray that I can finish this before Marie and I have any children.

I wouldn't want to bring a child into a world with an evil madman running around.

"You gonna check the time?" Steven asked.

"Huh? What?" I asked, looking at him.

"You took out your watch to check the time but you sort of drifted off," he said. Leaning closer, he whispered, "Did you have another vision or whatever you call them?"

"Oh, no. No, I didn't. I was just thinking of something Marie told me before I left. I'm not sure how I feel about it."

"What was it? She wants a puppy or something?" he asked, smiling a little.

I chuckled as I rubbed my neck. "No. She is pregnant. I'm going to be a father."

Steven stopped dead in his tracks. His face went emotionless as the bags he was carrying clattered to the ground.

"Uh, Steven? Are you okay? Sorry, didn't think it would freak you out?" I said, concerned.

Without warning, Steven ran at me and squeezed my body in a bear hug that lifted me from the ground. It caused some vertebrae and ribs to crack, hopefully into place and not out of. He shook me like a ragdoll and screamed at the top of his lungs. "You're going to be a father!"

After about fifteen seconds of jumping around with me in his steely grip, he dropped me back to the ground. I struggled to breathe, taking in huge lungfuls of the humid September air.

"Davey, I can't believe it! Can I be an uncle?" he beamed. "Uncle Steven, I like the sound of that."

"Yes, sure. You can be an uncle," I said.

"How far along is she? When can I start being an uncle?"

"I'm not sure Steven, I only found out just as we were leaving to come here to the United States of America," I said. "When we return, I will know. You'll be the first person I tell." I noticed my pocket watch was still clutched in my white-knuckled hand, so I popped it open to check the time. "By the way, it is 10:35."

"Friends! Friends! Friends! Come try this! You will love this!" interrupted Nikola.

"Okay, we're coming!" I yelled back.

Steven and I looked over towards the direction his voice came from. Nikola was standing near a small corner brick building surrounded by a few dozen people. Everyone looked to be enjoying an array of delicious-smelling food.

When we approached the building, we noticed that each of us needed to take a ticket with a number so they could keep the restaurant orderly. We all got in line and waited until it was our turn to order. When we chose something off the menu, we waited for a few dozen minutes and finally got what we wanted.

"You know," Steven started saying as he took another bite of his sandwich, "I don't care for this much."

"Really? I like it. I think it tastes pretty good," I said.

Steven took a few more bites of his sandwich before he continued talking with a semi-full mouth, "I honestly don't think they will stay open very long. The meat is dry, and the bread is soggy."

I shrugged, continuing to eat my own sandwich. "I don't agree with you. I think they will thrive." I turned to look at Nikola and spoke with a mouthful of delicious, salty pastrami. "So what are we actually doing here anyway? I know it has been hush-hush since we left London, but I kind of need to know what to expect."

Before Nikola could tell me why, I noticed something out of the corner of my eye. It was a soft, warm glow that beckoned me to turn to have a better look. At the edge of the crowd stood a man in black resting on a cane, lingering amongst the fringes of the stragglers enjoying their food.

"Steven, does that man look familiar?" I asked, cocking my head to the side.

He turned to have a look. "What man?" He mumbled, his mouth dripping with pastrami from his sandwich.

"That man," I said, pointing him out.

Steven squinted to see. "Umm no, why? Have we met him before?"

"Yes, I believe we have. I think he was at the scene of Mary's murder, and I think I also met him before all this happened," I said.

I looked back over at the man to make sure he really was who I thought he was. As I did so, he glanced our way, a sly grin stretched across his thin pale face. It was a strange look that seemed out of place as his crooked yellow teeth protruded from his lips as bright as a crescent moon.

"He has the yellow cane I remember seeing in the vision too. The one I had after touching Mary's body," I said.

My eyes were trained on his as I started in his direction. The smile never left his face, nor did he attempt to move as I drew closer.

"Davey, where are you going?" Steven asked. "We can't arrest anyone here."

I ignored his protest and advanced through the crowd of men, women, and children after the man. A few angry exclamations of frustration and shrieks followed in the wake of the path I was cutting through them. I got about five feet away when I was cut off by a stagecoach. It creaked to a stop right between us as if on purpose. The horse whinnied and snorted a few times, clomping its hoof on the hard surface of the cobblestone.

"Oi, I'm walking here!" I yelled at the coachman atop the wagon.

"Oh shut it, you limey! Go get some tea or something," the man retorted in anger.

"Get out of the way!" yelled a stranger on the other side.

"Mind your own business!" growled the coachman as he glanced to the other side of the stagecoach.

With a flick of his wrist, the reins cracked against the horse's back. It gave way to some more choice noises from the overworked animal as the stagecoach slowly lurched forward with the energy provided by the frustrated horse. When it was finally out of the way, I looked beyond to find the man had disappeared.

"Where is he?" I yelled.

Steven, who had followed me after I ignored him, now spoke. "Who, the man?"

"Yes! I just saw him, he was there. Right there," I yelled, pointing at the ground where he stood.

Steven and I looked around for a few minutes without seeing any more of him.

"I don't think we will find him, Davey," said Steven.

I shook my head and looked back toward Nikola. To my surprise, he was still where we left him, albeit arguing intently with someone. Steven and I jogged to him, wanting to prevent anything bad from happening.

"Alternating Current is far superior to the barbaric Direct Current!" Nikola said, chest puffed outward.

I reached for Tesla and pulled him away from the man. "Sorry, sir."

The man took another step toward us, lips pulled back in a sneer. Steven slipped in between the man and I, stopping his advance.

"That's far enough, mate," Steven said.

The man grunted and spat a loogie at our feet before turning and walking off. Steven and I watched for a second before turning back to Nikola.

"People are not very nice here in America," Steven said.

"Yes, yes, yes they are," replied Nikola.

I was going to ask Nikola why he was arguing with the man but wasn't able to on account of him wandering off immediately. I rolled my eyes and followed along like a good babysitter.

With the situation averted, we made a few stops at a couple stores and shops. I eventually decided on purchasing a journal of sorts to start recording memories and events of my time in America since I did not have my journal, which I had left in London. I would be a father soon, so I wanted to have something my daughter or son could look back at and see how different things could be just across the pond.

After that, we spent a couple of hours or so trying to find the man with the cane. Sadly, we had no luck. The local police were not as friendly as we hoped and didn't want to divulge any information on a natural-born citizen. We were told to drop the matter before getting into any more trouble. Steven and I agreed that he may not have even been the correct man. And we were in America, where we had no jurisdiction.

Nikola noted that the air in New York felt quite a bit cleaner and easier to breathe than back home in London. Eventually, Nikola wandered off somewhere once more, prompting us to follow behind like freshly hatched ducklings on the heels of their mother.

After a few hours, we came upon a market tucked deep into the heart of the city. I voiced my concern about getting lost, but Steven and Nikola both ignored me like I assumed they would.

Up ahead, I noticed there was a crowd centered around a stand in the middle of the courtyard. Men, women, and children all stood close as they listened to the man who paced on the platform. He held a megaphone near his lips as he spoke to everyone.

"Welcome all to the first Sotheby, Wilkinson and Hodge's public auction here in the heart of New York!" yelled the man.

"Hey, Nikola. Steven," I said as I tapped on their shoulders. "I think this is the auction Father Hubert wanted me to keep an eye on."

Steven and Nikola turned to see what I was talking about.

"Oh, oh, oh! How fun!" exclaimed Nikola. "Friends, I will buy you whatever you please!"

I turned to Nikola in astonishment, "What? Are you sure?"

He nodded. "Of course! Think of it as a gift from TEA."

"That is mighty nice of you, Nikola. Are you sure?" Steven asked.

"I am positive. What are friends for?"

Before we could object any further, Nikola marched off toward the crowd. We jogged after him and nestled ourselves on either side, still wanting to do our jobs of protecting him. I glanced at Nikola and saw a grin plastered across his face.

He certainly is something. Such a strange man.

"The first item up for auction is an original copy of *Le Morte d'Arthur* by Thomas Mallory. It is preserved quite well and has been painstakingly restored to its original self."

I chuckled to myself and whispered, "The whole book is quite a fabrication, of course. It isn't true whatsoever."

Someone near me looked in my direction, shushed me, and turned back to the front. I winced and decided to pay attention myself, not wanting to miss anything, just in case. Nikola did end up bidding on a few items, but it was mostly to rile someone up. I asked why he was doing so, and Nikola revealed it was because the man was actually the very same one he came here to talk to anyway.

"Harold P. Brown can suffer a horrible inconvenience," muttered Nikola under his breath.

"Yeah, you prove a point, Nikola," Steven encouraged.

It went on like this for a few hours. An item would come up for sale, a few rich people would bet on it, and eventually, some other rich person would swoop in and take it. None of which seemed to be the right thing I was looking for. Eventually though, we got to the last item that was to be auctioned off. I squinted at it as the man with the megaphone spouted off what it was.

"This is an ancient belt buckle from the second half of the sixth century," said the man.

Honestly, if the artifact were anything, that's what it would be.

Steven nudged me in the arm to get my attention.

"What is it?" I asked.

"Is that the man you saw earlier today?" he asked.

I peeled my eyes away from the buckle the auctioneer was holding and looked to where Steven was pointing. To my surprise and anger, it, in fact, was the same man. He had his eyes locked on the center stage with his hand in the air, bidding on the item.

"That's the artifact," I said.

"Are you sure? Why do you think that?" Steven asked.

"Well, if I was going to bind my heritage to an item, it certainly wouldn't be a book that told lies about my life."

Steven tilted his head slightly and nodded, "so what do we do?"

I was about to say that maybe we could scrounge up enough money to bet on it, but I then noticed Nikola was doing just that. Our jaws dropped as the amount of money continued to rise as the two duked it out. It leaped past the thousand dollar mark and eventually settled on fourteen hundred American dollars.

"Nikola, do you even have enough money for that?" I asked, worried we bit off more than we could chew.

"Why yes, yes, yes I do," he replied. "If it is something my friend wants, then it is something my friend gets."

I glanced off in the direction of where the man with the black cane was standing, only to see he wasn't there. It was as if he vanished into thin air the second he realized he did not win the auction. To be honest, it might be better that way.

I stood there in awe as a representative brought the buckle to us. Nikola promptly counted out the money in a slow but exact process. After what felt like ages, the man received and counted the cash as he handed the item off to us.

The minute he placed the item in my hand, I felt a slight surge of electricity course through my arm. It did not hurt, nor did the feeling stay with me for longer than a few seconds. I turned it around a few times and looked at it more closely.

Sitting in my palm was a pristine metal belt buckle that shone beautifully in the morning sunlight. The design was of what I thought to be Griffon with the edges carved out around it. That wasn't the most interesting part about it, no. The part that solidified my suspicions was the fact that Father Hubert's ring lit up when it came into contact with it.

"Thank you Nikola, you wouldn't know how much this helps."

Chapter 21

A Time to Remember

2nd October, 1888
The Atlantic Ocean
9:42 p.m.

It was the end of the trip, and we all agreed to meet for one last meal on the S.S. Britannic. The dining area of the saloon had a nice open layout, layered extensively with beautifully carved wood furnishings.

Small tables were placed against the walls, four against the east wall and four on the west. In the middle of the saloon sat three larger tables, one a smidge smaller in between the two bigger ones. A gramophone in one corner was playing soft melodic music, gently wearing away the stress and worries of the day. Before coming down tonight, I looked over the menu and learned it was the always delicious bangers and mash.

"What an adventure that was," said Steven as he sat down heavily in the chair opposite of me.

"It was. I am glad we are heading home though," I said.

Steven nodded in agreement. We both sat in silence, enjoying the dull moment for once in our lives.

Nikola finally found his way to the saloon, arriving late like usual. He took a seat next to Steven and began folding the eighteen napkins and placing them in front of him. Since we got used to this ritual of his, we waited for him to finish before we continued to talk.

"I cannot wait to go home and get some beans. I think food in America is okay and all but nothing will ever be better than some fresh, hot beans," said Steven.

Steven lifted his glass, and I picked up mine to join in the toast. Nikola followed suit with the glass of water he brought from his room.

"To long life and the prevalence of AC over DC, salute!" yelled Steven.

After a while, the night turned into a hazy blur. The food was delicious, and the night was one I would certainly need to remember. We decided to retire to our rooms after the well-deserved dinner. I had to steady myself with the walls or railings depending on where I was, hiccupping as I tried to keep the alcohol down. Our voices filled the halls as we sang familiar tunes, not caring if any of the notes were on key. Eventually, we reached our floor, and I said my goodnights to Steven and Nikola as I departed to my own room.

I fumbled with the key in my hands, now regretting the fourth, or even fifth, glass of brandy as I struggled with simple motor functions. Eventually, I was able to get the door open and stumbled forward to the desk that sat against the wall.

The waves rocked me around, causing my landing to be less than comfortable. But, I was well enough up a tree to not care too much. I reached forward to turn on the desk lamp in front of me, illuminating the top with the glow of a Tesla bulb.

"Ah, yes. The journal!" I mumbled aloud to myself.

I flipped open the pages to read over the last few days we had in America. Now that it was over with, I wasn't as frustrated with the situations those two got us in. I squinted as I focused on the words scribbled on the page.

Journal Entry 1 - 22nd September, 1888

The first day of our trip was interesting, to say the least. We ate some good food and found an artifact of one of the knights of the round table. Convenient, I think. Two or three later though, Nikola finally revealed why we were accompanying him. Apparently, in the United States, there are some people who believe very strongly that Alternating Current doesn't belong in the public domain in any capacity. There is one man in particular that seemed to oppose it fiercely. His name is Harold Pitney Brown. He has been holding rallies against the use of AC. His hatred of it comes from the multiple deaths reported from the AC power lines in New York City. Some reports, mainly from Nikola, say that Harold P. Brown is working with Thomas Edison. I have talked Nikola down from doing anything too drastic. Unpredictability is a very prominent feature of his personality.

Journal Entry 2 - 23th September, 1888

We are in jail today. Nikola tried freeing some animals from the menagerie located in Central Park. In the process of doing so, we were confronted by some police officers. Hopefully peacocks can survive in the urban environment.

Journal Entry 3 - 25th September, 1888

After two days in jail, I feel as if I have had enough. It is very exhausting keeping up with

Nikola. The surprising thing is that both Steven and Nikola get along great now. It's like trying to wrangle toddlers. I better get paid well for this.

Journal Entry 4 - 26th September, 1888

Did you know there is a part of New York called the Bronx? Yeah? Well, I didn't. While here in the USA, we heard from some locals of the new bridge they were building to connect Manhattan to the Bronx. It was named the Washington Bridge, originally planned to be completed for the centennial for the first president of the United States. Apparently, it also was to coincide with his birthday as well.

Journal Entry 4 - 27th September, 1888

It is our last day in New York, and we finally collected the gear and equipment Nikola said we came here for. I briefly mentioned to him that we did not confront Harold P. Brown like he originally intended, but he said I needn't worry. At the auction, he had enough fun bidding the man up for items that were worth quite a bit less than what he paid. If there is one thing I learned from this trip, it is that I wouldn't want Nikola as an adversary. In terms of sheer will and stubbornness, I would lose every time.

"This is all a little more entertaining in hindsight," I said to myself once more.

I laughed some more before shutting the journal in front of me. With my eyes already closing, I reached over and turned off the lamp as I laid my head down on the desk in the twilight. Before I could realize it, I was out cold.

Chapter 22

Homecoming

7th October, 1888
Richmond Borough, London, England
8:45 p.m.

We returned to London around four days after we left Liverpool. The return trip wasn't as horrid as the original ride there almost a month ago. All of us were tired, worn, and ready to be done with the world. Rick brought us back to the Temperate house to drop off Nikola Tesla first.

"It was a great pleasure to meet you, my dear friend. Please, if you ever need anything, let me know!" Tesla said, holding out his hand.

He must have really taken a liking to us. He wouldn't do this for just anyone.

Surprised, I took it, testing the waters with how hard I squeezed. After a moment of this, a familiar light glowed softly from the ring. Tesla pulled his hand from mine, and a look of curiosity sparked across his face.

A Dimmer? One day he might be someone we would need to bring into this. Maybe.

"What is that?" he asked, taking a closer look.

"Oh, that? It is just something a friend of mine made." I began to feel my face get red, and struggling to think of anything else, I told him, "It measures levels of electricity. When we work out the kinks, I'll let you know."

A mischievous look danced quickly over his ever-grinning face. "Okay, my friend, Rick will see you off safely. And Steven, stay out of trouble. Try and get your sea legs before we meet next."

"Will do, Nikola. Stay out of any more fights, okay?" Steven asked.

Nikola smiled and waved us off as Rick encouraged Jimmy to take us home.

8th October, 1888
Farringdon Borough, London, England
5:47 a.m.

I knocked on the very familiar wooden door of the church. After a moment, an also familiar face answered, a grin growing across it as he answered.

"Hello, Father, nice to see you," I said.

"Davey, how are you? Would you like to come in? It is awfully early."

"No, that is alright. I just stopped by on me way home to drop this off."

He raised an eyebrow as I held out the buckle. Before taking it, Hubert fixed the worn checkered robe that he had wrapped loosely around him, crossing it across his body and tying off the sash that hung in loops around his waist.

"You found one?" he asked.

I nodded. "I did. All thanks to the ring you let me borrow all those months ago."

He turned it over in his own hands, taking in the design for himself.

"I also ran into someone else while in America."

"Who?"

"I believe it is the man that killed Mary. I think it is the man that I saw in the vision I received by touching her body."

"Were you able to catch him? Talk to him?"

"No, I was not. I tried to, but he got away." I sighed heavily before I spoke again. "He is the reason I took the chance and bought that, actually."

"Really?"

"Yeah, I only started bidding on it because he was. It only seemed logical that someone involved in murders may have Jakobus in the shadows pulling the strings."

"I would say it was a good assumption. And you weren't able to catch him after all that?"

"No, when I realized we won the buckle, he had already disappeared."

Hubert clicked his tongue and said, "I suppose we will see him again, but it is a good thing you found this. It will help more than you know."

Spitalfields Borough, London, England
7:47 a.m.

I sat at the foot of the bed, Excalibur lying gently across my lap, reflecting in the budding sunrise. A subtle breeze squeezed through the partially opened window, causing loose fabric and strands of my hair to dance together simultaneously. I glanced over my shoulder at my wife, Marie. Her small frame was rising and falling with her rhythmic breathing, never missing a beat.

"You lied to me," she muttered.

The whisper cut through my spiraling mind from lack of sleep and general exhaustion. It jaggedly pulled me back to the surface of the present world.

"Hmm, what?" I asked, turning to Marie.

"You lied," she repeated in the soft, almost inaudible tone.

I thought for a moment, thinking of what she could be talking about. "What's that, my sweet pea?"

She stirred as she turned onto her back. We locked eyes before she spoke. "You said you'd be gone a month."

I sat for a second, wondering what she meant. I watched her caramel auburn hair sway with the breeze, joining mine at the winter ball. "I was, wasn't I?"

She inched forward, trying to get a little closer. "No," she paused. A mischievous smile grew on her face, "You were only gone for twenty-nine days."

An odd sense of relief fell over me. Part of me thought something worse was coming. By god, do I love her. It felt good to be home after a long and strenuous trip. America is definitely a wild frontier, all right.

"Sorry I lied to you," I said, chuckling, then embracing her.

"I suppose I will forgive you. Just don't ever again. It's more than just us now," she said, placing my hand on her stomach.

"Oh, good. I was worried you never would," I said, smiling.

"Love, I don't want to worry you, but I think someone is creeping around the hospital. I would even go as far as to say they are following me," she said, more worry in her voice.

"I thought I asked Father Hubert to check in with you once and a while. Did he?"

"He did, but he couldn't be there every second of every day."

"I suppose. Do you know who it may be? Has anyone else seen the person?" I asked.

"No, no one has. I just get this sudden feeling of dread and fear. It comes and goes during my shift. Deep and dark primal dread. Like all the light, all the joy in life will cease to exist. Like we may know exactly what the people of Pompeii felt when the earth spewed forth hell, and the end fell from the sky and flowed over them. I have been trying not to think about it, whatever it is. But it's like I know I should be worried."

"I will see what I can do. Maybe I can get the commissioner to place someone there during your shift. Especially since all the things that have been happening lately."

"Maybe you can get Jules to do it. He usually works the night shift, doesn't he?"

I thought for a moment. "Yeah, he does, I can see."

"Regardless, you are home now."

We sat there for, I don't know how long, holding each other, breathing in unison.

Chapter 23

Good Intentions

Field Notes Entry 8

The pressure surrounding the murders over the past year is mounting to the point of boiling over. So far in this investigation, there have been four murders, two of them attributed to the man known as Jack the Ripper. Dr. Thatcher was able to comb over the bodies of the victims and come to a more conclusive decision that they all only received damage by one person at a time. This is the running opinion by most physicians that I have talked to about the matter. But, I am certain Jakobus has been involved with all four at least. They all have had a missing liver along with the various damages done to not only their bodies, but their dignities as well.

The latest murder, which happened about a month ago, is the one that still haunts me. Her name was Annie Chapman. By far, this was the most gruesome yet. Her body was deposited in the backyard of twenty-nine Hanbury Street. An older resident of the lodging found her body early in the morning before six. He was terrified by the horrid sight to the point of not knowing what to do.

Luckily, two other workmen happened to pass by at the same moment. They were motioned over to help revive her under the assumption she may still be alive. Upon closer examination, they said she was covered in blood from what seemed like head to toe.

A few rumors have been making their rounds around the station about one of the small details regarding her death. Apparently, there was a handkerchief tied around her neck for the sake of fashion. But some people are causing panic by saying that the real purpose was to keep her head from rolling away after Jack the Ripper slit her throat. This, of course, is not the case.

10th October, 1888
Westminster Borough, London, England
9:29 a.m.

"Steven, Davey, how was your trip to the United States?" asked Commissioner Warren.

He motioned to the two identical chairs, insisting we take our seats. Steven and I followed his advice, slowly lowering ourselves onto the inviting cushions.

"It was nothing short of interesting," I said. I gave Steven a sideways glance, silently judging him for being such a child. He returned my look in his direction with an innocent response.

"What? I behaved," he paused before continuing with a smirk. "Most of the time."

While Steven and I had our usual spat of sarcastic remarks and our mocking statements, Commissioner Warren already had his pipe out. The dry stench of the burning tobacco cut through our conversation, winning the so-called argument.

"Boys," Warren said as he paused to take a long draw of his pipe. "Are you done?"

"Sure," we both said in unison.

Commissioner Warren chuckled at the response he received. He stopped after a few seconds, then cleared his throat. "Good. Down to business then. I got word from the crown that everything went well. What do you two think? Any complications?"

"I don't think so. We had some situations where we had to do some explaining, but for the most part, no," I said.

Commissioner Warren looked at Steven expectantly, checking if he had anything to add to the story.

"No, sir. Most things went well," Steven said. "Actually, there was one thing."

"What was it, boy?" Warren asked. Steven put on a serious face, looking the Commissioner in the eyes.

"They didn't have any beans," he said, feigning disbelief. "No one had any already warmed up. Not a one."

I rolled my eyes, letting out a laugh.

"Steven, can you do something for me?" asked Commissioner Warren.

"Yeah, what can I do for you sir?" he asked.

"Be quiet. Unless it is important. But besides that, be quiet," Warren said.

Steven began to open his mouth to argue, then decided against it. Instead, he gave a sheepish grin and shifted uncomfortably in his chair.

"Alright." Warren took another pull from his pipe. He exhaled a plume extending ever further. "Now, like I said, back to business. I have some good news and bad news to tell you two, so which would you like first?"

Steven and I traded glances before I responded. "Good."

Warren cleared his throat and spoke. "Your individual investigations into TEA have been concluded."

"Really? Why?" I asked.

"Since your departure to the U.S.A. a few other detectives looked over your findings and concluded there was no significant evidence to show anything to be weary over. Thus, not justifying any more of our time to be spent on it."

"Good. I agree completely," I said.

"So what is the bad news?" Steven asked.

Warren frowned and said, "There have been two new murders since you were gone. They happened almost two weeks ago."

Steven cut him off, launching himself from his chair to his feet. Before I could stop him, Steven began yelling at the commissioner.

"What in the bloody hell are you guys doing here, then? I thought you said you had it covered while we were gone?" Steven bellowed, inching closer to Warren.

I jumped to my feet moments after he started yelling, grabbing his arm. Rage boiled deep inside me, threatening to sear away the protective layer of common sense. It came very close to spilling over but was stopped by Marie's calm face in the back of my mind. I pulled Steven back to the seat, forcing him to sit back down.

"Steven, please," I said through clenched teeth. "Warren, who are they?"

The Commissioner didn't look shaken up at all from Steven's display of anger. He was still calm as he looked at us thoughtfully. Smoke from the smoldering tobacco collected in the air above him, like the sign of warmth from a chimney in the dead of winter.

"Their names were Catherine Eddowes and Elizabeth Stride. They were found on the same night," he said.

"Are. Their names are," Steven corrected him.

"Sorry, are," said Warren.

"How were they found?" I asked, frustration with the situation now overtaking the rage inside.

"The first was Elizabeth Stride. Someone found her body around one in the morning. We have a witness that claims to have seen her about a half-hour before the time we think she was murdered," said Commissioner Warren.

"What did he say?" I asked, feeling impatient.

"He didn't speak much English, if any. So figuring out what he saw was a little challenging," Warren said. He stopped and reached down to his right. The dry scraping of wood was followed by some clinking of what I assumed was glass. Warren leaned back upright with a bottle in his left hand and three tumblers in his right. "Whisky?"

"Yes, please," Steven said.

"Sure, I suppose," I said.

If I ever needed any, it would be right now.

Commissioner Warren pulled the cork on the whisky with an ear-piercing pop. He slowly poured the amber and brown liquid into the three glasses. Filling them about three fingers high, he finished and re-corked the bottle. His pipe glowed a lively orange and red with the inhalation of the smoke.

"Basically, all we got out of the man was he saw two people interact with her that night. One of the two men ran him off before he could do anything to help," said Warren.

I took a swig from the drink. The sweet burn coated my throat on the way down, doing its best to fight fire with fire in my gut.

"Any details of what they looked like?" I asked.

"Some, but like I was saying, he was run off. He believed one was about five foot five inches and middle-aged, surly. The other was around the same age but a little bit taller and quite a bit thinner," Commissioner Warren said.

A stout man and a beanstalk. Could they be the same men I have been told about before? If so, where is the other man?

The realization hit me, prompting me to hastily ask Warren a question. "Was there a man with a cane there? Anywhere at all at the scene?"

"Not that I am aware of, why?" he asked.

"I believe I have heard of these men before. I think it was connected to another murder not too long ago," I said.

"Yeah, who was it with?" Steven asked, snapping his fingers. "It was with Martha! It was her friend, Polly, that had a run-in with them. Are they all involved with Dr. Henry, you think?"

"I'm not sure," said Warren. "And speaking of the enigma known as Dr. Henry, or sometimes as Dr. Edward, we were unable to locate him or them."

I rubbed at my chin, then turned to the commissioner again. "You said two. What about the other victim? Catherine?"

Warren let out a sigh and tossed back the rest of his whisky. He exhaled loudly, letting the good kind of pain soak through to his weary bones. Picking up the bottle, he offered some to Steven and I before pouring himself some more. Steven and I shook our heads, and he put the bottle back down on his desk. Lifting the tumbler with his right hand, he took his pipe from his mouth with his left.

"That one is a little more tricky. The witness speaks English but is less credible in my opinion," Warren said.

"Why is that?" I ask.

"The, usually, local man that spends more time locked up than he does at home. But regardless, he is thought to be the last one to see her," Warren said,

"Well, get to it then. What was it?" Steven asked, leaning forward in his seat again.

"The lighting was poor. Too poor to make out much. All he could see was half of the man's face. Apparently, it was contorted into a painful-looking expression," he said.

"What was the second thing?" I asked.

Was it white shoes? Could it be Dr. Henry or Mr. Edward?

"He had white shoes on," he said.

Steven and I traded quick glances. We both somehow knew it was coming to this.

"Commissioner, we need to go do some digging ourselves. Thank you for telling us," I said.

I began to get up, wanting to leave. The anger was seeping back into my fibers, causing me to fidget and move involuntarily. Warren got up too, placing his pipe back in his mouth. His teeth clacked against the stem with an uncomfortable noise. He reached out to me with his free hand for me to shake it.

"We tried, you know. I will keep someone on it till we can figure this out. As of now, it is a joint effort between many law enforcement entities to end this menace. To stop this monster," Warren said.

I took his hand, "I know you had your men try. I'm just angry I wasn't here to help. I am invested in this wholly and deeper than you know," I said.

"I know, son, I know. We are going to do our best," the Commissioner said.

"One more thing," I said.

Warren raised an eyebrow. "Yes?"

"Can you have Jules stationed at the hospital? Me wife thinks there is someone following her lately, and I don't want anything bad to happen to her too. Especially since I am involved in this. She would be a prime target," I said.

"Oh, of course. I think I can swing that. I'll have him start tonight, actually," said Warren.

"Thank you, sir," I said in response.

Shadwell Borough, London, England
12:00 p.m.

I haven't been to see Dr. Thatcher since my run-in with Mr. Edward. Or was it Dr. Henry? We are going on a slim chance that the bodies of the last victims are still at the morgue. Our next stop was to speak with Dr. Thatcher in hopes she could tell us some helpful information.

"Dr. Thatcher, how is a charming and beautiful lady like yourself doing today?" I asked, knocking lightly on the door to the exam room as Steven and I entered.

"First, bugger off. Second, thank you for the compliment," she said, her voice muffled from facing the other direction. Metal clanked against other metal as Dr. Thatcher turned to look at us. The front of her bone-white linen gown was covered from neck to toe with stains of crimson.

"What's for dinner?" asked Steven.

"Really? That's disgusting," I said. I went to elbow him in the side, but he quickly hopped forward and to the left.

"Ha! Not today!" he hooted.

He was about to celebrate his narrow but daring victory when it was suddenly cut short. Dr. Thatcher was in range of an expertly placed hit to the kidney.

"Oww! What was that for?" Steven yelped.

Dr. Thatcher smirked. "You're not getting away that easy."

I let out a few chuckles, enjoying not being on the short end of the stick when it came to Dr. Thatcher for once.

"Doctor, thank you. Anyways, how are things?" I asked.

"Alright, I suppose. Just finishing up here. What brings you two by?" she asked.

"We got some news today about two murders we missed almost two weeks ago. I know it's high hopes, but we were wondering if you still happened to have the bodies here," I said.

"No, we don't. Sorry gentlemen, we only had them for about a day. We've been dealing with a batch of very incompetent nurses here," Dr. Thatcher said.

"Why's that?" I asked.

"They decided it was a good idea to wash them before I could take a look. So I don't have anything to go off of either. Sorry gents," she said.

"It's okay. We will find out who did this eventually. By the way, do you mind if we ask you any questions about Mr. Edward?" I asked.

"Uh, sure. What about him?" she asked.

"Have you seen him since the last excursion I had with you two about a month ago?"

Dr. Thatcher gave it some thought. She started to tap her foot, quick and light. It echoed faintly off the close walls, jumping around to its own beat.

"No I haven't. I think he went back to the city he was going to school," she said.

"Which is that?" Steven asked.

As she talked, the tapping stopped. "I think it was Oxford. Yes, that was it. He went back home the same day you ran past me like a madman."

Hah, me. Yeah, I am the madman.

"You know you never told me what was wrong. You two just ran off like the heavens were on fire," she said.

I need to be careful what I say. I don't want to get her too involved. That's the last thing I need, someone else on his list.

"There was no particular reason. I believe I needed him to help me with something. It really doesn't matter," I said, trying to change the subject. "Could you tell me more about the last two victims if you remember anything?"

"Sure, the two that happened in the same night?" she asked. "Elizabeth Stride and Catherine Eddowes, correct?"

"Yes," I replied.

"After closer examination of Catherine I discovered she was missing her left kidney while Elizabeth only had her throat slit," Dr. Thatcher said. "But it was also strange. Her ear was partially sliced off."

"Why the ear?" Steven asked.

Dr. Thatcher shrugged. "Unsure."

The kidney again, why?

"Thank you for your time, Doctor. Come on, Davey, we will let her get back to it," Steven said.

CHAPTER 24

Doctors Appointment

Field Notes Entry 9

Initially, we had two suspects we were attempting to keep tabs on in this investigation. One of which was the man with the black cane, seen in multiple places and multiple continents. As I began to think back, I realized I ran into him on several occasions. The first was on the night I received Excalibur from the strange gentleman by the name of Gregory Merlinus. Another, although indirectly, was on the night of Martha's murder. The last time, that I am aware of, was on my trip to America with Steven and Nikola.

Taking all of this into consideration, the current suspect is named Dr. Henry, or in some cases, Mr. Edward. With our return, Steven and I have had a few run-ins with him on multiple occasions, always seemingly unable to apprehend him. The last of which ended poorly, but not without progress.

Both the newspapers and professionals alike have given some predictions on how there are many people that could actually be involved. That of course is contradictory to what Dr. Thatcher has stated, as I mentioned before.

I have a suspicion that these are, in fact, the same person, but have no proof. Thus proving we may need an outside opinion of someone that may know more than we do. We decided to follow up on some leads that seemed promising.

Recently hearing of a professor giving a lecture at The University Of Oxford for the next couple of days, we thought it might be a good idea to go see what the class was all about. Some reports mentioned that the professor there kept an open mind to the odd and the strange. Mostly when it's involved with cases of diseases, but I thought he might have an insight that might help us in our endeavors. Both Steven and I have taken a few weeks off from TEA and the Scotland Yard to travel to Oxford.

31st October 1888
Oxford, England
12:45 p.m.

The smog and ash floated through the air like pollen carrying the last hope of the dying plant. Rays of sun fought their way through the fog in cracks and splinters, creating a jagged view of the polluted world. Steven and I weaved our way in and out of the crowds of women and children. The men sold baked goods and their kin offered to shine shoes for money to get enough for their next meal.

The leaves started to turn a multitude of colors ranging from burnt orange to crisp brown that mingled with the greens of the soon-forgotten summer promise. Most everyone we passed clamored and murmured about the killer that had been terrorizing London.

In an attempt to gain insight and understanding of the killer, or killers, we wanted to attend a lecture held at a local university. The speaker came highly recommended by Dr. Thatcher because of his evolved opinion on certain subjects pertaining to human behavior. Specifically, how and why people act the way they do, and the reasoning behind said actions.

As we climbed the steps of the lecture hall, I pulled out my pocket watch to check the time. Upon doing so, I saw that it was a quarter past one in the afternoon. Dabbing my brow with the muckender, I recounted the Christmas I received my watch as a gift. I slipped it back into my pocket and reached for the door, glancing around at the world around me once more. With a loud creak, we entered the lecture hall, quietly scanning the room. The light from the open doors bathed everything in a yellow shimmer, dust slowly drifting through the air.

Seeing as how the lecture was still in progress, we crept to a pair of empty seats in the front. Eyes from the current attendees bore through the backs and sides of our heads. They all silently judged and questioned who dared to interrupt their lecture.

We sat and listened for some time as he wrapped up his lecture about tuberculosis. My eyes drifted to the pile of books stacked up on the floor. By my count, there were eleven or twelve, edges and corners hanging over each other.

What information is between those pages? The best recipe for haggis you could imagine? The answer to the universe? Or perhaps something more modest like the comprehensive collection of lavatory stories.

Chuckling at the last thought, I tuned back into the lecture.

"Diseases as we know them today are the same as they have always been. The thing that has changed is our understanding. Humankind is finding the causes of these extreme sicknesses," The man said as he paced back and forth.

As I listened, I noticed that one of his feet dragged slightly with each step he took.

"Take tuberculosis, for example." He pointed to a poster hanging on the wall behind and to the left of the podium. "For centuries it was attributed to vampires. That the dead loved ones were actually still alive, taking life from the living. Can anyone tell me the name that we still use for this disease?"

Someone to the left of us raised his hand.

"Yes?" asked the professor as he pointed to the student.

"Consumption?" The student guessed.

The doctor stopped pacing and returned to the podium. "Yes, yes it is. But the symptoms of the disease have caused us to come up with an explanation for something we know nothing about. Our fear is supplementing true reasons with tales of the strange and fantastic," he continued, taking a small muckender from his breast pocket and wiping his face. "For the most part, this is radical thinking. Many still believe in these folklore stories, explaining away the issues thinking that a simple tonic of blood and tree bark will fix all their ailments." he said, walking back around the front of the podium. "That concludes today's lecture. Come back tomorrow for the last of it. Also, if you have any questions, you can come talk to me before I leave for the day."

With all the students leaving the atrium, we sat patiently until the last few stragglers that remained asked their questions and went on their way. When they finally did, Steven and I stood up and walked over to the professor.

"Sir! That was quite interesting and informative," I said.

"I appreciate the kind words, but I get the feeling you two aren't part of the university student body, are you?" he asked.

"No sir, we are actually detectives with Scotland Yard. We heard you'd be here for some classes and wanted to come talk to you about some things," I said. "Me names Davey and that's Steven."

"Nice to meet you two. I am Doctor Abraham Van Helsing," he said as he clapped his hands together. "I'm not quite sure how much help I can be, but I will do what I can."

"We wanted to ask for your opinions on some things that we've received in the mail. Also, we wanted to ask what you thought about Jack the Ripper."

A look of interest grew on his face. "Which opinion would you like first?" he asked.

Exchanging glances with Steven, he shrugged. "I suppose we can start with some letters and other items we got in the mail."

Steven and I walked over to a table near the podium and waited as Dr. Van Helsing hobbled to it.

He took a seat behind it and asked, "What might you have in there?"

I reached into the bag, pulled out a crinkled brown envelope, and placed it on the table. It was followed by a jar filled with semi-transparent red liquid that sloshed around inside as I set it down. As the liquid settled in the jar, it became more clear. Bubbles collecting on the sides and top.

Dr. Van Helsing picked up the jar filled with the red liquid and gave it a long quizzical look. As he focused on the jar he asked, "What is contained in the envelope?"

"A few letters were sent to us throughout the investigation," I said, picking it back up. "And some photos from the scenes of the crimes."

"I am assuming the pictures were not taken by the Scotland Yard, were they?" he said.

"No, all before we found the victims," I replied.

I unraveled the red tie made of twine on the back of the worn brown folder and pulled everything out. The pictures and letters scraped against the sides on the way out, cutting through the momentary silence.

Handing them to the doctor, he put down the jar while taking them from me. He shuffled through the photos first, his face contorting from the sight. It first turned pale, followed by the clear look of repulsion.

"To give opinions, I need to ask a few questions of my own. May I?" Dr. Van Helsing asked.

"Certainly," I said, nodding.

"Do you believe it is only one man?"

"The predominant theory is that it is only one, but some believe otherwise," I said.

He rubbed his chin, allowing the color to come back into his face. Putting the pictures down, he carefully unfolded the first letter and read the contents. Taking a few moments to read the second, he went back and forth between the two. "If it is one person, I believe it could be a strange case of multiple personalities. But it could also be two or more people, depending on how well they know each other."

"The main suspect of mine has behaved quite strangely on the occasions I have had the chance to talk to him. I think it would support your theory," I said. "I am the only one so far to have seen this strange behavior though, I was beginning to think I was just mad."

"I assure you that you aren't. I'm assuming that's why you came to me?" he asked, raising an eyebrow.

"Yessir. We heard you can come up with some outside-of-the-box thinking," Steven said.

"I would say it's the former then. From what I can tell with the letters, they both have differences. But," he said, clicking his tongue. "They are also similar."

I took the letters and photos back as he handed them to me.

"So what's in the jar you have there?" he asked, picking the jar back up.

"It's half of a kidney, sent through the mail to Mr. George Lusk. He is the head chairman of the Mile End Vigilance Committee," I said. "We believe it is from one of the victims of Jack the Ripper."

"Why do you think this?" he asked.

"The cut marks match ones found on one of the deceased," Steven said.

"Is that the only body part taken from a victim?" he asked.

"No sir, the fourth victim had her uterus taken," Steven said before pausing, a grim expression flowering on his face. "Never retrieved."

"Curious. Very curious," he said, "Maybe he believes in ritualistic sacrifice, or, he eats them."

Disgust flashed over my face. A pit in my stomach opened up and threatened to empty the contents from my last meal.

"One more thing that we have noticed over the duration of this investigation is that most of the victims have had their livers taken too," I said.

"Peculiar. Very peculiar," the doctor murmured as he stroked his chin.

I looked over at Steven then back at the doctor. "Why is that, sir?"

"Well, over the course of my many years of being a doctor," the doctor said before pausing to fix his eyeglasses. "I have found that many societies and groups of people believe livers are very good for memory."

"Memory? Why is that important? You're not the first person to say that either," I said.

"You would need to tell me. With the assumption your suspect has multiple personalities, he may be using them to keep the real him near and dear so as he doesn't get lost in the fold of everyone else in his head," he said.

I looked at the ground for a moment, pondering what he had told me. "Is there anything else you get from this?"

"What I can tell you is if it's multiple personalities, or two people, one of them is a doctor. Part of the work done seems to be surgically performed. Other parts seem rushed and sloppy," he said, putting the jar back down.

I looked at Steven silently, nodding.

"Well, thank you, Doctor, that helps a lot. It confirms some suspicions we've had," I said.

"Please, call me Van Helsing. If you ever need any help, you can come find me," he said, reaching out his hand to shake.

"Thank you sir, ehrm, Van Helsing," I said.

Shaking, the ring started to glow very faintly. It wasn't enough for him to notice but just enough for me to.

He's a dimmer. That must be why he is more in tune with what happens around him.

We said our farewells and thank yous to Dr. Van Helsing shortly before leaving the lecture hall. Everything we learned today will definitely help us. Steven and I stopped at a street vendor to get some food before heading back to London.

We walked slowly and talked about the information Van Helsing gave us. As we passed some brick fences that lined the very edge of the marketplace, we came upon a couple of young children playing hopscotch. They sang aloud in a semi-melodic fashion between jumps. The hairs on the back of my neck stood up, and my pulse quickened as I took in what they were actually saying:

Tap tap, it's Whitechapel Jack
Tick tock, wind your clock
Strike strike, turn on the lights
Knock knock, check your locks
Scrape scrape, you won't escape
Run run, he's out for fun

The song penetrated deep into my mind, pushing everything to the back. I tried to ignore what I was hearing to no avail. A slow buzzing filled my ears as the world around me went dark.

Scrape, scrape

A flash of lightning turned the darkness to light. Looking up into the sky, I saw I was in the eye of the storm. The wind was calm, and the smell of the ocean was very faint, not like the other times I've been here. The grass was still as it stood all around me, and the only thing I could hear was my heartbeat. I noticed the man I saw last time was still to my right, magnificent accented armor and all.

"You're King Arthur, aren't you?" I asked.

He didn't speak, only nodding his head.

"His name is Henry, isn't it. That's the one I'm after, or at least that's the name he's going by now," I said with curiosity.

He neither answered that question, nor did he nod to it either.

"I can't do this without any direction. I need help!" I screamed, anger growing in the pit of my stomach. "All of these puzzles and hidden messages are just a frustration!"

Off in the distance, thunder sounded, and as it startled me, the rage subsided.

"This is all the help I will get, isn't it?" I asked.

Feeling defeated, I looked at him for answers. Just wanting something to go off of or a hint in the right direction.

"Be wary Davey, he is more than just a person. He is a plague, an infection, bringing only death and pain in his wake," Arthur said.

The ground started to shake as the winds picked up again, pulling me and everything else back into the storm.

Black. Cold. Familiar.

Scrape, scrape

I stopped dead in my tracks, coming back to my senses. Turning to look at the children playing hopscotch, I asked, "Excuse me children, where did you hear that?"

The children stopped playing and looked up to me. "We heard it from a man, sir."

"What man? What did he look like?" I asked.

The children began to look afraid. "We don't know, sir, he just was walking past, and we heard it."

"Do you remember anything about him? Anything weird or special?" I asked, getting closer.

As I did so, the little girl on the right started to cry.

"I'm sorry, I don't mean to scare you. It's just, I need to know," I said.

The girl on the left said, "We don't remember, sir. He had really pretty shoes, though. They was white."

"White? Do you know where he went? How long ago did you see him?" I asked.

The girl on the right's crying subsided slightly. "We saw him a while ago sir. We don't know."

"Bollocks," swore Steven.

"Steven, watch your language around children," I said condescendingly. "Sorry girls, go about your playing again. I didn't mean to make you cry."

We started to walk once more, leaving the children alone. Our feet echoed off the ground and bounced off the brick fence.

"We must've missed him a while ago. Damn," I muttered.

"Watch your language, Davey, children are near," Steven said mockingly with a smile.

Like always, he was rewarded with an elbow.

Chapter 25

Like A Waterfall

1st November, 1888
Farringdon Borough, London, England
10:12 a.m.

The church seemed to sing, imaginary angelic voices mingling in the open, inviting space. They created an orchestra that greeted my ears as I entered through the large double doors.

The rays of sunlight broke through the shadow's grasp it had around the room. Like always, Father Hubert was off to the left, sitting in one of the seats in the first row of chairs.

"Oh Davey, how have you been?" Hubert asked, looking at me. "How was your trip?

"Not too bad, Father, just got back to London from a trip to Oxford," I said, letting out a sigh. "Just got back this morning, actually."

"Seems like you have been busy as of late. I haven't seen you or Steven in a little while, have I?" he asked.

I nodded. "That's true, sir. By the way, have you been able to find another Descendent for the buckle artifact?"

"No, sorry, my son. There has not been any luck on that front."

"Hm, it is what it is, I suppose. I am hoping to have someone else to help soon. Steven is enough to deal with by meself. It would be nice to have someone else babysit him."

Hubert chuckled. "Speaking of Steven, where is he by the way? You two usually aren't far apart."

"He went to go see the commissioner. After getting back from America, Steven and I have been trying to catch up with everything we missed."

"Like what?"

I sighed and rubbed my neck. "For starters, we missed more murders. I have been beating myself up over it ever since we returned. We messed up badly. Instead of galavanting off in America, we could have been here to prevent the last two."

"Davey," Hubert said, pursing his lips. "None of it is your fault. You know this. You *should* know this. It was not by choice. You were tasked to do this by the Crown. We have been playing catch up since the first time you stepped foot through those doors."

"It doesn't feel like we should be cutting ourselves any slack; we are the only ones able to stop him. How can we if we are too busy running around pretending we don't need to worry about it!"

The ever-present singing from angels of sunlight and hope paused with the arrival of my anger. The silence crashed through, causing the room to fill with an uncomfortable tension.

"Davey. Come here." Hubert motioned to the seat next to him. "You know how many years The Keepers have been around? How long have we been trying to stop him?"

I let out a long sigh, trying to calm down. "I don't remember Father." Rolling my eyes, I took a seat next to him. My shoulders sank as I slumped over, my elbows resting on my knees and my hands holding up my head. "I have been chasing him for a while, and I don't feel any closer to catching him. I am starting to feel hopeless."

Father Hubert placed a hand on my back, patting gently. "It's okay, Davey. I feel like we are the closest we have ever been to catching him. Over the last fifty years of my life, I don't remember ever getting as close as we are now."

With my face still resting in my hands, I asked, "Father, how did all of this even transpire? I have had visions of King Arthur and some of the other knights over the course of the last year, but it's fragmented."

"What do you mean?"

"Why are we around? The Keepers. Why are we here?" I asked.

"Ah, yes." Hubert paused, taking in a breath. "Many, many years ago, when King Arthur was battling against Jakobus, they spent years tracking him down all the while protecting themselves from his random attacks."

"So, what does that mean for us? Why have generation after generation tried to take him down then?" I asked, frustration creeping back into my voice.

"Arthur and Merlin originally thought with each new generation there would be different takes on how to prevail over Jakobus. Another reason was that each new set of descendants means more memories for the next to use to their advantage, regardless of the outcome."

"Do you know how they did it? Why do we get the memories from the artifacts?" I asked, beginning to calm down. "In the visions, Merlin used a ritual of blood to link them to the artifacts."

Father Hubert slowly rocked forward, pulling himself up. He began pacing back and forth as he continued talking. "You're right, that is how they did it. Since the times of King Arthur and the creation of The Keepers, a lot of information has been lost to time. Some have survived, but most have been forgotten, or the records have been destroyed. It was the best way to pass it on."

"What do you mean destroyed?" I asked, curious now.

"In the year 1543, this very monastery was badly ransacked. Half demolished by many godless people. It was part of the dissolution of the monasteries, a legal process started by King Henry the Eighth. The reason he started this was to fund the Crown, but most of the money went towards his military campaigns," said Hubert, still pacing.

"Davey! Hey!" yelled Steven, barging through the double doors. He stopped a few feet from me, leaning over his knees. "She's missing!"

"Who is?" I asked.

"I just got to the station when Warren told me she was missing!" he spat, trying to catch his breath. His face went white, color bleeding away from his features. "It's Marie. She's gone."

"Dammit, Steven, don't tell me it's her. Anyone but her!" I yelled. "What about Jules? He was supposed to watch her off and on when I couldn't. Where is he?"

"He wasn't the one Warren had watching her. Apparently, it was someone else at the time," he said.

My whole world began to spin, colors and lights blending into a swirling inferno and then slowly beginning to fade away into oblivion, away from the world of good and happiness. It was him. Henry, or Edward, whatever the hell his name was. We need to find him. For Marie's safety.

"But I got— I got an address," he said.

"An address? An address for who?" I asked, light and sound pulsing back into vision with the hope of good news.

"For Dr. Henry."

"Wha— how?"

"They were able to come up with one just this morning."

"How? We have been chasing him for a while now."

"Do we need to care? Come on."

"He has to have her. It has to be him!"

We ran through the double doors to get to Dr. Henry's house before it was too late. Not only to catch him but in hopes of rescuing Marie too.

Please be safe, Marie. Please.

Westminster Borough, London, England
10:45 a.m.

We ran to the address as quickly as we could. The thoughts in my mind started to eat away at the fringes of my sanity. Worry set in thick like flies in sweet honey. Thinking it would be less suspicious, we began to walk when we got closer.

I pulled out my pocket watch to check the time. "Good, it's still early in the morning. I think we may still have a chance to catch him," I said, clicking the watch shut gently.

Ever since receiving the pocket watch as a gift, I had been trying to preserve the springs and clip on the inside of it, only opening it whenever it was needed. I clicked it shut and noticed a small buzzing that started in the back of my mind. It was abrasive and annoying, almost a trilling-like noise from. It grew louder with my quickened heartbeat.

Steven was a few steps ahead of me, eagerly looking around for what I assumed was Dr. Henry. I paused for a moment and looked around, noticing that the street was pretty much empty. There were no people going to and fro for work, nor children playing tag accented by the fresh sprinkle of wildlife either.

"Come on, just up here! Commissioner Warren said Dr. Henry lives at 28 Leicester Square," Steven said, urging me to move again.

We walked up to the front door and knocked gently but with a sense of urgency. I took a few large steps back to look at how high the building stood. It was about six stories high, made from an elegant, cream-colored stone. I looked back at Steven and noticed he started to bounce his leg as he crossed his arms. Steven sighed as he gave the door another good knock, getting frustrated with being professional and all the procedures that went along with it.

"Should we just enter? If we keep waiting, he might have time to run off," Steven said.

"I don't know. I suppose we could. Probable cause? Someone might be injured since our knocks haven't been heeded," I said, shrugging.

The door creaked open just as Steven reached for the doorknob. He and I looked at each other with our eyebrows raised.

"I guess that answers that for us," Steven said.

Before we could enter, a voice from behind stopped us. Turning, I grabbed the hilt of Excalibur while Steven pulled his bio-electric rifle up to eye level. The gun produced a crackling charge from contact with his skin, filling the silence with an eerie uneasiness.

"What are you two doing here?" asked Jules.

Frustration and anger swelled in the surprise of seeing Jules. The feelings started to slowly recede from front and center, taking second place to confusion and curiosity. I then immediately remembered he was supposed to watch over Marie.

You are to blame. It's all your fault. Why couldn't you watch after her?

"What do you mean?" I asked, slowly letting go of my sword.

In the background, I could hear Steven's modified Mason model 1870 slowly discharge the built-up electricity, the snaps and crackles giving up and fading like the dying hearth of a fading flame. The hairs on the back of my neck and arms stood on end as I felt the static in the air build up. Filling the atmosphere with the lost energy seeping back into the environment.

"Well, I asked you first. But I suppose I can go." Jules chuckled. "I heard about Dr. Henry living here and thought I'd come take a look."

How? As far as I know, Commissioner Warren wasn't bringing him in on this investigation.

"Ah, well, we have it from here. I insist," said Steven as confidence and seriousness filled the tone of his voice.

Jules looked at us with a blank expression. As he was doing this, I suddenly felt a chill fracture down my spine. My mind began to fill with thoughts of hopelessness, and the world felt even colder than it ever had.

Jules cleared his throat. "Okay, I will let you two take care of this." He began to smile. Not a particularly happy or inviting one, but more a matter of fact one. "Keep in touch, boys."

Jules turned and began to walk off down the street.

I reached out and grabbed his wrist, stopping him from leaving. "Wait, why couldn't you watch Marie?"

Scrape, scrape

"The end is nigh," Arthur said.

A boom echoed through the air, reverberating through my body. It started in my spine and spread like wildfire through each of my vertebrae.

"I'm sorry, sir, I have failed. I haven't gotten any closer than I was in the beginning," I said, turning to see him. "And now Marie is missing."

His once young features, strong and stoic, began to fade with the storm. They were completely different from the first time I saw him as they began to turn worn, old, and gray.

"You have done the best you could have. That is more than what is expected of you. But don't worry, you still aren't finished yet," Arthur said.

"What if I can't do it?" I asked.

"Do to the best of your ability and pray that your children, or your children's children, can end it once and for all. Remember, evil is never really that far away."

The clouds in the sky swirled above, lit up by bouts of rage. The storm, no, my storm, was almost through. All I needed to do was try and weather it. Hopefully, everyone I know will make it too.

Scrape, scrape

"Who are you talking about, my boy?" Jules asked, turning back to me with a calm look on his face, absent of any reassuring emotion.

I shook my head to refocus myself. "Me wife. Warren was supposed to have you watch her. She is missing."

"Oh, I was unavailable at the time. I will get on that right away though. Hopefully she isn't missing for too long," Jules said, a sly smile forming on the edges of his mouth. It tugged at them, daring them to show what truly lies behind.

The tension of uncertainty and fear filled the air once more, pitching war against the leftover static electricity. As we waited for Jules to reach the end of the street, Steven slipped the bio-electric rifle back around his shoulder.

"What was that all about?" Steven asked. "It's almost as if he forgot he was asked to look after her."

"I don't know, Steven. I don't know what to think of him anymore. He is always in the wrong place at the right times like we always are," I said.

"Yeah. Maybe he is a lost descendent like us. Maybe he is brought to these places without even knowing. Maybe that's why though?"

I lifted my right hand up to see if the ring was glowing, noticing it wasn't.

I grabbed his wrist with my left hand. Does it matter which hand touches the descendants?

"Either way, let's get back to checking into this lead, okay?"

I began to enter the home of Dr. Edward and gently placed my right hand on the middle of the door, pushing it open. As it creaked open loudly, we could make out there were no lights on in the house, natural or otherwise. To help find the light switch, I pulled out my Embyr. I held it out above our heads as it cast the luminous light on our surroundings.

I held the Embyr up near the wall, looking for a Wavergy light switch. Finding it easily enough, I looked at the brass button encased in a brass dome, gleaming in the light from years of rubbing the oil of hands onto it. I pressed on it gingerly, not wanting to disturb anyone that didn't know we were there. In a split second, the whole house came to life with a vibrant and glowing light.

Not needing it anymore, I put my Embyr back into my pocket, so I didn't put it down and forget about it. The front foyer of the house seemed as if it was all carved from the same piece of wood, connecting to form a cohesive feeling throughout. Just inside to the right was the wall in which the light switch was installed. In front of that was the staircase to the second floor. To the left was a main level originally intended for a few businesses to be housed in. But now, most surfaces were covered in paint-stained linens and ladders randomly jutting out from the ground, like buttes in the great wild west.

"Where do we even start?" I asked, taking in the wide-open space.

"I can start on the first floor here," he said, looking at me. "You want to look on the second floor?"

I nodded. "Okay, I'll start there then. Yell if you find her, okay?"

"I will, don't worry. We will find her."

Steven and I split off, heading in our own directions. I looked at the staircase, squinting to see how far it went up. A moment of staring gave my mind enough time to imagine a shadowed figure standing at the very top. The seconds slowly dripped past, giving my imagination time to see everything that wasn't there.

"Come," said the shadow.

Its form morphed into a slithering black blob, quickly shifting and wavering back and forth.

What in the bloody hell is going on? It was actually there? Who is that? Why does it want me up there?

Before I could think, my body made up my mind for me. My foot began to lift itself onto the first step. I tried to resist, straining from the otherworldly force pulling me upwards. I couldn't stop myself from ascending the staircase. All I could do was turn my head from side to side.

About halfway up the steps, I looked at the wall to my right. Picture frames of all sizes dotted its surface, randomly placed at bizarre intervals. In all, there were about a hundred. At first, I couldn't make out why they frightened me, but I finally realized what it was that made me feel that way. Each was either a photo or painting of a man by himself. But the strangest thing about them was the fact that all of the faces had been burned off at some point. The feeling they reflected back toward me in the glass was anger and frustration.

What's going on? Why is his face gone?

When I finally reached the top of the steps, I regained control over my legs once more. The second floor widened to a large open layout. The light was out on the second floor as well, prompting me to find another Wavergy switch. Feeling like it was a waste of time to take my Embyr back out, I just groped the wall helplessly for it. With a click of the button, the room sprang to life.

In the far corner opposite of me was a well-stocked bar, wood countertops sparkling and gleaming back at me. The wall behind was equipped with mirrors taking up the corner. It reflected reality back, making one wonder what was real and what was an alcohol-induced stupor. Bottles lined a shelf that hung about waist height, accompanied by glasses. The odor of the room made my nose tingle, and I rubbed it in response. It smelt like freshly dried paint mingling with newly layered varnish.

I looked to my right and noticed it was set up like a parlor, complete with a red, velvet-lined lounging chair. Next to it sat a small coffee table covered with an array of liquor bottles and papers. Against the right wall closest to me sat a lavish causeuse, a french loveseat. It was made from a cream-colored cloth decorated with *fleur de lis*. Pearls lined the seams of the cushion that met the beautiful dark brown wood frame of the feet.

A flash of light coming from the left caught my attention, causing me to turn to see the other side of the room. As I looked to the left, it helped me discover where the new paint smell originated. Everything on this side was white, reminiscent of a new snowfall covering the death and decay of the world, fooling our senses with false beauty and hope. The stark contrast between the two sides was bizarre and disorienting, creating a sense of inanimate bickering.

I scanned over everything for a moment, eventually not seeing anything that could have caused the flash of light. All of the furniture was removed from this side except for a long metal exam table.

I looked closer and saw that a body was lying across it, covered with a linen sheet. As I ran to the exam table, my heart began its crazed effort to leap from my chest and break through its cage of ribs. To leave this place of misery and dread.

Oh God, please don't be Marie. Just don't be her. Anything but her.

"Marie! Oh God, Marie. Is that you? Are you okay?" I yelled in a panic.

Anxiety and worry fought fiercely with my sanity. They threatened to overwhelm my mind with images of things unthinkable.

I reached the table and pulled the linen free, hoping it wasn't her. Underneath, in the pale light, I could make out the body of a woman. Her torso was cut from the sternum all the way down to her hips. Her ribs were cracked and split open outward to provide access to her internal organs.

It isn't Marie. Thank you, God.

The woman was unknown to me, but it was all the same. Another person I wasn't able to save. I slammed my fist down on the table next to her. I didn't know anger could do this to me, grow so much in a short amount of time.

I realized the cool steel was clean and free of any blood, her body patted down dry. At her feet were her organs in a neat pile, glistening in the light. I scoured them with my eyes to see if her liver was among them. I couldn't tell if it was or not, but I could only assume it wasn't.

Another burst of light came from my right. I turned and centered my gaze upon the bar, seeing the corporeal shadow.

"Davey," said the figure.

My head snapped to the front of me, straight at the bar in the corner.

"Who are you?" I asked.

After the words left my mouth, my legs began to move again. Starting off slow, they pulled me towards the source of the unknown voice. It pulled me away from the unknown woman and the stench of cleaning solutions and death. When I reached the counter of the bar, the shadow started to swirl and form into a semi-transparent form.

"I thought you had this handled," said the figure.

"I– What?" I stammered, confused.

The features of the figure solidified, changing to the face of someone familiar.

"Gregory? How—" I continued to stutter.

"This is all I can do to help," he said.

"What do you mean? How can you?" I asked.

Gregory put his left hand on my shoulder and looked at me for a while. Sorrow and pain swirled through his eyes, making me feel as if he had more than his fair share of losses. His form began to slowly dissipate, phasing back to translucency.

Before completely disappearing, he told me one last thing. "What has passed is never done."

With his form fully gone, I looked down on the countertop where his right hand was placed. Underneath it was a white envelope with a wax seal stamped onto it. I picked it up, opened it and began to read.

> To Whom It May Concern:
>
> My name is Doctor Henry Jekyll. I am writing this letter as a form of confession to my sins. I was offered a chance of a lifetime. I thought that joining him would help me understand the mysteries of the human mind and body. At first, that was exactly what I re-

ceived, knowledge of things mankind had only dreamed of.

As a man of science, I thought I could change the world one patient at a time, hopeful and innocent in my ignorance. After a while, I began to notice small things here and there that didn't quite add up. An inkwell in the wrong spot; one of my pillows on my causeuse turned the wrong way. Eventually, bigger things piled up. Decent sums of time were missing from my daily schedule, along with some people I knew starting to treat me differently.

I eventually found that in joining this man, I wasn't myself anymore. I was no longer just Dr. Henry Jekyll, I was also Mr. Edward Hyde. When I am in control of myself — in control of him — I try to atone for our sins. I have tried to prevent him from taking control by harvesting the livers from his victims — no — *our* victims.

From years of research, I learned livers have properties that promote a healthy memory, and my hopes were that it would help me know who I was. *Who* I am. I fear that the times I cannot be in charge, I simply don't remember. I beg that whoever finds this letter, please stop us. I fear the next time he breaks free, I will no longer be here. Jakobus isn't through, he has taken another victim, but I am unsure what he has done with her. He may just be biding his time, and I don't know when he will strike

next. All I know is where. It will be near the
Spitalfields Market. Please, anyone. Help.

6th November, 1888
Farringdon Borough, London, England
8:09 a.m.

"Father, Steven and I have kept an eye out for about a week now. I don't think he will show up again," I said.

"Patience, Davey. I believe he will come back in due time," said Father Hubert.

"I can't! He has my wife! He has my unborn child!" I yelled.

"You do not know it is her that he has. It could be someone else," Hubert said.

I stopped and stared at him for a moment, using my demeanor instead of my words to tell him what I thought of that statement.

Steven came over and patted me on the back, trying to help me stay calm.

I turned to Hubert and asked, "And who is this other man he speaks of? Do you think that Henry is not Jakobus?"

"Honestly, if Arthur and Merlin were able to preserve not only their memories but everyone else's in all the bloodlines, then I fear Jakobus was able to do something like that as well." He paused for a moment. Continuing, he said, "Or I fear something worse."

I finally sat down in one of the old chairs. My chair. It creaked and groaned underneath my weight, complaining about the added stress it didn't want. Even though I sat, I began to bounce my leg, nervousness always present in my mind.

"I suppose we will have to keep up with the searching then. Thank you, Father, I am hoping that we are close to the end of this," I said.

"Don't worry, my son, we will find her. She is strong-willed," said Father Hubert.

Chapter 26

Eye Of The Storm

8th November, 1888
Spitalfields Borough, London, England
12:00 p.m.

A melody floated through the air like a mid-fall lullaby. It spread far and wide, weighing heavily on sober eyelids of the men and women roaming the streets at night.

Father and mother, they have passed away.
Sister and brother, now lay beneath the clay.

The woman sang, walking down the street. The night slowly changed from one day to the next, fading to the quiet and usual bleak night. Energy from all around began to slow as people started off to their beds and homes. But, on this night, a beautiful tone decided to break up the monotony and revolt against what normally blanketed the streets. The woman continued to sing once again, acting as bait for the foul creatures lurking in the shadows, slinking and creeping around, ready to take advantage of the gift she was giving their ears.

But while life does remain,
to cheer me I will retain.
This small violet
I plucked from Mother's grave.

She was blissfully unaware that the last song she would ever sing almost sounded like an apology. An apology that she would never be enough. Never do enough to be what her parents wanted her to be.

Field Notes Entry 10

About one week ago, Steven and I stumbled upon Henry's place of inhabitance as well as learning of my wife's abduction. I haven't slept much, unable to find solace in the empty sheets next to me. All this time not knowing if she was still with us or if she was having a reunion with her parents.

Sadly, when we arrived at 28 Leicester Square, Dr. Henry had already disappeared once again. Upon entering, I encountered another ghostly figure lurking in the shadows. At first, I feared the apparition, not knowing it was just helping me find my way through this bizarre journey of mine.

At the end of searching the premises, the shadow led me to a note left by Dr. Henry. I read what the good doctor left only to find out some shocking news, though we already had a hunch for part of his confession.

I have been posted in the area by
Commissioner Warren after I revealed
some of what I found out to him. I
have told him that another victim
would be taken from the Spitalfields
market area but left out any mention
of Jakobus since Warren had no idea
who that was. Steven was able to
get transferred to a day shift for
maintenance, making it easier for the
both of us to keep together during
most of the last week.

9th November, 1888
Spitalfields Borough, London, England
10:45 a.m.

"I'm sorry, Steven. It's just really hard keeping my mind on all of this," I said.

"I know. It's okay, Davey. We'll find her soon," he said.

"I just want her home. I want to find her."

We both worked in silence for a minute or two while frightful things filled my thoughts with dark and depressing pictures.

Why did it have to be her? It must be because she is pregnant. Jakobus could be cutting—

My train of thought was now fully engulfed in flames, threatening to become more sinister by the second. Thankfully it was derailed by a man calling out to us.

"Oi!" shouted a man from across the street.

Looking down from the lamp post I was working on, Steven and I said, "Yeah?" in unison.

"We gotta stop doing that," we both said again.

"You see a bobbie around?" The man asked.

"No, just a detective, but I can help," I said as I screwed in the bulb

I stepped down off the ladder and walked toward the man.

"Hey Steven, come on," I said as I looked over my shoulder.

"Fine," He grumbled.

The man gave us an odd look as he said, "A lady over there. She owes me rent. I checked her door, but she won't answer. Thought I'd try and get a bobbie to come take a look."

"Since we are detectives we can try. Why don't you show me to her?" I said, thankful to divert my attention to something else.

The man led Steven and I around the street corner and past a few decrepit buildings. At the end of the next block, he led us into Miller's court. We followed him under a covered tunnel that opened up into a relatively small courtyard. It was longer than it was wide, doors closed, and windows shuttered to keep out the honest light.

He stopped and turned back to us. "This is it."

"Okay, do you have keys?" I asked.

"I already unlocked it, just didn't want to go in. As I was about to earlier, I yelled to her, but she didn't answer. I got a strange chill. Ran all the way up me back. Thought I should leave it to someone else," he said.

"What's her name again?" I asked.

"Mary Kelly is her name," He said, "You mind checking for me then? Since you volunteered?"

"Okay, um, yes, I will," I said.

I swallowed hard and reached for the handle, turning the knob slowly. The springs and pins began to groan with the added tension. Angry, I awoke them from their slumber. As I did so, I inched the door open, being careful and mindful if she may be indecent.

"Hello? Mary Kelly? Are you here?" I asked through the crack.

I waited a moment without receiving any reply. Shrugging, I pushed the door open the rest of the way. Immediately, my nose was overwhelmed with the scent of freshly butchered meat. A metallic taste laid siege to my tongue and taste buds, coating them with death. The stench of blood-soaked cloth and bile coalesced into a cloud that hovered thickly in the air.

The change in light made it hard for me to make anything out, causing my eyes to struggle as they adjusted. Out of reflex, I readied my stance, remembering what it was like during the war. My mind was reeling from knowing that within seconds being ready was the only thing that may help me make it till the next sunrise.

I looked over and saw something lying on the bed, knowing that whatever it was, it was long gone. It bore no resemblance to a human, as if it never was. The sunlight from the window glinted off of the gore and viscera, like a gruesome chandelier that hung true for a nightmare masquerade.

I quickly scanned the room and looked to the right as my world seemed to stop. I felt my blood drain from my face as it inched down every fiber of my muscles, every vein on the verge of collapse, eventually pooling at my feet, threatening to join the mess on the floor.

Laying in the fetal position next to the bed was Marie, my sweet Marie. My love, my life. The mother of my unborn child, still and unmoving. I felt like collapsing, and my will to live was expelled with my ragged breath.

Marie, why did I let this happen? Why didn't I find you sooner?

I ran to Marie and collapsed to the floor next to her still form. My hands feverishly felt for a pulse, and I checked for any cut or slash from a blade. She was covered in blood as well, dress clinging to her body as it dried and cemented itself to her.

"Please! Marie! Stay with me. I can't do this without you!" I yelled.

As I found the vein in her neck, her pulse slowed to a crawl. It stopped within seconds of me feeling for it, proving to me that nothing in this life was fair.

A low chuckle filled my ears, purring with enjoyment. I snapped to the left and flew to my feet, Excalibur drawn, blade razor-sharp with my rage. In the windowsill was a man crouching, getting ready to jump. The low vibration of the laugh turned to a playful growl. Marie lay at my feet, but it felt like there was nothing I could do to make it better. I saw red, and before I could even think about what I was doing, I sprinted at him.

"Hey! Get back here!" I bellowed.

Before I could get any closer, he was over the edge. I crashed into the windowsill and looked over it, shaking my head trying to rid myself of shock.

I freed myself from the window and pushed past Steven and the man as I shouted at them. "Steven, he jumped out the window!"

"Who?" Steven asked, already on my heels.

"I can't tell, but he killed that woman! He killed Marie!"

"What? Marie was in there?"

"Yes, he killed her, Steven. She was breathing but it stopped as soon as I got to her!"

The man kept ahead of us by about thirty feet. Trying to stay with him, we picked up the pace. My body moved quickly as we tried to catch him and make him pay for what he had done for taking Marie from me.

"You killed her! Stop, now!" I bellowed.

I started to hear a familiar buzz and crackle fill the air right next to me. In the next second, a brilliant blue ball of electricity whizzed by my head. It crashed hopelessly against a stack of crates against the left wall, sending rats scurrying in every direction.

I ducked, almost falling to the ground. "Bloody hell?" I yelped in horror, feeling like I dodged a bullet.

"Sorry," he said with an apologetic tone.

Focusing back on the man in front, we kept with the chase. Steven pulled out ahead of me to take another shot. With the buzz and the glowing light, he let off another charged bullet. The projectile hit our assailant square in the back, pushing him forward about six feet. The man's body crashed to the ground as it landed next to one of the Tesla coil substations.

"I hit him?" Steven asked as he cleared his throat. "I mean, I hit him!"

We slowly came to a stop and walked closer to him, watching him dubiously.

"You think I killed him?" Steven asked as he held up his bio-electric rifle, reading another charge.

I crouched down to grab his shoulder. "I don't kno–" I began to say.

I was cut off and pushed back. The force was so strong it felt as if an elephant pushed me off my feet with his trunk. Hitting the ground, I tried to roll to my feet but only got halfway. I looked back and saw the man was on his own feet now, torso slumped over his legs with his arms dangling at his sides. A slow and melodic tune escaped his mouth. A whistle.

Straightening his back, he looked at me and laughed. "You really are stupid."

My muscles went still, locking in place. The realization of what was happening caused my body to dump adrenaline into my veins creating an overload of thoughts and impulses.

"Jules?" I asked in disbelief. I shook my head, trying to let it all soak in.

This can't be true. It can't be real. He killed Marie.

I looked closer at his clothes, noticing the whites of his shirt were stained red, blood smeared onto his hands and face.

"You stupid mortals. All this time, and you couldn't see it in front of you. You're just like all of the ones that came before you, Davey," he scoffed. "Trying so hard to stop me, but not actually thinking of how to do it. It was all set in motion before you even had a clue."

"What do you mean? We were together the night of the first murder! I thought it was Henry that hurt her. She said it was the awful white shoes!" I exclaimed.

He grinned. "Yes I was with you that night. It was Henry that perpetrated it. But in a way, it was me that hurt her. What a loop I've thrown you through. Always one step ahead. She wasn't the first one though. This started before you could have even done anything."

"Emma wasn't the first?"

"No, you idiot, why would I want it to be that easy for you?"

I shook my head in disbelief, not knowing what to think. Jules' back straightened as he reached behind his head, pulling a sword from a sheath in between his shirt and jacket.

All of the visions came to me when I ran into him. They warned me of how he was no man. I thought it was Henry.

"Why are you controlling Henry?"

"It's simple. I found the ones with evil buried deep inside. Ones that could be persuaded easily. All they needed was a little push," he laughed.

"Then why kill all of those women?" I exclaimed.

"At first, it was just to kill the true-bloods. You know, kill who threatens my own life before they kill me. Eventually, through the years I started to enjoy it. Now it's for fun. Now I kill anyone that could be a descendant, true or otherwise. Another good thing is that it takes care of the filth that's spreading disease in the streets," he sneered.

"They were innocent! They had families! What kind of monster are you?" I yelled, anger growing in my stomach.

The answers have been in front of me the whole time. How could I not see it before? Every time there was a death, he was there.

"The kind that lives on!" he cackled, readying his sword.

Just like that, he was on me. With a flash, I drew Excalibur just in time to parry his blow, knocking it out to the left.

"He knows how to fight!" Jules barked in a crazed voice. "Too bad you're just prolonging your pain and demise."

His sword came down hard on me once again, and I caught it with the edge of mine, forcing myself in close, causing our blades to meet at the hilt. A grinding and vibration started in the spot where the swords touched, building to a crescendo. With an explosive force, we were both knocked back a fair distance, our feet skidding as we both tried to keep balance. Faltering slightly, I was rushed again with his relentless anger.

"Why do you need to do this?" I demanded through gritted teeth. I used my whole body to prevent another strike that would've turned into a pissing contest.

"Because Davey, why would I live life going by the rules? Why bow to kings and gods when I can make them grovel at my feet?" He laughed.

Pushing me back, he broke the locked blades. Out of the corner of my eye, I saw Steven run to the control panel for the Tesla coil. My attention was brought back to the fight as Jules came back in with a jab to my stomach. I quickly jumped to the side, narrowly escaping a punctured kidney but not a graze to my clothing.

While he followed through with his jab, I brought Excalibur down on his extended arms. A few seconds later, I was looking up at the darkening sky, laying on my back. I was dazed from what felt like being blown off my feet.

What just happened?

"I can finally rid myself of Arthur's dirty bloodline. Eventually, you'll understand. It was never just me, I can't be killed or defeated that easily." Jules grinned, looking down at me.

He readied his sword in both hands, positioning it over my heart. Knowing this could be it, tears welled up in my eyes, keeping the storm cloud from being lonely.

I wonder what awaits me on the other side? I hope I see Marie. I hope she is there, along with my child. At least I have that to look forward to.

"Please, don't," I said.

Marie wouldn't want this. She wouldn't want me to just give up. I can't let him win. I can't let this go.

With a flash of lightning, a figure bolted into Jules, throwing him away from me before he could bring down the sword into my chest. I jumped to my feet and looked at what had just happened. Tears fell to the ground with the rain as I did so. On top of Jules was Dr. Henry, fighting to keep him on the ground.

"What are you waiting for?" Henry yelled.

Glancing back over to Steven, I realized he wasn't ready. I needed to keep Jules busy a little bit longer. Just enough time for Steven to finish messing around with the Tesla coil.

Jules managed to knock Henry off of him. They both squirmed on the ground, writhing at unnatural angles. While Henry was still on the ground, Jules slowly dragged himself up.

"What do you think you're doing? I made you!" Jules bellowed, thunder booming around us. "You are a part of me!"

"I can't do it! I never wanted this!" Henry yelled.

"Yes, yes you did. You'd be nothing without me!" Jules roared once more. "I made you who you are. Powerful! You are free of the restrictions pressed upon you by the mortal coil."

"Stop! Stay out of my head!" Henry cried in pain, clutching his skull in both hands, collapsing to the ground.

Staring at him for a moment, I shouted, "Henry! Are you okay? Get up! Just fight it. I know you are good!"

"Now, where were we?" Jules asked as he started to walk towards me, picking his sword up in the process. His arms swayed back and forth as he started to whistle more. "What was that delightful song they sang about me? Ah yes, I know. Scrape, scrape you won't escape. Run, run it's time for fun. Come on, Davey, why don't you run?" he mocked, an unnatural grin forming from crooked white teeth splintered into my mind.

It pierced through me, threatening my body to freeze once more. Off in the direction of Dr. Henry, I heard some rustling and murmurs.

"I'm with you now. I am still here. No matter how hard you try, it's time to kill." A voice whispered out of Henry's body.

"Yes! That's it! Come join me, Edward, let's finish this together, as one." Jules called back to Henry, still walking towards me.

"Henry?" I asked, backpedaling from Jules' advance.

Henry slowly got back up and turned in our direction. The look on his face flashed back and forth, between an ear-to-ear grin and a look of deepened sorrow.

"Don't listen to him. You can fight it," I pleaded.

Jules advanced closer, singing that damned tune. Before he could get any closer, Henry tackled him from the side, throwing both of them off closer to the Tesla coil. He had Jules in a bear hug, struggling to break free. In a flash of the sky, I saw the look of regret on Henry's face as he fought Jules for control.

"I can't fight him back any longer!" exclaimed Henry.

"No, you can't. Oh, no, no. Just give in and let go!" screeched Edward. The expression Henry's face momentarily flashed to something more sinister.

"Please! I can't hold Edward or Jules off any longer!" Henry cried, tears streaming down his face.

The storm grew with intensity, lightning arced across the dark clouded sky. Thunder crackled and boomed a few seconds following each bolt. The Tesla Bulbs in the lampposts flashed with each surge of extra electricity, adding more light to the area around us.

Steven looked at me, and we both knew. We knew it came down to this one last moment. With Henry still holding Jules in a bear hug, I started to run in their direction.

"No! Don't! I can't go this way!" screeched Jules, struggling to knock Henry off of him.

Henry continued his grasp on Jules. "I am Henry Jekyll!"

I only had this one moment to take them. I centered Excalibur at their stomachs and ran both Jules and Henry through, pushing them closer and closer to the Tesla coil.

"Steven, now!" I yelled over the thunder, hoping he heard me and knew what to do.

As we locked eyes, Steven flipped the switch, and the coil roared to life. A deafening buzz filled the air as electricity arced off the top of it. Within a second, all of the power focused on Excalibur's blade, electrocuting Henry and Jules where they stood. The surge of energy pushed me back, toppling me head over heels.

I landed on my side next to Steven, knocking the breath from my lungs. The wind slowed as the sky lightened, thunder subsiding and the rain stopping. The buzz from the coil still droned the air like a biblical storm of locusts.

Looking at their bodies, I yelled to Steven, "Turn it off."

As the coil powered down, the last tendrils of mobile lightning dissipated into thin air. Jules' and Henry's bodies started to crack and crumble as parts fell off in jagged chunks. The light leftover breeze started to pick up the particles and dust of the remains, taking them with, destination unknown. Excalibur clanged to the ground with the last speck of Jakobus being swept away.

It's finished. It's done.

"Are you okay?" I asked Steven.

He stared at me wide eyed. "Yes," he said, patting himself up and down, checking for holes as a smile crept onto his face. "Yes, I am."

CHAPTER 27
Never The Same

1st April, 1889
Spitalfields Borough, London, England
5:00 p.m.

The scrape from the door against the frame created cracks in the thin wall of silence that fell over the room. I turned to see Steven sneak through the threshold, silently trying to close it behind him.

"How is she?" Steven whispered, trying to be quiet.

"She is doing alright. It was a very long night. Up for seven hours straight. She's stuck in there, though," I said.

"Who has come by?"

"Father Hubert came by not too long ago. He wanted to be here for support," I said. "Thanks for coming by. You really didn't need to, though."

Steven blew raspberries. "And miss the birth of my niece? I wouldn't dream of it!"

I gave Steven a stern look. "Technically, you already did. And stop yelling. We wouldn't want to wake them."

"Oh, sorry. I am just so excited. Where are they?"

"They are in the other room. Wait here. I will go check if you can see them."

Steven patted me on the back with care, a grin stretched across his face. I nodded in appreciation and tiptoed past him to the doorway that separated the front door and the lounge.

"Marie, how are you feeling?" I whispered through the crack of the door.

A faint rustle of linen and pillows came from beyond. It was followed by someone talking to another, too quiet to hear what they were saying. After a few seconds, I pushed the door open slowly.

"Come in," said Marie. Her voice was hoarse, raw, and strained from the long night.

I opened the door the rest of the way as I tried to keep the noise down. "Steven is here. Can he come see her?"

"Of course. I bet he is excited."

I walked back to Steven and said, "She says you can come see her. But make sure you are gentle, okay?"

"Yes, of course. I will be as gentle as I can be," he said.

We both walked to the lounge where they were lying down. Last night we covered them up the windows with blankets to keep the glare and light from being too much for their eyes. What little light there was in the room was provided from a small Tesla bulb lamp in the furthest corner of the room. It cast shadows over part of the wall opposite to it, creating a pitch-black mountain.

"Hey, Steven, nice to see you again. Thank you for coming by," Marie said.

"I wouldn't dream of not being here," he said. Steven took a few steps closer to have a better look. "What is her name?"

Marie looked down at the baby in her arms, swaddled cozily in a small blanket. Some of the light lit up her face, revealing a look of bliss. Marie looked up at me with a wide and beautiful smile, sending a tidal wave of emotions rushing through me.

"Her name is Eleanor," Marie said.

"May I hold her?" Steven asked.

"Yes, just be careful," Marie said.

Steven walked around to the right side of the bed and took Eleanor into his arms. He stood up and rocked back and forth slowly.

"She is perfect," Steven beamed.

Steven looked at me and smiled some more before letting it falter. He handed Eleanor back to Marie and pulled me to the side, away from their ears to hear us. Marie took our baby in her hands with a gentle care I would only expect from her.

"Steven, what's the matter?" I asked.

"I know this may not be the time to bring this up, but I will be leaving."

"Leaving? What do you mean?"

He put a hand on my shoulder. "Do you remember the man you saw in America? The one with the cane?"

The man with the cane. Of course. I let him slip from my mind as I cared for Marie after the attack.

I nodded. "Yes, what of him?"

"Hubert and I agree that I should go after him. Maybe we can also find the two men that were with him. The Harvesters."

"Why?" I shook my head. "Regardless of why, I will go with you of course."

"You can't."

"Why can't I?" I asked, anger starting to swell.

He squeezed my shoulder, as if he knew I was getting frustrated. "You just had a kid. How could you abandon that?"

I can't just leave them.

"You are right, but why then?"

"Hubert and I agree that this may not be complete until he is apprehended and taken care of, that's why. He could be a part of Jakobus, and we do not know it. Like how Henry was."

"You'll be back though, right?"

He nodded. "I will."

He squeezed my shoulder again before returning to Marie and asking to hold Eleanor once more.

"Marie, where did Hubert go?" I asked, looking around the faintly lit room.

"He was in the kitchen. He said he needed to talk to you when you came back in from the foyer," she said.

"Okay." I paused and looked at the three of them. "You going to be okay for a few minutes?

Steven was too busy cooing sweet words of love to Eleanor as Marie nodded silently, radiant and beautiful but visibly drained. Feeling satisfied with the responses, I turned to meet the Father in the other room. He was in the kitchen like I was told, standing in front of the window and looking out over the small garden Marie had started earlier that year.

"Life can really change in the matter of a year, can it not?" asked Hubert.

I looked out at the bees floating around the plants. They were buzzing here and there, doing the only thing they knew how to do, care-free and content with their small little world but unaware of the truly horrible things that could happen.

"It certainly can. I still am having a hard time believing it," I said.

Father Hubert let out a chuckle. "That's what makes it the stuff of legends."

"I suppose you're right. Thank you, Father. For being here to help with Marie and for helping me find my way," I said.

"Not a problem Davey." Father Hubert let out a sad-sounding sigh. "I have a feeling it wasn't as easy as this, though." He turned to me, a look of concern and dread creeping in on the edges of his face. "Let us hope it is, but I fear it isn't done. Not completely."

"The same feeling crossed my mind a few times since the incident. I was hoping it was residual, left-over from the year of chasing him." I paused and looked back at Father Hubert. "I never could track down the man with the cane. I know he is involved. Steven said he would return to America to look for him."

"I agree. I did talk with him. Regardless, I think your story is complete, my son. That is all we can say. But we will need to prepare for the future. You may need to join Steven at some point. We may never know." he paused. "Do you still have that trunk you received the sword in?"

"Yes, it is in my room. Why?"

"It is time to put Excalibur to rest for now. You have a family to care for in the time being."

"Okay, just follow me then. We will do it now."

We made our way to the bedroom, sneaking past the lounge where everyone else still was. Entering, I looked down at Excalibur leaning against the chair next to the doorway.

"It's right there," I said.

I bent down and pulled the trunk from its hiding spot underneath the bed. As it touched the rays of light cutting through the window, the hardware started to glow with a copper and gold sheen. I crouched, flipped the latch on the lid, and opened it up slowly.

"I will be closing a chapter of my life on the same day I will open a new one. I just have to make it the best I can and never miss a second of it," I said.

"Wise words. It should be the only way anyone lives their life," said Father Hubert.

I looked at the ring still on my finger, taking in the scuffs from the hundreds of years of memories it held. I eased it off slowly, being careful for no particular reason. After it was off, I placed the ring in its respective spot in the plush bed of velvet.

This feels like it was a huge part of my life for a very long time. It will be hard to go back to a humdrum existence after this.

"Now for the sword," I said, standing up.

Hubert already had Excalibur in his hands. It was laid out across his palms, mirroring the offering of how Merlin did to King Arthur. I took it one last time, turning the magnificent blade over in my hands.

"So much power and good in this sword. But I fear there is more pain to be shared as well. Hopefully, whoever must take up this story next will be able to finish what I couldn't," I said. "If it truly isn't finished now, I hope I can finish it before I die."

Hubert nodded at the sentiment.

I turned to him and asked, "What will you do, Father?"

"I will do what is tasked to all who came before me and all who come after."

"What is that?"

"Look for descendants and look for their respective artifacts."

I nodded in acknowledgment as I leaned down on the floor. My hands gingerly guided the sword to rest in its bed of crimson. Eventually, I found the strength to pull away for what hopefully was the last time, my eyes still staring in awe.

As I shut the lid on the trunk, I said aloud, "To end the wicked, it must be in the dead of night. You must fight for what's right with all your might. Farewell and good luck."

EPILOGUE

16 July 1937
Spitalfields Borough, London, England
6:45 a.m.

Today is just like any other day.

Deckard reached into the shower and turned the knobs. With a creak and groan, it spat to life. He stepped in and shuddered, not from the chill of the icy water on his bare skin, but from a sense of dread that washed over him. He tried his best to scrub the grogginess away as he thought about the last time he saw his grandfather, Davey.

Maybe I should visit him today.

Deckard finished, turned off the water, and stretched for the gritty towel that hung on one of the three tarnished hooks, all worn like so much of the well-lived-in flat. Wiping the beaded condensation from the scratched mirror, he found himself staring at the reflection in some sort of sleep-deprived daze. He rubbed his face and could feel the built-up stubble as it scratched and tugged at his hands. He decided he hadn't shaved in a few days, so he thought that maybe he should today. The image in the mirror was deceiving, reflecting something different than the way Deck had felt.

Today is just like any other day. It must be.

7:15 a.m.

Ring, ring, ring.

The noise coming from the rotary phone brought him out of his trance. He ran to the kitchen to answer, being mindful his soaking feet could slide out from underneath him at any moment.

"Hello?" he answered, grabbing the phone on what he thought could've been the last ring.

A moment of silence followed by a small shuffle came from the speaker in the cracked receiver.

"Hey Deck," said Drow.

"Oh, hey Woodrow," Deck replied, rubbing his eyes, squeezing out the last traces of sleep.

"Deck, when will you listen to me and just call me Drow? Is that too much to ask for?"

"Sorry, it's just hard to get used to it. I've been calling you that me whole life. Anyway, how are you?"

"I suppose I'm decent. I'm assuming mum hasn't called yet, has she?"

"No, she hasn't. Why, what's going on?"

Light rustling came from the earpiece on the other side of the line. It was followed by a silence that felt as if it carried something heavier in the absence of noise.

"She called me this morning, oh about an hour ago." Drow sighed as he paused. "Grandad passed away last night. She said that he had a heart attack. Bloody old man, always seemed like this would never happen."

Leaning over, Deck grabbed a kitchen chair and pulled it close to take a seat. He felt a rush of emotions cascade through him, like the sudden crash of a cannonball through his hull.

His brother's voice droned and then faded after a moment, turning to a soft buzz. It grew with every second that passed, eventually turning to an unwavering and persistent ringing. The only thing Deck could focus on was the nauseating, vertically striped wallpaper that consisted of a horrible mustard brown sandwiched between an unappetizing pea soup green.

The sense of vertigo made his world spin, turning the stripes into a swirl of confusion. He tried to take hold of his thoughts, knowing he needed to hear what else Drow had to say.

Regaining his composure after a moment passed, Deck tuned back into the conversation at hand. "We just got done visiting him last weekend. I didn't think anything was wrong."

"Yeah, neither did we. Mum was crying and barely got the words out when she called me. She wants us to go by later today to talk about the plans. You know, when we are gonna go through all grandad's stuff," said Drow.

"I can't believe it." Hot tears welled up in Deck's eyes, churning his stomach and bringing forth feelings of anger and sorrow. He started to bounce his leg in a vain attempt to keep his mind preoccupied. "When will you go by?"

"I was going to go by around one this afternoon, give her some time with dad and go through a couple of things."

Deck's leg was still hitting the floor like a jackhammer.

"I'll probably see you there around then. I'm just gonna head that way now, I still–" He paused, a lump forming in his throat, hard and impassable.

"I– I get it. It'll take me a little to get there. We all loved him, and I know you two were really close. I'll meet up with you there, Deck. I'm hoping Mum is okay."

"Me too, Drow. See you then," Deck said, struggling to squeeze the words out. He could feel the tears running down his cheeks, starting warm then growing cold.

Getting up to hang the phone on the wall, he leaned over to push the chair back in. Deck stood there for a moment as he took it all in.

I guess I should go get dressed. Standing around here won't help me none.

7:45 a.m.

Deck leaned over and grabbed his wrist-watch, a gift from his grandad, and rubbed at the cracked face. He placed it gently on his wrist, slowly guiding the brown leather strap into place. A memory of when his grandfather gave it to him flashed through his mind, and he remembered that it was actually not too long ago. It was on a weekend that he spent most of a Saturday with Grandad, going to the outskirts of town to a swap meet. They spent the whole day looking for oddities and collectibles.

Almost forgetting about his well-worn black wallet, he reached down to grab it from the small corner table near the front door. Looking at the time, he shook his head as the watch read 7:45 a.m. and started to wind it, stopping right where he wanted it to be."

"Uh, thirteen. Good, just like it should be," he mumbled to himself.

He didn't know why, but he had just always been like that. As long as he could remember, he liked to be early.

Deckard reached for his tweed fedora and tan trench coat, teetering on the ball of his left foot as he tried to keep his balance. As he threw them on and walked outside, more dread washed over him.

8:32 a.m.

The only way to get to Deckard's grandad's house was past the farmer's market. Normally this would not be an issue, but his girlfriend ran a fruit and veg stall very close to his grandad's house, and the last thing he wanted to do was talk. A sudden spark of sorrow jolted through him, reminding him of the most recent news.

Lost in thought, Deckard sulked his way past the old rickety wooden carts and stands filled to the brim with fresh fruits and vegetables. There were green cabbages lying next to vibrant orange and red peppers while large watermelons and cantaloupes teetered on the edges, ready to fall. Ignoring how far along he was, he knew he wasn't looking forward to this. He didn't even know if he could tell her about Grandad Davey. He hoped she wasn't working there today.

"Hey there, Deck!" squealed Hope, pulling him from his depressing thoughts.

The sudden gesture startled Deckard.

"Oh. Hey, Hope," Deckard said half-heartedly, which sank ever further. This was exactly what he didn't want.

Tilting her head, Hope scrutinized his appearance. She kept her eyes on him for a moment as they stayed silent. Deckard was worried he probably looked as bad as he felt.

"Deck, what's wrong? You don't seem yourself," she said.

"I got bad news from Drow earlier," he breathed in deeply. He felt a shudder splinter out from his spine as he continued to talk. "Me grandad passed away last night. It's so sudden, I'm still just trying to make sense of it all."

Deckard looked at her just in time to see a cascade of tears fall from her hazel eyes, slowly staining her porcelain cheeks with a reddish hue. "I— I'm sor—" is all he could get out before she embraced him.

Deck nodded in understanding, feeling the tears form in his own eyes.

"I'm– I'm so– sorry, Deck," she struggled out, trying to form the words through her tears. She buried her face in Deckard's coat, still sobbing softly as he wrapped his arms around her.

"Will you be okay?" she asked as the tears sunk into her skin.

Deckard slumped over as well, putting his face in the crook of her neck as he sighed. "I don't know, but I need to be strong for me mum. I'm going to meet up with her and me brother to help go through Grandad's belongings."

She let out a little sigh herself. "Hopefully the sorting goes well, and it brings up fond memories, not bad ones."

Deck squeezed Hope once more before letting go of her loving embrace. He departed and continued on his way.

8:44 a.m.

Deck climbed the steps to his grandad's place, step by step. There were so many memories that belonged here, and one of them came to mind in a heartbeat. It was a sunny summer day when he and his brother were just a few weeks shy of eleven. They just came by to visit their grandad to get early gifts when one of them tripped on the second to last step near the top. Drow ended up skinning his knee and elbow when he hit the stone.

Deck shook his head and cleared his mind as he reached for the door and went inside. As he stepped in, he closed the door quietly behind him, not wanting to disturb his mum. Truthfully though, she might have welcomed the distraction from that moment.

Deck saw his mum in the foyer looking through some papers in her hands. She reached up and wiped away a loose tear as she looked over them. He cleared his throat to get her attention.

"Hey, Deck," said Mum as she looked up at him. She set down the stack of loose papers she had in her hands on the crowded living room table, adding to the cluttered mess.

"Hey, Mum," Deckard said. Taking his hands from his pockets, he reached to give her a hug. "How are you holding up? How's the cleaning and sorting going?"

"Well," she began, sighing, rubbing her eyes sharply and shuddering. "It's been stressful. It just happened out of nowhere. I was talking to your grandad yesterday. I'm still in shock. I was up all morning calling the funeral home, flower shops, and the church for arrangements. He just has a lot of clutter. It's a bloody mess with paper everywhere. I don't know what he thought was important and what he just forgot he had."

"I know, Mum," Deckard said, letting his arms go slack a little while still holding onto her. "I'm sorry about it all; it is a little unreal. It seems like just yesterday I would ride with him to town in that beat-up buggy of his. I feel really awful about this whole mess. I haven't been by to see the old man in a while. Makes me regret it a little."

She smiled at the last thought, remembering her two sons and her father from times past.

Deckard sighed, his shoulders slumped a little more. "Hey, where is Drow, by the way? Wasn't he supposed to be here too?"

"He hasn't been here yet. When I called him this morning, I asked him to go to the print shop to make sure I could get the funeral programs printed in time. He'll be here in a little while to help with more things. I'm sure you'll catch him in a few hours," she said worryingly.

Deck nodded and rubbed his mum's back to help console her.

"I've been going through all his old stuff. I've learned quite a bit about your grandfather. More than I thought was possible. I mean, I am his daughter for God sakes, and I'm finding out things I've never heard before," she said, chuckling softly.

Shrugging, she walked to the dusty kitchen to have a seat at the old, metal-trimmed kitchen table. As she sat, she looked near the window at more envelopes and mugs filled with pens and pencils. Multiple picture frames with older photos still standing were covered in the golden haze of mid-morning sunlight.

She reached over to grab one of the photos, and, with a smile, she noticed it was of her and her father in black and white. She looked over at Deck and said, "You only really knew Grandad with gray hair. It was actually dark brown. When he was younger, he always had one of those handlebar mustaches; always dressed well. Close cropped hair with a little bit of a wave to it."

Deck followed behind and took a seat across from her. Looking down at the worn, cracked plastic top of the table, it reminded him of a drought-stricken desert hoping for rain. Some spots had started to peel, while other spots had chipped off and shown the wood layer underneath.

He looked up at her and said, "Mum, you going to be okay?"

She seemed to visibly shrink from the question right in front of him. She grabbed more tissues from the half-empty box on the table and blew her nose. "I don't know, Deck, I just don't. We knew it was going to happen but chose to act like nothing was wrong."

"What was wrong? Last time I was here he seemed just fine," Deck said.

Crying, she continued. "He didn't want you to know."

I wish he would have told me. I would've made the best of the last few weeks. I would've visited more to help him.

"What was wrong?" Deck asked as he closed his eyes.

Her lip quivered as she spoke. "He had pneumonia. It got out of control, and took him from us."

The news hit him as a surprise. Like Deckard said, the last time they spoke, his grandad seemed to be fine. Great, even. But he supposed that like all things in life, they often go in ways you do not expect.

He felt his mum's hand touch his face, bringing him back to here and now. "It's okay, Deck, we will all make it through this."

He nodded and opened his eyes as he took her hand. She started to cry again, tears rolling down her cheeks slower than before. He let go of her hand to let her wipe at her face once more.

She regained some composure and said, "By the way, this morning when I came by to start going through things, I moved some papers in the living room, and I found an envelope with your name on it. I didn't open it because I figured you'd want to read it first."

She handed it to Deck with her left hand, still holding onto the tissues with her right. Deckard took the letter from her and turned it over in his hands a few times, feeling the folds in the thin golden stained paper and thinking what it might say. He looked up at his mum, but she already got back up to go sort through some more papers in the living room.

Feeling anxious, worried, and a little confused, Deck turned it over one last time and opened it up. He pulled out the papers and unfolded the letter to read what it said.

> Dear Deckard,
>
> A long time ago, I was a young man like yourself. The year was 1888 or so when it all started. This far along now, and the dates all meld together. It was a lifetime ago, but I feel like it's best that I tell you this. There is something that I'm going to need you to do. I have

lived a long life, mostly filled with happiness, and in my later years, all because of you.

There is, however, one thing that has haunted me since I was a young man. A task which was bestowed upon me from an unlikely stranger to do the impossible. I was unable to complete this task, but that isn't without saying I tried. By God, did I try, but I fell short of finishing it and ending it all.

I have left to you something very important. You will understand everything soon enough. Your life will forever be changed by what will come next and once you touch what is contained in this trunk you will understand. It will be difficult, but I believe you can do what I was not able to. After all, you are your mother's son. I love you more than I could ever say.

Just remember one thing Deckard. What has passed is never done. I wish you luck and God be with you.

Best Regards,
David O'Shea

Deck thought about that last sentence, wondering what it could mean. He looked at the envelope again and noticed there was a key inside. Confused, he yelled out to his mum, "What's this key for? Does Grandad have any chests or boxes around here that are locked?"

"I don't really know for sure," she said as she popped her head around the corner with a puzzled look on her face, tissue to her nose.

"If he did, it's probably in the basement or upstairs. I could go check in the attic if you'd like."

"Okay, I'll go check the basement."

Deck hopped to his feet as he grabbed the back of the worn chair. As he did this, he noticed that the spot he had his hand on must've been where his Grandad touched a thousand times. It hit him as to how real all of this was. This spot was a lighter tan instead of the darker stain on the rest of the chair, almost as if it were speaking to him. He slid it back into place and took his hand from the backrest, patting it once for good measure.

Looking at the key one more time, he noticed it was very ornate, old, and slightly oxidized on the surface. It was molded into a design of a medieval dragon with the tail wrapped around the start of the key spine and extended to the end of the teeth. Stamped, or forged, into the top where the dragon's body occupied was the Roman numerals for thirteen: *XIII*.

Lightly tossing it into the air and catching it, he decided to make his way from the kitchen to the basement. He passed the cluttered foyer, scattered with stacks of books piled two feet tall and leaning every which way. Pictures hung on every square inch of the walls, covering them almost entirely. Some of them were of Deckard and his grandad, while others were of Mum and her siblings. A few were of him when he was younger, standing with a few people he knew once upon a time.

Most of them were of him, and another man that Grandad always said was his best friend. One was of him and his mates in the 21st Regiment of Hussars. Deck's grandad always told stories about when he joined the military and was sent over into Sudan in 1884 to 1885.

Deck entered the living room, passing more pictures. This room connected to another hall leading to the old Victorian staircase. It was made of beautiful mahogany, flowing upwards in a spiral, hugging the wall. Built into the staircase was the doorway that led down into the basement.

Deck opened it and reached in the dark for the wireless button to turn on the Tesla Bulbs. The gesture made him remember when he was just a lad and how he always felt that at any moment, a monster would reach out and bite his hand right off. Now, being grown, he knew that it was silly to think that way. Monsters don't exist. At least in any way that you can plainly see.

His blind fingers hungrily found the button as the panic set in, causing him to feel like a famished dog looking for every last morsel. Still thinking of when he was young, he hastily pressed the button to illuminate the dark abyss in an attempt to rid his imagination of dreadful thoughts.

Seeing that there were, in fact, no such things as monsters, and that young Deckard had nothing to worry about, he chuckled a few times as he shook his head. With the light shining, warding off the dark, Deck slowly took the stairs down, step by step. He thought of how many times his grandad did the same thing, most likely without the being scared of monsters bit.

The steps opened up to a fairly large basement, a fact that one wouldn't know by seeing all of the piles of junk scattered everywhere. He surveyed the mounds covered with off-white linen sheets, reminding him of snow-capped mountains.

There were Tesla Bulbs hanging from the rafters shining over the mass of clutter that was before him. Unsure of where to start first, his eyes fell on the center pile as he pulled off the first sheet. A thick cloud of dust filled the air as if a gust of wind swept through an abandoned mining town in the dust bowl. Underneath was an array of cardboard boxes neatly taped closed, accompanied by others that were hastily folded shut. Deck sighed as he moved them around to look for a chest or case, not finding anything of such description.

"On to the next pile," Deck muttered to himself as he tossed the sheet half-heartedly back on top.

His eyes looked over to another stack, equally as unpromising as the last. Deck made it through about three mounds of rubbish before he came to another pile in the far-right corner, tucked underneath some old brooms and mops. This last pile was covered with linen, like all the others, but it failed to send out a shower of dust mites ready to assault his olfactory receptors when pulling it off.

Thinking this was odd, Deck looked back and saw that there was, in fact, a wooden trunk underneath everything. Bending down to pull it out into the light, he started to drag the trunk inch by inch, trying to be careful not wanting to disturb anything inside.

With the incandescence of the Tesla Bulbs now showering warm golden light on the trunk, Deck started to make out it wasn't as simple as it seemed. First off, it looked very old but oddly immaculate for its age. The hinges on the back of the trunk were shaped like claws, and the lock was in the shape of a family crest.

To Deckard's dismay, the crest was unrecognizable, as if something had rubbed the etching away. Reaching for the key in his pocket, he pulled it out and turned it over in his hands a few times.

"If there is a dragon on the key, then the claws on the chest could be dragon claws. Huh, that's actually pretty ace," Deckard thought to himself.

Starting to feel the collywobbles, he whispered, "Let's see if this key actually works."

Deckard knelt down and slid the key into the keyhole, feeling some resistance as he did so. Grimacing, Deck pushed a little harder as it slid the rest of the way. He did this gently, trying to be careful not to break it off in the lock. Turning the key, he was rewarded with an audible click.

Adrenaline rushed into his body as he thought about the contents inside. He corrected the key and pulled it back out before doing anything else. Deck placed it safely back in his pocket and reached for the brass handles.

Upon opening the lid, he saw a tray on the top containing old rolled-up papers, some leather-bound journals, and tarnished metal utensils. The metal instruments appeared to be an old compass and something else he wasn't familiar with. The underside of the lid had a description etched into the wood.

Deck squinted as he read aloud, "To end the wicked, it must be in the dead of night. You must fight for what's right with all your might."

I wonder what that's all about.

Attached to the tray was a red silk tassel at the back edge near the hinges. With great care, he pulled it up to remove the tray, revealing what lay below. Laying upon a bed of red velvet was a sword along with a simple golden ring resting next to it. The sword, most likely a double-edged one, was about three feet long from the hand guard to the tip of the blade. Looking at it closer, he noticed the hilt was made of a dark brown leather wrap starting at the pommel and interwoven with a single dark, almost ruby red stripe crisscrossing to the top near the crossguard. The pommel was what he guessed to be a dragon claw clutching a red stone the size of an apricot. The sword's scabbard was the same dark brown as the wrap with a golden inlay from one end to the other.

Of course it's a dragon claw. Gotta keep up with the theme.

As Deck kneeled, staring at the sword that lay in front of him, he noticed the nervousness was gone from his mind. It was replaced with a calm sense he had never known, almost as if his whole life led him to this moment.

Deck leaned forward and reached out to the sword with his right hand. His fingers curled around the worn leather wrap of the sword. It was warm to the touch, crackling visible with small arcs of electricity that arced to his hand. Everything went dark, followed by a flash of light through his mind.

Deck saw many things as images flashed in front of his mind's eye. At first, he heard muted and muffled noises and saw streaks of light, followed by large masses of dark. He could eventually make out his surroundings a little more clearly, focusing as he did this.

The ground was well-worn cobblestone with ruts from many years of carriage wheels. Off in the distance was a man at the top of a ladder that leaned against a lamppost talking to a man near him. He could not make out what they were saying from this far away; all he could hear were mumbles and grunts.

Deck willed himself to take his hand from the sword, to stop whatever he was seeing. Just like that, he was kneeling in the basement once more. Dust floated lazily around him, lighting up as they crossed the rays of sunshine that cascaded through the windows.

Deck thought about what he just saw. What he *thought* he saw. It was something he didn't recognize as a memory of his own, or of a time he had been in. He thought about the note his grandad left him and how it said when he touched whatever was in this trunk, he would understand. He knew the note, the key and the sword were important. He just needed to find out why.

He needed to see what the sword had to tell him.

He closed his eyes and decided to take the leap, to see what he could. Deck reached for the sword one last time.

16th July, 1937
Spitalfields Borough, London, England
2:11 p.m.

The sword tingled in the palm of his hand. He looked up from the trunk and gasped.

"What was that?!" Deck said, feeling his whole body shake and shudder.

Looking back down at the sword, Deck turned it around in his hand a few times as he lifted it from the bed of soft, red velvet. His mind kept racing faster and faster, and he didn't know what to make of it all.

Was it a dream? Did that actually happen? What did it all mean? Am I to believe that Grandad and I were actually descendants of knights from the round table? And chasing Jack the Ripper, for that matter? I need some answers, and I need them now. Is there anyone left?

Looking back in the trunk, he saw the gold ring resting in its own spot next to the impression where the sword rested. He grabbed it as he stood up, carefully closing the lid on the trunk.

He looked one more time at the sword in his right hand and the ring in the other, giving off an effervescent, golden glow.

But this means he's back. That grandad wasn't able to do it. It's now up to me.

Deck heard some rustling behind and flung around to see who was there. Out of pure reflex that wasn't his own but somehow was, he pulled Excalibur from its sheath. In a fluid motion, he rose to his feet in a readied stance, steel gleaming in the sunlight. His mum yelped, jumping back a few steps. He lowered the sword as he realized it was just her, exhaling his held breath in the process.

"Um, Deck, did you find anything? I've been yelling at you for five minutes." She glanced down at the sword, then back up at Deck "I couldn't find anything upstairs. Did you have more luck?"

Deck looked down at the sword in his hands and then back at his mum.

"I did."

"Why do you have a sword in your hands?"

I smiled and said, "You'll never believe this."

Acknowledgements

I would like to give thanks to all who were involved in this long process. A thanks to my parents, David and Kim, for being the best they could be. Another to Ward for fueling the fire. A thanks to Cole, my editor, for putting up with all the questions. I also want to express gratitude to one of my old English teachers, Mr. Fiene. A thank you to my friend Donn, for the help at first. And last but not least, Bryan and Eileen for reading the first few drafts.

Thank you all for the support.

Author's Notes

In the novel, there are a few chapters, nineteen, twenty, and twenty-one, that may seem out of place or that they hinder the story slightly. I understand that I could have done them a different way, but keep in mind that the victims I depict in this novel were real people. At some point, I almost lost track of this truth and decided to go a different route and relay the story in another way than I did during the beginning. I also decided to modernize the style and mannerisms of the characters for the time periods to make them more relatable and easier to understand.

Thank you to all that picked this book up and decided to give it a read. My main goal was to write the story I wanted to write, and I hope you enjoyed it as much as I did.